The Jumbie Bird

Ismith Khan

Longman Group UK Limited,
Longman House,
Burnt Mill, Harlow,
Essex CM20 2JE, England
and Associated Companies
throughout the world.
Published in the United States of America
by Longman Inc., New York.

Cover photograph of auther by David A. Buxbaur

First published 1961
This edition 1985
Eleventh impression 1993

ISBN 0 582 78619 3

Printed in Hong Kong
WLEE/11

Introduction

The Author

ISMITH KHAN was born in 1925 in Port of Spain, Trinidad, in a house that looked out on the famous Woodford Square where much of the action of *The Jumbie Bird* takes place. Indeed this is where much of the drama of pre-independence politics in Trinidad was enacted through the years that Khan was growing up. His grandfather, Kale Khan, on whom the character in the novel is based, was a Pathan, one of the fiercly independent, mountain-dwelling people whose ancestral homelands straddle what is now Pakistan and Afghanistan. The Pathans are renowned for their courage and military prowess: they resisted the British in India for generations and are presently involved in another colonial war, fighting the Russians in Afghanistan. They are a proud people with a strong sense of their own traditions and culture.

Like the fictional character, the 'real life' Kale Khan was very conscious of his Pathan background and tried to instil the values of his culture to his only grandson. In a letter to the critic Arthur Drayton, Ismith Khan wrote of his grandfather that he

> was ever involved in all things anti-British . . . his was a rebelliousness, his life was one of dissent, he ridiculed the Raj, [and] chastised fellow Indians for being run over rough shod by the Sahibs.[1]

Ismith Khan grew up then in a family dominated by this larger-than-life character who was something of a legend in the Indian community at that time.

Despite his Muslim background Ismith Khan was educated at

Queens Royal College, one of Trinidad's leading secondary schools, almost exclusively attended by children of the plantocracy and upper middle class. As Arthur Drayton comments,

> It is not inconceivable that like Jamini, the young protagonist in *The Jumbie Bird*, he experienced there (at school), or knew others who did, the uncomfortable sense of *not belonging* socially and economically.[2]

So far so much like the novel, but it is important to understand that *The Jumbie Bird* is *fiction* and that although many of the characters and several of the events of the story can be traced to people and incidents in Ismith Khan's boyhood it would be a mistake to read *The Jumbie Bird* as simply an autobiographical account. For example, Ismith Khan points out that his own father, unlike Rahim in the novel, was a strong authoritative personality. What Ismith Khan has done is to use the scenes, characters, life style and language of a community he knows intimately to create an authentic location for his fiction. *The Jumbie Bird* utilises the perspective of a child growing to an understanding of *his* world to allow the reader insights into the nature and working of a particular community.

Ismith Khan worked as a reporter for the Trinidad Guardian for a time, before leaving Trinidad to study sociology and creative writing at American Universities. He has lived in the USA ever since, teaching and writing. He has published another novel, *The Obeah Man* (Hutchinson, London, 1964) and several short stories as well as academic and critical work.

Context

The Jumbie Bird is one of several Caribbean novels which are set among the East Indian community in Trinidad. It is the only one, however, to examine in any depth the issues of indenture and repatriation.

Those two terms, the fact of indenture and the dream of repatriation, stand like book-ends at either end of the East Indian experience in Trinidad. The destruction of the dream, which *The Jumbie Bird* chronicles, perhaps marked the moment when the East Indian community (by then mostly second and third generation born in Trinidad) began to regard itself as *West* Indian rather than as an embattled enclave of temporary migrants.

With the final abolition of slavery in the 1840s the plantation owners in Trinidad were unable to obtain sufficient labour, at a price they were willing to pay, to run the sugar plantations efficiently. They tried importing indentured labourers from many places, but it was in India that they found thousands of people living in destitution who were willing to risk emigration to a distant and unknown land in the hope of being able to make a better life for themselves and their families. For most, however, the experience proved far from liberating, the conditions they were required to live under were little different from those the slaves had endured.

The indenture terms stipulated that for three or five years they would work as a chattel of the plantation owner, being paid barely enough to subsist on. They would be denied the right to change employers, to live away from the plantation or to demand higher wages. After ten years of working in the island they were entitled to a free return passage to India. However, few had amassed sufficient money by then to enable them to return to anything but the destitution they had fled from. When, in the 1890s, the right to a free passage was withdrawn even the possibility of repatriation was lost for most of the community.

Despite the poor conditions in Trinidad, Indian indentured labour continued to pour into the island for a further seventy years, until 1917. By that time it was estimated that 143,000 people had made the crossing. The East Indian community including of course those born on the island amounted to one third of the island's total population.

Despite their significant presence the Indian population had little in the way of civil rights. It was not until 1946 that Muslim and Hindu marriages were recognised as valid under Trinidadian law. Prior to that date all children of such 'unregistered' marriages were deemed illegitimate and had no inheritance or property rights in law. Hence the significance, in the novel, of 'The Red House', the registry where their 'illegitimate' births were listed in red ink, as a symbol of colonial exploitation and Indian resistance (pp. 61–2). The Indians' right to vote was similarly limited, as Kale Khan explains to the more politically innocent members of his community (p. 152).

Partly because many in the Indian population resented such treatment and hankered to return to India, and partly because the 'African' and Indian population hardly mixed, the East Indian community retained many of its distinctive cultural traditions. The shared experience of indenture broke down some of the cast and religious divisions that had existed within the community itself, so that the festivals of the Hindus became occasions for celebration by Muslims too, and vice versa. The Hussay festival, which features so prominently in the novel, is a *Shia* Muslim celebration which became a key festival for the entire Indian community. Essentially a celebration of the end of an old order and the dawning of a new, the Hosein Festival became, symbolically, a focus for 'demonstrations of Indian national feeling which culminated in the Hussay riots of 1884.'[3]

The gradual decline of sugar as a cash crop increased the exodus of 'worn out' or discontented Indian field hands to the city. Without family or friends, with no prospect of work and no hope of return to their ancestral Hindustan they were the most obvious victims of a labour policy designed solely to serve the interests of the planter class and the 'mother country' (p. 18). The malaise ran deeper however. Economic and industrial developments were undermining the traditional crafts and businesses of the urban Indian population and threatening the cultural cohesion of the community as a whole.

Against such a background Kale Khan's obsession with repatriation to an India that would respect the skills and tradition of its exiled children is not just the sentimental dream of a nostalgic old man. It is an attempt to save a cultural tradition that he sees – in the emasculation of his son and the confusion of his grandson – to be disintegrating. Far from being the self-aggrandisement of 'an enormous ego' as one critic has read it, Kale Khan's quest, and the manner of his death, can be seen to have been an heroic attempt to restore his people's essential dignity.

Character, Imagery, Themes

Though spanning only a few years of a boy's development the story of *The Jumbie Bird* encapsulates three generations of the East Indian experience in Trinidad, represented by the three male members of the Khan family and their 'womenfolk'.

Kale Khan (his first name being pronounced Kal/ay – the second syllable rhyming with 'say') is a dominating and domineering figure. Significantly the novel opens with him rapping on the ceiling of his room demanding the attention of his family. He seems a gruff, stern, isolated character, certain of his own values and uncompromising in his disdain for those who live by less rigorous codes. Our first impression of him is defined by the list of things he hates (p. 2). He seems, in every sense, a *hard* man, even down to his insistence on sleeping on a solid board with a block of wood for a pillow. The impression is heightened by the images associated with metal and strength that surround his person: he has 'bright metallic grey hair', he carries an iron-rod walking stick and wears a 'great brass buckle' on his belt. He despises weakness and vacillation. He is proud of his own independence, of the fact that he has 'never work for nobody', that he came to Trinidad a free craftsman, not an indentured labourer. Most of all, he is proud of his Pathan ancestry; his stern independence of spirit is an expression of the Pathan code of manliness. He is out of step with the attitudes of the East Indian community gradually assimilating itself to a creole society still under British rule.

Kale Khan's ambition to lead his people back to India is an attempt to regain a world ordered by that Pathan code. When Rahim seems to be heading for self-destruction in a world of corrupt values, Kale Khan wishes that he and his son could be back 'wrestling with the elements side by side with the hill tribes of Hindustan' (p. 89). If he seems constantly to be looking back to the past it is in order that he might shape his own, his family's and his community's *future*.

Kale Khan's philosophy of life is 'proved', as it were, by experience. It served him well in times of crisis, like the Hussay riots when he *acted* without hesitation and became a hero. All the great men of history, he insists, have been armed with such a moral code. His son's attempts to adapt seem to Kale Khan a sign of weakness; he is disappointed in Rahim and pins all his hopes on his grandson, Jamini, whom he sees as both the hope for his personal immortality and of the regeneration of the community as a whole (p. 11).

His love for Jamini drives Kale Khan to turn a generalised

resentment of colonialism and the indenture system into a specific campaign for mass repatriation. Jamini becomes 'the closest symbol of the ruin that this land had brought upon them'. His love for Jamini, his compassion for the homeless old men in the square and what we learn of his youthful passion for his latterly estranged wife Binti (p. 37), modify our initial impression of Kale Khan as a hard, unfeeling man.

As we see from his exposure of the voting franchise limitation (p. 152), Kale Khan is a politically sophisticated man, fully aware of the exploitation and deception enacted on his fellow Indians by the indenture system. His political acumen is an aspect of his 'cunning', a character trait that is brought out several times in his dealing with his family. His understanding that the visit of the Indian High Commissioner will put pressure on the Trinidad government leads him to time his campaign for repatriation to coincide with that visit (p. 151). He hopes that pressure from both sides will forces the government to agree to his demands: 'It does take two hands to clap, you know, well now is we chance.' (p. 67) Kale Khan's tragedy is that the other hand will not 'clap'. When the Indian High Commissioner rejects his plans, tells him he has been foolish and misguided in rousing the Indian community, Kale Khan's 'heart broke like the calabash that had swelled in the rain' (pp. 169–70). He is betrayed by Hindustan.

The manner of his death is an expression of his adherence to the Pathan code: having annointed Jamini as his spiritual as well as his physical successor, and tried once more to instil some of his own steel into Rahim, he chooses a fighter's end.

Rahim is overwhelmed by his father's strength of character. Our first image of him is of a dutiful, rather frightened, child running to do his father's bidding. Kale Khan still speaks to him and treats him as if he was a boy even though he is now the family's main breadwinner and has a child of his own (p. 4). Unable to prove himself in the Pathan tradition of rebellion and combat he is trapped between loyalty to his father and a feeling that, in order to make a life for himself and his family in the changing circumstances of *his* society, he should embrace a more flexible moral code.

Despite his own achievements as a craftsman he sees that the society is changing and that his skills may soon become redundant. He resists the idea of compromising his standards but fears, even before the destructive partnership with Hardaker, (itself perhaps a metaphor for the colonial relationship) that such an insistence on quality may be self-destructive. He is in a very real dilemma and is as much a victim of circumstances as of any genuine defect in his character. Both his father and his wife repeatedly tell him not to worry so much, but he understands, perhaps better than they do, the problems that may lie ahead for the family. 'What goin' to happen to us? We aint belong to England, we aint belong to Hindustan, we aint belong to Trinidad.' (p. 54)

Rahim is under great psychological pressures, and when Kale Khan tells Jamini that 'God is dead' the idea terrifies Rahim and reinforces his growing sense of the futility of his own aspirations. Tricked out of his business by the unscrupulous Hardaker and let down by the snivelling lawyer Salwan, Rahim becomes, effectively, a 'drop out', drifting aimlessly around the bars of the town, loosing touch with his wife, his father and his son. Haunted by his own sense of inadequacy, he fears that the fate of Sookiah, who has lost his name, and Hop-and-Drop, the drink-cadging cripple who has lost all dignity, will be his (p. 128). He reaches rock bottom when, tortured by his sense of having let his father down, he takes his anger out on Jamini. This is the ultimate admission of weakness in Kale Khan's eyes and he dismisses Rahim as a 'good for nothing' (pp. 137–9).

Before he dies Kale Khan makes a final attempt to restore some sense of purpose to his son's life by avowing, despite everything his love for Rahim and his certainty that his son *will* make something of himself (p. 162). When the American who wants to buy a set of jewellry that is 'the finest work from this area' (Trinidad was famous for the quality of its jewellry, made by East Indians, in the first half of this century) commissions Rahim, it seems that Kale Khan's belief in his son has been rewarded. The restoration of the relationship of trust between Jamini and Rahim in the final scene of the novel suggests that Rahim's period of struggle may not have been all waste. Unlike Kale Khan, Rahim can understand *his* son's confusions and feels that he *can* guide him towards personal fulfilment precisely because he, too, has had to adapt his cultural inheritance to the contemporary situation in Trinidad.

If Kale Khan represents the Indian past by his insistence on the Pathan code, and Rahim represents the wavering generation of assimilation and compromise, Jamini is the symbol of the future. The novel follows his growth into manhood, suggesting the pressures that bear on the kind of man he will become.

As a child he is a dreamer, absorbed in his grandfather's tales of romantic Hindustan and a noble ancestral tradition. He lives as much in imagination as in reality: the early scenes in the novel depict him day-dreaming round the statue of Sir Woodford in the square, fantasising that the bust of a white man in the chemist shop is God (p. 30), or subject to bad dreams in the night (p. 18). That capacity to dream suggests his innocence, which underlies the purity of his childhood love for Lakshmi.

The central section of the novel sees Jamini going through the awkward years of puberty when he must lose that innocence about the world. He begins to understand, through his relationship with Lakshmi, that the face people show the world may not be a true expression of their inner feelings (p. 43). That sense of the isolation of the individual, 'locked up within themselves and quite alone' is an aspect of the confusion which overtakes Jamini as the certainties of his childhood start to disintegrate. Kale Khan's brutal destruction of the boy's idea of a beneficent God shatters the 'order' of the world that his childish mind had build up. Kale Khan's Pathan code seems inadequate to the kind of life Jamini must lead. He cannot explain this to anyone and as the novel proceeds we find him 'growing away from the people closest to him'. It is a time of great agitation and distress, of unfocussed anger. The relationship with Lakshmi becomes a torture, he is alienated from his parents, who regard him as 'idle', and he feels that the world is conspiring against him.

Jamini is saved from despair by his recognition of the depth of his affection for his grandfather, who has been ailing and close to death. Kale Khan seems to understand the trauma Jamini has endured, to recognise the boy's sense of his own isolation in a hostile world. He asks him no questions but gives him a shilling to spend on himself. It is a gesture that restores Jamini to a purpose in life; to assist Kale Khan in the return to India (p.

140). What would the 'return' to Hindustan mean for Jamini? In his grandfather's imagination it would give him a certainty of purpose, a tradition in which his role and his duties would be clearly defined. An escape from confusion – it is the dream of all teenagers in every culture. In fact Jamini hardly thinks about it, so bound up is he in his role as his grandfather's assistant.

The day of the Hussay procession proves to be a crucial one in Jamini's development. It is a rite of passage from one state of being into another. First the brutal and loveless consummation of his relationship with Lakshmi severs the last bonds of his attachment to the innocence that was his childhood (p. 166). Then his grandfather's death, after Jamini has felt himself to be 'anointed' as Kale Khan's successor, shatters the dream of escape forever. He is thrown back on his own resources. Though Binti arranges for him to go to the secondary school and Rahim seems to convince him that he should stay there, we are left at the end of the novel wondering what will become of Jamini. The secondary school must lead him towards the kind of cultural alienation that Kale Khan was so scathing of in Dr Gopal and the lawyer Salwan. But what alternative does the society offer now the dream of repatriation has died with Kale Khan?

In a sense that question is answered by Binti, by the manner of her life after her separation from Kale Khan. She is perhaps the most sympathetic and 'whole' character in the story. As proud and self-reliant as Kale Khan, she has not allowed the many trials of her life to make her bitter. She is a symbol of creative endurance in the novel, suggesting by her energy and independence that there *are* ways for individuals to adapt to changing conditions without losing their cultural identity, without abandoning their heritage.

Throughout the novel she is a figure of great dignity, even though she is involved in menial and seemingly demeaning work like hawking her two gallon drums of coconut-oil around the streets of Port of Spain. She has chosen this work as a means by which to assert her independence from Kale Khan, from anyone. She wore a heavy silver bracelet to let the world know that 'she was a woman of respect', who 'vended in the streets not from poverty . . . but because she set her life in the balance, and made it hold its equilibrium.' (p. 25) That is her answer to the dependence Kale Khan would wish on her (p. 24) Her Pathan steel shows too in the burial scene where she seems 'suddenly to possess the fire that Kale Khan had had in him' (p. 180).

In a less dramatic way Binti is associated with resistance and renewal *throughout* the novel. She urges Rahim to resist his depression when it seems he has accepted that his fate is sealed by the call of the Jumbie Bird. She forgets her antagonism with Kale Khan when he is ailing and secretly massages him back to health, and in the final phase of the book she reunites the family after the old man's death and restores their sense of purpose.

Like Binti, Meena maintains both her dignity and her principles through times of stress. She is self-effacing, respectful and dutiful, in a traditional way, to both Rahim and Kale Khan. She is resentful, though, of the old man's influence over her husband and Jamini, fearing that he will turn them against her. Kale Khan's dislike of women, his abandonment of his daughter and dismissal of his wife, haunt Meena. She is both pious and pragmatic, a foil to Kale Khan's dogmatic individualism. She respects Kale Khan's principles but is more of a realist about the future of the Indian community in Trinidad, '*Barp*, where we have to go? We done born and live here, what we go do in Hindustan?' (p. 90).

She supports Rahim in his period of confusion and self doubt, urging him to 'take courage'. Finally, however, when he seems to blame *her* for all their troubles she loses patience and attacks him for his loss of faith, and ironically for his lack of principle, the same weakness Kale Khan bemoans in his son (p. 120). After this argument Meena leaves Rahim and returns to her parents' home, but with the death of Kale Khan she returns to the family and again tries to support and encourage Rahim in his new enterprise. She even offers to sell the jewellry he made her as a wedding gift. We have little sense of Meena as an independent character, she appears only in the traditional role of the supportive, conscientious wife and mother.

We have even less real sense of Lakshmi. Although her relationship with Jamini is an important strand in the story she hardly features in her own person. All the images we have of her are of an isolated, lost, frightened figure, a victim. As a child she was 'always afraid, something was always going to happen'. As a young woman she seems 'cold and evasive'. She has no mother and her father's work means that she must spend much of her time alone and must make her way without any real guidance. It is little surprise that she becomes a victim of her own fundamental loneliness and insecurity, or that the relationship with Jamini breaks down.

Loneliness is an important theme in the novel. All the major characters, except perhaps Meena, endure degrees and varieties of loneliness: Rahim is struck by the 'gnawing loneliness' of his father's life; Binti weeps in the night for her lost daughter and her broken dreams; Rahim feels that the world has conspired against him and Jamini believes no one can understand the confusion and isolation he feels. The minor characters too are examples of different kinds of loneliness and alienation. Mongoroo and Kareem, the old men in the square, have no family, no hope, no identity except as derelicts. Lawyer Salwan and Dr Gopal are alienated from their ethnic culture and isolated within the middle-class creole culture they aspire to join, men whose 'bones had tautened too long, [so] they could no longer cross their legs and eat on level ground like their parents did, (p. 154). Sookiah and Hop-and-Drop are lost in a different way. Without real names, without dignity, they represent the society's 'failures' – to be patronised, ridiculed and kicked around. If most of the minor characters in the novel seem little more than caricatures held up to ridicule, Sookiah, who weeps because he has lost his name, and Hop-and-Drop, the cripple who is ridiculed, are figures that haunt the imagination (p. 115–16).

Death is another theme which pervades the novel. The call of the Jumbie bird, a type of owl, is considered to be a 'message of death'. It is a 'fearful reminder' of mortality to everyone, provoking curses and oaths from those who hear it. This ominous, haunting cry forms the Prologue to the novel. Thereafter, the Jumbie bird's sinister night time presence is never far away.

This image of death that recurrs through the narrative refers symbolically to many issues: the death of an old way of life to make way for the new (Kale Khan's death seems almost sacrificial); the death of the dream of repatriation; the decay and impoverishment created by colonialism; and the death of childhood innocence.

Despite the emphasis on loneliness, isolation and death the novel is not finally pessimistic. With the revival of Rahim and the renewal of the relationship between Jamini and his father the theme of regeneration, of death leading on to rebirth and renewal, is the final image left with the reader.

Kale Khan and all that he stands for has gone, and with his death comes the possibility of growth. The pressure is taken off Rahim who has come to terms with the conflict he feels between his traditions and the values of the society he *must* think of as his own. The old man's death releases Jamini, despite the confusions of boyhood and the difficulties of his life at school, to make the best use of his talents in the uncertain world of the *future*. In a sense he is equipping himself for self-reliance and independence, the essential Pathan qualities that Kale Khan held so dear.

A Note on Language in the Novel

The *Jumbie Bird* is full of 'nuances of language that are at once Trinidadian and particularly East Indian.'[4] One of Ismith Khan's particular achievements in the novel is to locate and *describe* characters very precisely by the language they use. His ear is finely tuned for distinguishing the variations in register and tone which are important in determining the class, background and relative status of a character. The confrontation between Dr Gopal, with his patronising anglicised way of speaking (pp. 103–5) and Kale Khan, irritated into a particularly earthy dialect by the upstart's lack of respect, suggests the range of registers within the East Indian community '. . . you lick Englishman boots over there, an' now you want to come back here an' you want to talk more big big English than Englishman he self eh?. . . You gone England, put on bow-tie an' collar an' come back here callin' me 'Old Man'? That id what they teach you over there?. . . An' what the hell you is pissin' tail son-wa-bitch, get the hell outside my door.' (pp. 103–5)

In the novel, as in life, a character's language changes with his situation, depending on who he or she is speaking to, and over time, with changes in his social position. For Jamini, however, that process is formalised by his shift from one cultural environment to another. The dialogue between Rahim and Jamini that concludes the novel suggests all that is bound up in that shift.

Rahim asks Jamini what is wrong in a relaxed, familiar, natural version of the creole the boy has been brought up in, the language of his *home*. Jamini replies, talking about school, 'I just feel as if I don't belong there' (p. 187). After only a few months at the prestigious secondary school, he is speaking is more or less standard English. Such careful and significant distinctions of language are typical of Ismith Khan's handling of dialogue throughout the novel.

Suggestions for Further Reading

John La Guerre, (ed.) *Calcutta to Caroni: The East Indians of Trinidad*, Longman, 1974.
Eric Williams *History of the People of Trinidad and Tobago*, Andre Deutsch, 1964.
Ralph de Boisiere, *Crown Jewel*, Allison and Busby, 1981.
Ismith Khan, *The Obeah Man*, Hutchinson, 1964.
V. S. Naipaul, *A House For Mr Biswas*, Andre Deutsch, 1961.
V. S. Naipaul, *The Suffrage of Elvira*, Andre Deutsch, 1958.
Samuel Selvon, *A Brighter Sun*, Alan Wingate, 1952.
Samuel Selvon, *The Plains of Caroni*, MacGibbon and Kee, 1970.

References

1 Quoted in 'Ismith Khan', an essay by Arthur Drayton in Daryl Dance (ed.), *Fifty Caribbean Writers; a bibliographical and Critical Sourcebook*, Greenwood Press, USA, 1985.
2 *Ibid.*
3 J. C. Jha, 'The Indian Heritage in Trinidad' in John La Guerre, (ed.) *Calcutta to Caroni*, Longman, 1974.
4 An unpublished paper on Ismith Khan by *Rhonda Cobham*, to which this section of my introduction is much indebted.

Glossary

Baba (p. 67) Elder or father, a term of respect
Barp (p. 90 etc) Father, a term of respect for the head of the household
Chelars (p. 80) The supporters or 'seconds' of a stick-fighter
Flambeaux (p. 152) flaming torches
Hussay (p. 15 etc) The annual Hosein festival, introduced by *Shia* Muslims to commemorate the struggle of the

	Prophet's grandsons, it became a focus for demonstrations of Indian nationalism
Hindustan	(p. 16 etc) Strictly the area of northern India occupied by Muslims, but in the novel another name for India
jaldi-jaldi	(p. 105) Quick-quick
lathi	(p. 78 etc) The stick or baton used by the stick-fighters, a heavy, wire bound pole four or five feet long
lolo	(p. 127) A slang term for penis
Nancy story	(p. 152) A fairy story, fantastical tale, nonsense
Orhani	(p. 25) A kind of head scarf
Pathan	(p. 2 etc) The people of the hills of what is now Pakistan and Afganistan. Noted for their courage and fierceness in war
Rajah	(p. 90) A prince or local ruler
Sahib	(p. 64) Usually a term of respect for a European in India, but also used as an honourary title in deference to the authority of an elder or superior
Stickfighting	(p. 78–81) Traditional form of man-to-man fighting with sticks or lathis (see above). Symbolic of a warrior tradition in both the Indian and the African community in Trinidad, but also very much a *real* test of courage and skill. The stickfighter is an important figure of courage and resitance in Caribbean literature, see Bolo in Earl Lovelace's *The Wine of Astonishment* for example.
Sure	(p. 86) A verse from the Koran, the Muslim holy book

Stewart Brown

Prologue

THE JUMBIE BIRD called in the Calabash tree, it darkened the night with its twee-twee twee-twee twee.

The night was filled with curses and oaths ... hurled at the unseen bird, its twee-twee-twee calling a message of death.

In the beds of the young, between the white sheets of lovers lying in slack nocturnal embrace; all around the Town Hall, through the Trinity Church, the Red House and Woodford Square went this fearful reminder ... awakening the sleeping night. With the twee-twee-twee of the Jumbie bird calling.

Measuring out Time for some unseen listener tossing in the dark somewhere. Whose silent thought now played on violent acts ... wickedness, and errant deeds; who feared that it came calling on this night for him.

Bird go away ... you who are cast-out of the stone bowels of your mother's insides. Bird go away ... you are the bastard child of devil and whose ... drown your calls in the bottom of the Caribbean Sea ... do not come perched in the Calabash tree with tidings of death crouched in anonymity. Muffled voices in the pillow-sacks ... sure that it was not for them, hurled curses at the unseen bird.

Come out here if you devil or whore. Come out here if you are spirit or stone ... I will plant a rock in your black throat, Bird show your face in this night you profane. But the Jumbie bird sat in the Calabash tree on Frederick Street along Woodford Square ... came night after night with its message of death and its twee-twee-twee, its melancholy cries of twee-twee, twee-twee-twee.

Bird why do you come in the middle of night, to hide your

black feathers in shadowy leaves? Show your face once ... and death will be stuffed into your own throat ... Bird, death does not hide in the Calabash tree ... it walks on open ground. It fears not stone nor man nor light of day. What cowards' eyes hide between the leaves ... and will not take the challenge on this night ... Bird come down from that Calabash tree.

The curses flew, the nights turned day, the threats went past the Jumbie bird's ear but the Jumbie bird came each night to cry ... to warn from the Calabash tree. Bird here I am ... come down with your wicked claws ... scratch out your companion's name ... let us know for whom you issue foreboding calls of twee-twee-twee in these waiting nights. Bird you're formed from the droppings of devils. The bitter gall of rubbed cucumber edges flows in your poisonous veins. Why come to these nights and blacken the moon, hiding in the Calabash tree?

But the Jumbie bird hid in the Calabash tree to count out for one pair of ears, for one sick soul lying alone somewhere in the night, one heart that knew the Jumbie bird calls would never cease *this* time in his ear.

The moon ducked under the clouds those nights, pulled the sheets of its halo's ankles tight, and in the darkness across Frederick Street, between the half-open jalousies, Jamini peeped, his eyes searching the Calabash tree in Woodford Square for the Jumbie bird's perch.

'An old man once threw a stone at the Jumbie-bird and the next day he died on the Town Hall steps.'

So a voice reminded him as he held his hands across his chest ... to press the loud flutter of his heart ... looking for the Jumbie bird in the Calabash tree ... the Jumbie bird whose voice he heard but never could see, the Jumbie bird that ran away by day and buried itself in the heart of the jungle ... but returned with its reminder, with its haunting twee-twee-twee.

1

HE WAS rapping on the landing of the dark stairway with his iron rod walking-stick that morning, the thin iron rod he used as a walking-stick.

'Boy, ay boy,' he called, then knock-knock-knock, his walking-stick struck the landing again. The tight breathing in his throat seemed louder in the dark and silence of early morning between his calls and the rapping on the stairway to awaken his son upstairs.

'Rahim, Rahim, wake up, wake up, the old man calling you,' Meena whispered.

'Wha . . . what . . . who?' Rahim's senses struggled to pull away the veil of sleep.

'Boy, ay boy.' The voice called up through the darkened stairway.

'Oh, the old man, how long he been calling?' he asked Meena.

'That's what I been trying to tell you in your half-sleep, where you put the matches?'

'Where I always put them, Meena, under the pillow.'

'Calm yourself, Rahim, you still sleepy. I already look for the matches under the pillow, but I couldn't find them, see if they didn't fall on the floor.'

Rahim swept the dark floor with the palm of his hand, the scritch-scratch sound of his palm against the rough wooden floor stopped, he found the matches, and suddenly the dark turned light, the black floors were white, and the sheets, and Meena's night-gown; and Rahim was awake, walking over to the kerosene lamp on the grey marble basin-stand.

The shadows of the rungs along the banister of the stairway swayed and see-sawed in the glow of match-light, they settled down straight up and down when the pale yellow tongue in the kerosene lamp stood still, its chimney throwing a large circle of orange light on the ceiling and Rahim went downstairs, followed by his son Jamini. The little boy pulled at the cloth braces of his little home-made trousers, trying to get one over each shoulder. His trousers pulled off to one side as he descended the stairway, side-stepping, one by one down the steps, his eyes intently fixed on the braces, his mouth puckering in and out as if his lips too tried to unravel the tangled braces.

'Come on, boy,' Rahim called angrily, 'hurry up before your Dada gets vexed.'

He let go of the braces and hurried down the steps to his grandfather's room, which was on the street level, behind the jewel shop on Frederick Street.

The old man slept on a straight flat board, an old signboard with its advertisements rubbed off, its letters worn down, its sides still framed with moulding, making it seem like an old framed picture. Meena, his daughter-in-law, used to laugh at him behind his back:

'That old man still think the Sepoy barracks outside the door . . . still keeping himself in shape in case of a skirmish . . . he goin' to kill himself sleepin' on hard-wood.'

But no one questioned Kale Khan; he hated beds, he hated women, he hated women's hands touching his clothes, his food. He hated India from which he had fled, and he hated Trinidad to which he had come to find a new life.

Somewhere in every man, etched out upon his soul, is the one resentment, one love, one hate that his days have pressed out of him. Whether it's written harshly upon the surface of his wizened face, or pierces out from the deep within his yellow eyes, it's there! It tells his story. It's in the timbre of the voice, the off-guard laughter, the hair that grows upon the mole; for so it was with Kale Khan, the mole upon his cheek that sharpened his cheek bone, the veil of dirty soapy water that spread across his tired eyes the meaning of his name . . . Kale . . . black . . . dark.

The Khans, the Pathans, the rebels of the hills were all fair, so fair that one could see the swallow of the betel juice as it coursed through their throats; but Kale Khan was dark, and with it there was something strange, some greater temper of the Pathans that came to nestle in the corners of his brain, some strength that set him apart from the tribe, some constant rumbling of the soul that looked at all that was thus, and had the fire left to say that it should not be so. These fires burned through his eyes, they jerked his face up swiftly when his body slowed, and with his large hands that had not shrunken like his body with the flow of time, he spoke his life in single words. One movement of these cold, slow-moving hands, one touch of the queen upon the checkered chess-board, one piercing angered stab from those frozen eyes, one sudden turn of the face that showed the double-haired mole caught in the halo of lamplight, and it spelled out his life, that he was a man who walked the night with no-one, that he saw the world and kept it to himself, that he laughed at it when it came to threaten him with time.

'Jamini, you listen to Dada. You not come here like the rest of these low-class coolies in bond, you hear!' he said, referring to Meena's family who had come like thousands of other Indians to Trinidad since 1845 as indentured labourers on five and ten year contracts to work on the fields of the sugar-cane plantations; and had never made enough money to return to India.

'Take-um more than God, British Raj and *Devil he-self* to kill-um this old Pathan,' he groaned, as Rahim grasped his flesh, squeezing one spot, then another, to relieve the pains that made him bang on the stairway landing with his iron rod walking-stick at night.

Jamini sat on the square block of wood he used as a pillow, watching the contortions his grandfather's face made as Rahim grasped the old man's loose flesh, squeezing one spot, then another. His face creased with the same contortions twisted out on his grandfather's until, with each grasp of Rahim's hands, with each groan and sigh of relief, Kale Khan seemed to come back to life. His eyes no longer tightly pressed together, his heavy breathing slowed and he started smiling, looking at the boy out of the corners of his eyes. His four or five blackened teeth showed between his thin dry lips, then he hung down his head again, his large ears sticking out, his bright metallic grey hair cut short, looking like a spinning ball, starting in the centre and growing off in tangents, thick, strong. His hair seemed to have the same firmness that his voice did; they were staunch refusals to lie down and die, defiantly laughing in the face of time, which must have tired and gone on its way to gnaw and wear on other bones, leaving Kale Khan quite to himself to decide when he was good and ready to retire from the battle that he constantly fought with everything about him. He looked at the boy again.

'*You* Pathan son . . . Pathan grandson . . . mus' never be coward . . . born to fight and fight like LION . . . don't forget.' His head lowered again.

'Lower down, boy . . . lower, in between shoulders, *jaldi-jaldi*, (faster-faster),' he said to Rahim, who started a fast pat-pat-pat-pat-pat massaging of his shoulders and shoulder-blades. He cleared his throat, looking at Jamini who faced him.

'Saturday today, boy?'

'Yes, Dada.'

'An' we goin' to the Square? We goin' to the Square, you an' me today?'

'Yes, Dada, soon as we finish breakfast we goin' to the Square, . . . an' we going to Hindustan too, Dada?'

'Yes, boy, Dada carryin' you back to Hindustan, get away from all these worthless scamps and vagabonds, but you mus' learn good, good, good in school.' Jamini's large black eyes opened wider as he spoke.

'Dada, we goin' back to Hindustan and never come back to Trinidad when I grow big, only you and me, Dada, and get a sword like yours.'

'Good man . . . good man . . . good man, boy,' the old man guffawed in the still and silent dawn with only the far cock's crowing somewhere in the darkness. 'Rahim, you get nice clothes for this boy to wear, and strong shoes for his feet, tall Blucher boots for this boy not to sprain foot. All right now, next side, next side, boy. If you rub one side only next side gets jealous, get different, different pain . . . don't sit down and rub, boy . . . stand up, you not old man like me,' he said angrily to Rahim, who scrambled to his feet and went around the bed to rub the other shoulder.

'*Jaldi-jaldi*, boy.'

The darkness of early morning was beginning to steal away into the shadowy corners of his room, and the light of early tropical Trinidad morning began peeping through the cracks and crevices of the wooden partition and the doors beyond, that separated his room from the yard. Now the designs, the letters and pictures on the walls came to life, making the tiny tongue of light from the cup flame which lit up his room seem weak and dull against the slowly spreading brightness of morning.

The walls were an incongruous jig-saw puzzle of large colourful cinema posters. He had paid twelve cents to have his room papered by one of the boys who went about with a large pail of boiled starch and a wide brush, sticking posters of coming attractions on old fences around the city. There were incomplete words on different pieces of posters, BOD or SOU, and a small upside-down trade mark of Paramount Pictures in one corner, with its sharp mountain peak forked by lightning, and circled by a ring of stars in black and white.

At one side of his bed on which the bed-board lay was an old counter with dust-covered objects on it: jeweller's tools, files, several sizes of hammers, a snuff-box, pliers, the traced-out patterns of pliers which had been removed, leaving their stark impressions on the dusty counter, and a pair of oval steel-rimmed bifocal spectacles, wound over and over at the bridge with black thread, the edges of the smaller lenses traced out in brown upon the surface of the larger lenses.

Jamini's eyes fixed on another item, in the corner of the room, that looked as though it were currently in use; it was an old bent-wood rocking chair, its arms and seat shone with a polish of use and wear. He had sat in it, given himself a sharp rock backwards, and the thing went arching through the air in the most spine-tingling way, carrying him backwards, heading for the ground as if it were going to somersault in a complete circle. Suddenly, it started coming back to earth again. He had sat in it, told himself over and over that it would go only so far, but each time he had hurled himself backwards, he had the most hilarious, frightening joy within that fraction of a second when it was uncertain whether the thing would capsize carrying him over with it, or whether it would start forward again.

The sun was well up now and two chickens scratched in the

dirt outside the door, cluck-clucking, waiting for the handful of corn the old man threw to them every morning.

'All right, boy . . . go on now,' he said to Rahim, who sniffed the flavour of fried onions and eggplant frying in coconut oil which Meena was fixing for breakfast upstairs.

Jamini watched his grandfather prepare for the morning. He put on his sleeveless green flannel vest, pulled on his loose pair of trousers bunched up at his waist by a wide cracked leather belt with a great brass buckle, then hooked his iron rod walking-stick to the foot-bar of the rocking chair, and backing out of the room, dragged the chair out into the sunlight, where he sat in it, pulled his feet up, tucked them under his legs, and hung his walking-stick off to the side of its handle. He unfolded an old newspaper he had under his arm, placed half of it on the ground where his feet would rest later on, and put on his 'specs,' peering over the top of them as if to make sure that all was ready for his retirement into the old newspaper.

'What you lookin' lookin', boy . . . never see a man read newspaper before?' he said to Jamini, who was watching his movements curiously.

'Yes, Dada.' The boy hardly heard what the old man said, his scrutiny of the old man's movements made him think of so many things. 'Dada, you think we could carry anybody else when we go back to India?'

'G'wan, boy . . . g'wan upstairs, time for you to eat breakfast, before your mother start callin' you . . . and make haste if you want to go to the Square today.'

'Oh, all right,' he said disappointedly.

Upstairs Meena was turning the last flat bread (*roti*) from one side to the other: she turned her head to the stairway and called,

'Rahim . . . Jam . . . breakfast.'

'All right,' Rahim answered from the bedroom where he had gone back to lie down until breakfast was ready.

'Jam . . . Jamini.'

No answer.

'Rahim, where that boy? He living downstairs or up here? If your father want to take charge of the child why he don't cook for him and feed him as well?'

'*Jamini*! Come here, boy, why don't you listen to your mother?' Rahim shouted down from the window to Jamini, who was throwing corn to the chickens, grain by grain. He threw the whole handful to them, dusted off his hands on the sides of his trousers and came running up the steps.

'You want to carry your clothes and shoes downstairs and live with your Dada,' Meena said angrily. 'Tell me . . . you lost your tongue now . . . you want me to put your food on a plate and send it downstairs for you? Or you want your Dada to teach you how to cook and wash your own clothes? I really don't know what get into this boy.'

'Leave the boy alone, let him go and wash his teeth,' Rahim said, coming out to breakfast, putting his other arm through his shirt-sleeve. 'If the boy want to play a little before breakfast let him play.'

'Now look at that. Now you accusing *me* of not wantin' the boy to play. Is play he playin' when he forget about eatin' and sleepin', talkin' all kind of nonsense with the old man downstairs?'

'Come on and eat, boy, and listen to your mother. I'm tired of hearing complaints about this idleness of yours.'

Jamini went to his room after breakfast. His bed lay ruffled in the gallery that overhung the sidewalk of Frederick Street below, and the window looked out into the Square, with its eight foot high iron bars in the shape of pointed spears painted red, and weathered to a dull brown, the tips of the spears touched with yellow. From beyond came the sweet smell of the Calabash, their large shiny green shells flashing like mirrors on the tree in the morning sun, the almost sickly-sweet odour of one shell which must have ripened and broken open, spilling out hundreds of sticky wet seeds. He listened to his parents still arguing outside.

'You lettin' that old man rule your whole life and the child's life too, why you don't give him the child, is that what he want?'

He heard his grandfather's voice shouting into the stairway which he never climbed, but used only as a tunnel which carried along his needs, orders and complaints.

'Woman don't know how to bring up Pathan child. You want to make *woman* out of this boy?'

He had heard all the way from downstairs, the boy thought. 'Pathan have-um ears like telephone,' he remembered his Dada saying some time ago, and he had imagined him putting his ear to the ground listening for hoof-beats in the old days when he was in the Royal Pathan Regiments of Her Majesty.

'You hear how the old man ready to 'buse me so early Saturday mornin', Rahim, you hearin' my troubles so soon in the mornin'.'

'Don't argue with him, Meena.'

'Don't argue with him—don't argue with him, don't argue with him. Is that all you can say?'

'Jam . . . ready yet, boy?' Rahim called.

'Yes, Daddy.'

He came into the kitchen, both hands stuck into the side pockets of his new trousers, the first pair of short pants that a tailor had made for him with side pockets and a fob. Meena had made all the others on a Singer sewing machine, which they called a 'hand machine'. Only tailors had foot machines, and the boy had thought that one had to have a foot machine to sew 'pocket pants' until his grandfather got him the first pair of pocket pants from a tailor who worked with a hand machine.

'All right, go downstairs to Dada, and take your hands out of them pockets when you go down the steps,' Meena said.

'Don't turn 'round an' say is I who spoilin' the boy when you good and ready, you think he know what it is to bring children in this world . . . why he don't make his own child . . . tell me that?'

Rahim still sat at the table drinking black tea from a large chipped enamel cup as Meena removed the other dishes and put them in the sink.

'What you want me to do, Meena, you know the old man ain't have too much longer to live: let him enjoy his only grandson.'

Meena stood winding the long braid of hair which had come loose from her bun; she complained as if speaking to herself as she moved back and forth between the breakfast table and the sink.

'That old man's goin' to live longer than anyone in this house, he ain't have strength in his body, but when he ready to 'buse . . . well . . .'

'You have a clove to put in this tea, Meena?' Rahim asked.

Without looking at him, without answering, she took a small tin from the shelf and while her eyes were set on opening the can of cloves, Rahim put his arm around her waist, pressing his cheek against hers. He inhaled deeply the sweet smell of dried herbs from Meena's blouse, which she always stored in a chest made of cedar.

'Meena, Meena,' he said slowly, consolingly, 'he won't kill the child, is his own flesh and blood.'

She stood somewhat abashed in his embrace, like a child who had done some misdeed and wanted to say that she was sorry, but couldn't, and hung her head low, not knowing how to say that she was sorry that she spoke so sharply, how to let her eyes meet his.

'No, he won't kill the child, Rahim,' she said, resting her head on his shoulder, her voice almost down to a whisper, 'but sometimes it frightens me. I don't want the boy to grow up and turn out to hate his mother, you know how your father took you away from your mother when you was just a boy. He never even let your own mother come to see you,' she said, almost in tears.

Rahim held her face in both his hands, looking into her eyes as intently as he looked at a fine piece of filigree jewellery he made, and he saw the black irises of her eyes opening and closing like a strange species of a black flower beneath the surface of water, pleading to be allowed to come to the surface, to the air and the sun, and the hissing of insects' wings in the fields of morning, pleading to break out of the numb silence in which it wavered and wavered. With the tips of his thumbs he touched her eyelids, they closed, and he held her in his arms again, saying:

'Meena, Meena, don't cry, don't mind too much.'

'Bring coconut oil for this boy's head, you want him to catch sick in this hot sun?' the old man shouted up the stairway.

Rahim had tried to explain to Meena that the old man shouted because he had become accustomed to the ways of his army life, yelling out orders from horseback as they rode in the open plains. Meena always felt that the old man's voice was cold, and hard, and filled with anger.

Rahim poured some oil into the top of a Nugget shoe-polish tin and took it downstairs.

'You want me to put oil in the boy's head, *Barp*?'

'No, no, leave it there, go on, you have work to do.'

'Dada, you think I could have that Nugget tin when you finish with it?' Jamini asked. 'Dada, they give away valuable prizes for it, Snakes and Ladders sets, and a puzzle with a clown's face in a glass box with two fast-moving steel balls for his eyes, and you have to get them in, and big toys too and wind-up trains . . .'

'Hold up—hold up—boy. First coconut oil on that head, then you can take tin,' he said, laughing, as he left the room to go out and fill his cup with water from the pipe in the yard.

'Sometimes I wish that that boy was a girl-child,' Meena was saying upstairs.

Jamini peeped through the crack in the door to see what his grandfather was doing, he was glad that he had not heard, then there would be another argument, and they would never go to the Square.

'Your mother,' Meena was saying to Rahim, 'does grieve for her daughter. Every Sunday when she come here to see you, I can read it in her face. If only she had her daughter today. You think your father had any right to give away his own daughter to a total stranger in the Cawnpore Railway Station? You think I would like anybody to do that to me?'

'Meena, he didn't give away the child to a stranger, he left my sister with a doctor friend of his.'

'No, no, Rahim, your mother saw all this with her own two eyes. The old man think girl children is too much trouble, and when he got ready to leave India he gave away the child.'

Jamini went over to take a closer look at the tin; if it was a small four-cent size they wouldn't give prizes, it had to be a twelve-cent size, and only the rich people used that much shoe polish. It was strange seeing a large Nugget cover in his home; he looked carefully, 'Nugget Ox-Blood, six oz. net wt'. He smiled and put it back on the counter, right in the circle the coconut oil had made, so that his grandfather would not know that he was prowling about, he never let anyone come into his room, far less start touching things on his counter. Through the peep-hole he saw his grandfather coming back with the water in his cup, still muttering curses in Hindustani under his breath; Jamini tip-toed back over to the bed where he sat on the bed-board, both his hands in his' pockets, his legs swinging to and fro, looking fascinated at the pictures on the wallpaper.

The old man poured some of the coconut oil into the palm of his hand and began slapping it into the boy's head; he could feel the thick skin of his grandfather's hand, hear the strands of hair mashing together between the old man's fingers, and he saw the fine corrugation of his close-cut fingernails. Then the old man passed his hand, wet with coconut oil, across the boy's face, looking into his eyes, as if saying:

'This is my blood and bones . . . this is my flesh, sewn together with the mystery of unending time. This is the seed of the unknown that I have drawn out from the soil . . . the seed that knows no end . . . that bears the name of Kale Khan . . . the darkness shall not fall upon it.'

And he rubbed the boy's face again, his hands sliding slowly across his forehead, pressing his thumb, his hardened hands upon the muscles of the boy's neck, whispering to his soul alone that this seed must grow, that he was putting into it in his own being so that it might not stumble in the rocky soil, he was moulding it so that it would be nimble, and bend and sway away from the hard ground, go deeper and find nourishment and life, and never die. And the boy's eyes looked into his as if he understood, as if he knew that his grandfather lived for him, that after all the deeds he'd done, after all the tools of his trade had become idle, in the end it was he, Jamini, in whom the whole universe of his Dada's life had come to centre, to find its one reward.

'Boy . . . ay boy, we goin' to the Square now,' he called to Rahim, and the two of them started down Frederick Street, hand in hand, the old man dressed in his black serge suit which had fallen on the stoop of his shoulders. He wore large heavy Blucher boots, the thongs by which he pulled them on sticking out above his heels. He had on his white shirt, worn only when some one had died, washed with his own hands. Unironed, unstained, and lily-white, its small collar points curled and crimped about his loose throat, its top button replaced by a large brown trouser button, which he had sewn on with brown thread, to match the button, and slit the button-hole of the shirt to allow its passage.

2

THE city of Port of Spain had already sucked in its flood of employees into the shops and stores along Frederick Street when the old man and the boy walked out into the sun. The old man peered up at the bluish hills of St Ann's at the end of Frederick Street, sheltering his eyes with one hand as he scoured the hills; Jamini imitated him.

'It look as if is a dry day today, boy,' he said; then looked at Jamini. 'And what news that mountain have for you today, rain, or no rain?'

'I think,' the boy placed his hand over his forehead again, looked towards the hills, then faced the old man, 'maybe tomorrow a little shower, but dry today.'

'Good man, boy, good man,' the old man laughed, then they both laughed.

A late employee of the Frederick Street shops came tearing down, ringing his bicycle bell all the way, and when that was insufficient warning to pedestrians, he shouted.

'Out 'er the way, man . . . you can't see bicycle comin' through?'

He almost hit a woman carrying a basket on her head, on her way home from the market.

'Ah hope your boss fire you for oversleepin', you damn rascal.'

'Go to hell,' the cyclist shouted at her over his shoulder, as he pedalled on down Frederick Street, his hips swaying from left to right, his feet pumping hard on the pedals.

'These blasted bicycles is only trouble . . . trouble-trouble-trouble-trouble . . . that is all,' she muttered to herself as she shifted her basket of provisions to a more stable balance on her head, and climbed on the sidewalk at the entrance to Woodford Square, followed by Jamini and Kale Khan.

The paths of the Square were laid out like the lines of the Union Jack, in the centre of which stood the statue of a stooped old man, Sir Ralph Woodford, standing in a large basin of water splashing up to his knees. In his damp tall boots he stood all day and all night, one hand gingerly feeling his stomach between vests and coats, his right knee bent slightly forward, and his other hand resting in the small of his back, fingers curled, half-closed. His face and head were smudged with bird droppings, left as they tired of flight and perched on his head, or came there to flit and flutter their feathers amid small rainbows in the cool spray of water. Unmoved by their visits, he kept a constant vigil over the Square, looking out into nothing. It was he who had suggested bringing Indians to Trinidad after slavery was abolished, and they had started coming in 1845.

'Dada, don't you think that Sir Woodford is lonely up there? You think that he's thinking something whole day, whole night?'

'That damn rascal standing up there still wonderin' if he do good t'ing, bringin' all these people from Hindustan. Go on and play, boy. Dada goin' down this side.'

Jamini stood directly in front of the statue, then looked at the spot where its eyes focused, there was something special about that spot, he thought, then dismissed it, looking into the eyes again.

'Sir Woodford, Sir Woodford sir . . . I bet you don't know me.'

The statue looked at him, in austere silence, beginning now to look more severe, until he could tell what Sir Woodford was thinking.

'Boy . . . I know you . . . your father . . . and your father's father.'

His Dada's friends had said this to him when he became too playful and too familiar with them; he ran quickly around to the back of the statue.

'Sir Woodford, Sir Woodford, I bet you don't know who is hiding behind you,' he said, tip-toeing cautiously as a cat, his head tipped to one side, his ear cocked in the direction of Sir Woodford's lips. As soon as he saw the side of his face, and the rims of his eyes, he could tell that the statue was playing a game with him, that Sir Woodford was laughing quietly all the time, holding his breath to keep from laughing out loud.

'You knew who it was all the time. You're just pretending,' the boy said, laughing hysterically as he came back into Sir Woodford's full vision.

The statue stood in a basin, which four half-fish, half-women with swollen iron breasts supported on their shoulders, staring down at the tiny fishes in the water which were put there by the City Council to eat the breeding mosquitoes. Their tails curled around, and were covered with large thick scales up to their waists.

Jamini closed his eyes, turned his face away with a cringing expression of disgust, as he put out his hand and touched the ugly green scales, then he stood looking at the woman's faces.

'What awful awful, terrible things you've done,' he whispered to the busts. 'Dada says that people who do bad things are turned into all kinds of things.'

Perhaps theirs was not too bad a sin, he thought, since their upper half was very pretty, the lips smiling, the eyes not at all like Sir Woodford's that pierced the tree behind which one was hiding.

As he walked away from the fountain to join the old man, he watched the water fall on Sir Woodford's head, dripping off in hundreds of tiny trickles around the rim of the basin, so that the women below were always half dry, their awful fish-tails, wet green and slimy, glinted in the sun.

'Dada,' he went running to his grandfather, 'why did they put Sir Woodford to stand in that water all the time?'

'That poor man standin' up there all day and night thinkin' something, he need water to keep his brains cool. What else you think he up there for?'

'You think he knows me and you, Dada . . . you think he knows Mongroo and Kareem?' The boy pointed to the two old men who played chess with Kale Kahn; they were smiling at the earnestness with which he asked these questions, and took a kind of vicarious pleasure in the way Kale Khan spoke about Sir Woodford.

'He know well what wrong t'ing he gone an' do . . . bring all these people here to work and sweat in hot sun. Worthless scamp like that . . .'

'Dada, I bet it's you who shot him down that time at the Princes Town Hussay.'

Mongroo put his hand to his mouth to keep from laughing, and buried his face in the grass. The old man was laughing too.

'Don't talk nonsense, boy. Good t'ing he wasn't there, otherwise I shoot he, he moomah and he poopah too.'

The Square was a place where tired shoppers from Frederick Street came to rest their feet, to refresh themselves by laving their faces with the water in the fountain. Often they were dwellers from the hidden hills and hamlets, tucked away in forgotten corners of Trinidad, who know no one in the great city, and went to Woodford Square when the heat of the pavement scorched their bare feet. They had their shoes strung about their necks as they squatted in the shade of a great sweeping Saman tree, unfolding their lunches from large-sized handkerchiefs, pulling at the knots with their fingers, unconcerned with the city dwellers' laughter and humouring.

The city people went there only during the very hot days of August, and in the evenings; nurses in uniforms promenaded with the children of wealthy people, warning the children not to notice or attract the attention of the country people, particularly not to eat anything they might offer.

The bells of the Trinity Church tolling out the hour from its tall steeple broke into the silence of intense meditation with which the old men watched the chessboard as they became more and more engrossed in the game. Jamini stooped, balanced on his feet, his two hands below his chin and about his face, as if waiting for a break in the game when conversation would start again.

'*Rajah Rani*,' the old man said as he cornered Mongroo's queen, and the boy's hand slipped from his chin, causing him to fall sideways into the lap of the old man, and a break in the dead silence livened the group again.

Kale Khan took out a red clay pipe from his jacket pocket, and from the inside breast-pocket a creased envelope, almost cream-coloured with age, from which he shook, little by little, some black and brown herbs into the cup of his palm, tapping the envelope with his index finger.

'Khan Sahib,' Mongroo said, 'even if we ain't go back to Hindustan, these children should go. I does feel too bad when I watch them and see that theyis I ndian. I does say, "But what right these children and them have to stop here?" We old people was foolish, man, but the children an' them shouldn't have to suffer for we wrongs.'

'This boy have to go back, mus' go back to learn what kind people he born from . . . one day . . .' Kale Khan's voice trailed off as he passed some of the herbs to the other two men.

They massaged the herbs in the palms of their hands, the two men pressed their thumbs upon their palms with the herbs between, and Kale Khan pressed the herbs from one spot to another until he had a flat disc, which he rolled into a ball, and pressed it out again, doing this over and over. Then they put the three wads together, and Kale Khan stuffed it into the clay pipe with three or four quick sharp nudges with his finger. A look at the mouth of the pipe, a few more quick nudges, this time his finger entered the mouth of the pipe, then he set it down at his side in the grass.

'You mean to say all you boys didn't have sense to know it was only dry, dry lies those rascals tell you when they say that you would get rich and make plenty money plantin' sugar cane in Trinidad?'

'Baba,' Kareem said respectfully, addressing Kale Khan, 'we was young boys, we thought we would run away from home, make big fortune, and then we go back to we village; how we could ever know that when we come here they would give we cutlass and hoe to work in this hot sun? First day Mongroo get so much big, big blisters on his hands, he couldn't even hold the hoe the next mornin'.'

'You hear that, boy . . . you hearin' well what that worthless scamp Woodford tell these boys? Fool them and bring them come Trinidad side, you ain't go learn all that in History book. Listen good so you will know what you come from. You goin' to see your grandmother tomorrow . . . don't let that worthless woman put foolish idea inside your head . . . you tell her you *want* to go back Hindustan side,' the old man said, as he took out a large red handkerchief from his breast-pocket, folded it in four, and placed it over the mouth of the pipe.

With both palms together, fingers locked, he then inserted the top end of the pipe between his palms, its thick, blackened, resined rim sticking out below, and with his eyes closed, his head cocked on one side, Mongroo put a match to it for him. He hauled the rich brownish-greyish smoke directly into his lungs in deep long draughts, which hollowed out his cheeks, making the most pained grimaces as the pipe's mouth smouldered and darkened, livened and cooled, with each filling of his empty lungs with the wet-looking smoke that he emitted; flat, pale, and thin, their substances and resins soaking into his bones and marrow before the emission of the limp smoke. The boy, sitting to one side, imitated the pained, twisted expressions he saw on the old man's face as he inhaled, pressing his eyes tightly shut.

'Hey,' the old man said, tugging sharply at his ear, a wide smile on his face.

The boy's eyes jumped suddenly; saw his grandfather grinning.

'Don't make a monkey face like that. Want face to stop like that, then nobody want to watch your face.'

'Dada, you are a monkey face, you,' he giggled, pushing at the old man. 'You monkey,' he screamed, laughter curling and twisting his body as the old man reached for him and rolled him in the grass, pressing his knuckles against the boy's ribs.

As the old men became engrossed in their chessboard again, Jamini wandered off to one side of the fruit trees beyond. He looked about for the watchman, who was his grandfather's friend and came over occasionally to play chess; no watchman in sight. It was easier for boys like Tommy, the neighbour's boy, they could throw stones at the fruit trees and run when they saw the watchman coming. Jamini could never get away with things like Tommy. There was the time when the watchman chased Tommy and he stood behind a tree singing:

Watchie, Watchie,
Don't hold me,
Hold the man behind the tree,
He stole money and I stole grass.
Watchie, Watchie.
Haul your arse.

No, that would never do for Jamini, he had to be cautious.

The benches in the Square were painted green, to disappear into the colour of the surrounding grass and trees, yet most of the year the grass did not grow at all in the heart of the city. Then, when the rainy season came it shot up so fast over night that the old watchman who scraped the dry leaves from the lawns all year was lost trying to cut the grass with his yard-long scythe, while it grew faster and faster, always springing up behind him as he went from one spot to another.

It became one of the dreams that haunted Jamini those nights. He dreamt that he was lost in the tall grass, stumbling around, trying to find his way out, but the grass grew taller and taller, becoming thicker and harder to spread apart with his hands as he called 'Dada . . . Dadah . . . Da . . . Dadah,' knowing that no one could hear him. Then it became dark, and he could hear them searching for him, but he knew that they could never cut away the grass fast enough to reach him, to reach him before Sir Woodford did.

'Boy,' he heard Sir Woodford say. Then his head, with hair like a pack of snakes, popped up from the grass, his curly fingers milling around in his fists.

'Boy, you are going to stay here with me, and stand up in that water. Do you hear me, boy? I know you, boy, and your father, and your father's father; and I'm not afraid of you, nor your father, nor your father's father.'

'Dada . . . Dada,' he screamed, those nights, until Rahim came and woke him up, shivering and wet with tears, his hair soft and wet with the sweat of night; and he was so happy, he laughed and cried at the same time, when he looked through his window and saw the Square across the street, and felt Meena's hand stroking through his hair.

Around the benches on which he sat the earth was red, and nothing grew. With the warm, pleasant climate of Trinidad the outdoors became the home of the old and decrepit Indians like Mongroo and Kareem, to while away their time, their entire lives, what was left of them. Many of them had left the sugar plantations long ago and come to the city. They had lost their trade, their ways of ploughing and sowing, they had come to the city to wander, to spend the rainy nights under the Town Hall, curled into the stoops of the buildings across from the Square, dreaming dreams of rains falling and monsoons pelting at their eardrums somewhere in Hindustan, only to be awakened by boys of Jamini's age who threw stones at them from behind the bars of the Square at night, or the steel-heeled policemen who stomped and clack-clack-clacked at their ears, moving them on into the lonely wet corners of night that wept with them till morning came.

The old men sat in the park from day to day. They mended their trousers with scraps of cloth thrown out by the stores on Frederick Street, sometimes they shaved and cut each other's hair, sitting on old wooden condensed milk boxes; and when any of the festivals came around when people made offerings to the poor, they, as though they were trying to store up food for months of barren times, kept going back to the Square with the smell of curried lamb in their beards, their pockets filled with sweetmeats. Looking through sad eyes as they hung about Woodford Square, they themselves never troubled anyone, but their vacant faces disturbed the delicate feelings of the passers by who made protest after protest to have them banished once and for all from Woodford Square.

At one time it was a kind of Tourist Bureau which tried to uproot them; they felt that they were an eyesore to the tourists who came from America, England and Europe to visit this beautiful tropical paradise which they had photographed beautifully and advertised in travel magazines. The old derelicts in some way marred the scenery by littering the park with their soiled shreds of clothing, their sad eyes filled with a strange yearning and discontent that everyone shunned, but had to put up with, since they had abandoned the last vestiges of life when they left the sugar cane plantations and came to the city to wander.

The newspapers joined in the attempt to comb them out of the corners of Woodford Square. Some laughed at the newspaper article, others felt that the paper was justified in calling them 'A band of rogues and vagabonds . . . the ranks of the self-determined unemployed . . . who were a public nuisance, chewed betel-nut and spat upon the walks, leaving the most nauseating stains on the cement.'

The news went on for some time, Kale Khan went to the

Square to read the developments to the old men, most of whom were illiterate; then the attack upon the old men came to its climax when the case was taken up by one of the most prominent lawyers of Port of Spain, whose father, together with others who like Kale Khan, had homes, incomes and families, also went there to revive and exchange tales of the old country.

The most scandalous of all the protests, complaints and attempts to regain Woodford Square started when a new Governor, a young man for his position, instead of helping to find laws which would gaol the squatters and park-dwellers, took sides with them, and the same paper which hurled insults at them before, now had to print the speech of the Governor.

'The people of Trinidad, and the citizens of the capital city of Port of Spain, have all benefited from the labours of these lost souls in one way or another. They have made with their very hands this island which we call home . . . it is their home, we should be glad that they will let us share it with them. It is most dishonourable to spurn these men now that their youths and strengths and energies are spent in building up the colony. These are a race of uprooted people thrown into a vacuum now that "Sugar King has become Pauper".'

The old men wanted to write a few slogans on banners and go to the Red House, proclaiming the fair play of the new young Governor.

'Is just another trick . . . wait an' see . . . wait an' see', Kale Khan warned.

Many people disapproved of the young Governor's ways; he was seen in public walking about in shorts, talking to everyone; some said that he even went to Woodford Square to chat with the old men.

'He jus' don't behave like a Governor man, how we go have respect for him? He is just a boy, he must be have a father who do some great thing for the King and they send him out on this job,' the rumours went about; and soon afterwards he was sent back to the Mother Country, and an older man was sent to take his place. A man who was seen only at public functions and who dressed in official uniform.

The old men still had the Square, they waited for someone to come by and pay them three or four cents to carry heavy loads and bundles, which seemed to the chief source of commerce that the perpetual residents of Woodford Square carried on, and since no one wanted to share the Square with them, they carried on in their accustoned way. At night they spread out their thick sheets of cardboard, placed several sheets of old newspapers on it, and went fast asleep on the benches. The rest of Port of Spain used it only as a 'short cut' to cross diagonally from one point to another in going about the city.

'Wait an' see, next t'ing they go lock off the water in that damn fountain,' Kale Khan warned his companions that Saturday in the Square, as the boy took his hand and they walked toward Frederick Street.

'An don't forget, don't eat when you go to that old woman house,' he grumbled to Jamini, 'she go feed you poison just to grieve me, watch what she put in the food. I don't know why you poopah and moomah does let you go to see she at all.'

3

SUNDAY is not a day for crying, he thought, looking out of his window into the Square. A woman was pulling a child by his outstretched arm. They were both well dressed, perhaps on their way to Sunday School at the Trinity Church beyond. The child did not want to go with his mother; his crying sounded sad coming from the deserted Square.

A quiet empty feeling lay along Frederick Street, its shops and stores shut tight; no one crossed in the Square, and when the trams passed by he could see the conductor, from upstairs, sprawled out on the back seat of the tram, the brass buttons on the coat of his uniform loosened, his cap in his hand, fanning himself slowly with it as the tram grumbled past, empty.

'Don't eat anything in that old woman house, she go poison you,' he remembered his Dada saying, as he waited for her, looking to see when she would enter the gate to the Square beyond, after she had made her rounds of the city with her two gallon cans, one in either hand, containing coconut oil. Through the streets of Port of Spain, Binti went on Sundays, one gallon can in each hand, a funnel made of tin and an inch-tall pitcher-shaped measuring cup, with a handle so small that it would fit only fingers as tiny as hers. From a string around her waist the funnel and measuring cup dangled in front of her, clinking softly in rhythm with the slip-slap-slapping of her open slippers.

Through the Sunday-quiet streets of Port of Spain, and deep into the residential suburbs of Woodbrook, St James and Belmont she went on foot, shrilly calling out her home-made product in a tiny voice:

'Get your coconut oil—cooooo—cooooo—nut oil—' she called through the empty streets and alley-ways, stopping at her regular customers, advertising to would-be buyers the quality of her goods.

'Mummie, mummie, what's happened to Dadie? Isn't she going to come today?'

'I don't know, Jam, I don't know, son, perhaps she ain't well today.'

The boy said 'No . . . No . . . No . . .', and he cried out loud.

'What that boy cryin' for, anyt'ing wrong with the child?' the old man called up through the stairway, knock-knock-knocking with his iron rod, and with a cough he cleared his throat.

'It's his Dadie he crying for,' Meena said, 'it look as if she ain't comin' today.'

'Police must be lock she up, she sellin' without licence on Sunday. Tell him dat. She only makin' dat boy grieve an' grieve just to make me suffer. Better dey put she in gaol.'

He saw the day moving as he kept looking out of the window, moving up on the iron rails of the Square as the sun rose higher in the sky, and the pictures of past Sundays ran across his mind; the way Kale Khan had shouted up the stairway when Binti came to visit.

'Let them put that worthless woman in gaol, then we go see who she workin' for when Court House eat up all the money she make walkin' about Sunday 'pon Sunday. They go lock she up one day when she poison somebody with all that rubbish she fixin' up. They go lock she up one day . . . one day . . . an' throw key in the sea.'

In its vague and mysterious way word got back and forth between the two; somehow Binti heard his remarks about imprisoning her. She said,

'He still playin' soldier. Now he playin' British spy; let him report me to police, the damn good-for-nothing man.'

Through the air, through the distance between Quarry Street and Frederick Street the remark came back to him.

'Don't eat any rubbish when you go to that house, you hear me, boy. She go poison you just to see me suffer,' he warned his grandson.

'You see how the old man settin' up the child against that poor old lady for nothing at all, why you don't talk to him or something?' Meena pleaded with Rahim.

'The child have more understanding than all of you people put together,' Rahim told her, tired of the constant bickering.

The old man said, 'When I die, is that worthless woman who kill me; she say they go put me in the grave before she, but I tell you, when they put me in grave, and they lock she up in prison for poisoning somebody with all that rubbish she sellin' without a licence . . . Sunday 'pon Sunday . . . ants will bring the message to me from six feet below the ground.'

'Co-co-nut oil . . . Co-co-nut oil . . . Get your nice co-co-nut oil.'

Jamini thought he heard her voice calling. His ears were so attuned to the sound of her calls, he wasn't sure that he heard her calling, for all morning he kept thinking he heard her voice in the street.

'Co-co-nut oil . . . Co-co-nut oil . . . get your nice co-co-nut oil.'

He listened again, then rushed to the window. She was entering Woodford Square through the gate by the Red House.

'Dadie just crossed the street,' he said, as he rushed past Meena.

'Oh!' Meena said, 'I'm so glad nothing ain't wrong with the old lady.'

Kale Khan heard the boy's anxious voice from downstairs and muttered:

'I don't know why we can't give that worthless old woman somet'ing every week. She have to go all over town disgracing the family name.'

Jamini waited at the top of the stairs, watching her mount them slowly.

Her eyes caught his once, she smiled at him, then looked back down to make sure of her footing on the steps.

In the centre of her forehead, where every married woman wore a bright spot of colour, usually red, Binti had hers tattooed in blue-black. It had faded, and worked into her skin. It shone on the surface with the oil and sweat of warm Sunday mornings, the sidewalks and the alley-ways she had left behind before she came to Rahim's house to take her grandson to the Coal Shop for the day up Quarry Street.

She stopped at the landing between the two flights of stairs and put her cans in the corner, took the edge of her white *orhani* and wiped her eyelids, lifting her thick spectacles to her forehead.

She wore a discoloured skirt of white, drawn tight about her waist; an apron made of flour sacks, with faded letters of pale pink and blue, "Harvest Queen Flour." The letters circled a picture of a maid, her arm filled with sheaves of wheat.

'We was just sayin' it look as if you take sick today, *mai*. This boy start cryin' an' cryin'.'

'Poor people can't afford to take sick, Meena . . . what to do,' she said haltingly, coming up the second flight of stairs.

She sat down on the top step next to the boy and placed her arms around him.

'So yuh cryin' like if you is a girl-child?' She kissed him on his forehead. 'Mustn't cry, you t'ink that I forget you?'

He felt her arm about his neck, her heavy silver bracelet. It had rubbed against the marble-shaped bones of her wrists and made them blue. She had worn it for the world, for the world to know that she was a woman of respect, of a higher cut and class; that she laboured and vended in the streets not from poverty, nor want, but because she set her life in the balance, and made it hold its equilibrium. She smelled faintly of coconut oil, of the delicate aroma that floated out of the large cauldron with grated nut boiling and bubbling; and on the right side of her nose was a tiny hole where she had worn a beautiful nose-ring long ago. It had closed up now, it had sealed itself tight, with only a faint pin point showing. Unlike other women, she had not placed a thin bit of wire, or wood, or a piece of thread to keep it open. The nose-ring that Kale Khan had made, 'so fine that the spider in all its mystery would look upon it with wonder' now lay in a matchbox in Quarry Street. Not for *her* daughter, the lost daughter at the Cawnpore Railway Station long ago. For her grand-daughter? No, there was only Jamini . . . but perhaps for his bride . . . perhaps she'd live to see his bride.

'You must be tired, *mai*. Come, sit down, let me gi'e you some tea.'

'Not now, Meena, I just come to rest these oil cans here, I want to go see Bissoon, that Government chemist man in the next yard 'bout a li'l business. When ah come back . . . all right?'

'I want to go too,' Jamini said, 'I want to go.'

'Come,' Binti said. She placed her *orhani* on her head, and took him by the hand.

'Tell Rahim ah want to talk with him soon as we come back, eh Meena,' she called from the foot of the stairs.

As Binti and Jamini came out on Frederick Street a little boy came running out of the gateway next door, screaming with laughter.

'Hold 'im, hold 'im . . . somebody hold that chile,' a heavy voice called from the gateway.

'That is Bissoon voice?' Binti asked.

'Must be,' Jamini said, 'every Sunday when he tries to give Bolu a bath he has to chase him down like a deer.'

'But that child worthless so. He is a spoil chile 'o whar?'

'Boy, when ah catch you ah go cut you tail. Come back here,' Bissoon shouted as he came out on the street. He was fat, and wore his loin-cloth tied below his huge abdomen, his breast hung heavy like a woman's.

Bolu stood some distance away, giggling at him, waiting to dodge about again.

'Ay Bissoon,' Binti called.

'Didi, hold that boy for me, hold 'im.' Bissoon shouted anxiously.

The boy turned to run, but ran straight into Binti and Jamini. Binti caught him firmly by the arm, he looked at her abashed.

'Listen to you poopah, boy,' she shook him by his thin arm, 'you too spoil.'

Bissoon came trotting up to them, his large stomach shaking, his heavy breast jumping as he moved. His outstretched, stiffened palm came hard behind the child's neck.

Slap. The boy winced.

'Yuh too harden, cry.' Slap, Slap, 'Let me see yuh cry, you l'il bitch.' Bolu stood still, looking at the ground, still not crying.

'Boy, don't hit the chile so hard, you go make the child neck twist,' Binti pleaded.

'Didi, yuh don't know how much trouble ah does have with this scamp, every Sunday ah have to chase behind him to get 'im to bathe,' Bissoon complained wearily.

'You forget how to cry, eh?' he tugged hard at Bolu's arm.

'Ah go break these two match-stick foot o' yours . . . then we go see how fast you could run.'

Binti and Jamini smiled at each other.

'Didi, you don't know how this vagabond 'fraid water,' Bissoon went on complaining, as they walked into his yard. He stood the boy in a wooden tub, and poured water over his head from an enamel bowl which he dipped into the tub of water from time to time. As the cold water splashed over the child's shoulder, running down his back, it made him flinch and shudder. Bissoon struck him on the head with the bowl.

Pock, *pock* . . . 'Yuh lil bitch . . . yuh 'fraid water . . . you is a cat o' what?' *Pock*, *pock*. The bowl sounded on his head again. 'That go teach yuh not to run 'way when I call you.'

Binti said, 'Boy, ah hear you teach a man in Tunapuna how to make vinegar fom some kind of recipe, ah t'inkin' of startin' a li'l Sunday business.'

'Didi, ah does charge fifteen.' *Pock* went the bowl on the child's skull again, it sounded hollow; the boy's eyes winked with each blow. 'Fifteen dollars . . . Boy, why you don't stay still, every Sunday ah have to catch cold from the wettin' you does give me, just to keep you clean. Go on now.' Slap, he struck the child on his wet skin.

'G'wan an' dry you skin quick-sharp before ah blows you some more.'

The boy stuck his tongue out at Jamini, then disappeared.

'Fifteen dollars—two whole weeks food money, just for you to tell me a li'l somet'ing 'bout makin' vinegar,' Binti said.

'After all, Binti Didi,' he addressed her respectfully, 'we have to go to College to learn these t'ings, we have to go to America and England to study hard, it does cost plenty money, somebody have to pay we for our services.'

'Look here, boy, I ain't born yesterday nuh! The Government payin' you good money for all kind of idleness, and you want we poor people to grease your palm every time we come to you for a li'l advice . . . you boys who gone England and study all kind 'er t'ing, instead of comin' back here and buildin' up the island, you tryin' to milk we poor people.'

'Didi, but why we Indian can't get along . . . I tell you a price and right away you want to call me a robber.'

'Now look at that . . . now listen to you . . . but is who call you a robber boy? All I say is what right you have to charge we poor people so much. Look, I give you ten dollars, take it or leave it. What good all this l'ornin' go do you? *You* want fifteen dollars, all I willin' to pay is ten, an' is a strain for a poor woman like me. If you don't want to give me the recipe, you lose ten dollars. If you give me it, the two 'er we stand to gain.'

'But Didi, you does drive a hard bargain man, a real hard bargain. Ten dollars—only because is you—only because is you Binti Didi.'

As they walked away from the chemist she murmured to Jamini,

'Only because is you, humph. My ten dollars better than anybody else's? Other people money have hole in it or what? That damn rascal mus' be expect ten dollars all the time, that's why he start out with fifteen, what to do with these people, Lawd?'

She shook her head from left to right, in consolation, as she looked at the recipe for home-made vinegar, which called for burnt sugar, water, and acetic acid.

'Ten dollars for recipe, another ten dollars for licence to buy acids; this business go eat up all my capital before I even sell a penny vinegar, an' where to get this acid 'bidout licence, Lawd—where?'

When they got back upstairs Meena brought out some tea to the table where Rahim sat.

'You ready for a little tea now, *mai*?' Meena asked.

'Yes,' she said dejectedly. She sipped the tea in silence, looking out into space, a blank look on her face.

'Anyt'ing wrong, *mai*?' Rahim asked.

'Boy, I know you have to contend with that old man, and I is not one to bring troubles on your head, ah like to be independent; you know that, but I want to start a li'l Sund'y trade, a li'l somet'ing besides the "coal shop" an' the coconut oil, and I wonder if you could talk to Innis in the drug store to sell me a kind of acid.'

'*Mai*, you know how these t'ings is . . . is government business you talkin' 'bout; you know I have to get a licence to buy acids and so on for the jewellery trade; they have to register your name in the Red House and that kind of t'ing. Is serious business, they does put people in gaol and court house for that kind of t'ing.'

'Yes, is true, is true—but I gone and give that rascal ten dollars for a recipe to make vinegar, and now . . .' she stopped, sipped her tea, and went on, 'is not a strong acid you know, since you have all kind of your dealin's with Mr Innis, you don't think he might do a li'l somet'ing for you?'

'Rahim,' Meena said, 'if *mai* want to try she hand at some'ting, I think we could at least try to help she, after all, you know that she would never come to ask you for somet'ing so long's she could do it herself . . . at least try, Rahim, send a li'l note with Jam to Mr Innis, and let *mai* go with him. You never could tell.'

'All right, *mai*, we go try an' see, carry Jam with you when you get ready to go home. See if he ain't go sell without a licence.'

Mr Innis' Drug Store was at the corner of Prince and Henry Streets. During the weekdays, clerks, and housewives on their way to the Eastern Market made a 'short cut' by walking through the store. Jamini also used the 'short cut' on his way to Miss Lambert's school four times each day.

On Sundays, however, the drug store was closed, and in order to get in, Binti pressed a small button around which was written 'Night Bell,' a red electric bulb lit over it.

'Dadie, you know Tommy next door?'

'Yes.'

'Well, you know how tall he is; he like to come here and ring Mr Innis' bell and then run.'

'You sure you don't do worthless tricks like that too?'

'No Dadie, not me, I can't even reach the bell.'

'I don't know what devil does get into these children . . .'

'Y'ace,' the old druggist stuck his head through a half-opened door. 'Come in, come in.'

He locked the door behind, then went over and stood behind the counter.

'Well, what can I do for you?' he asked, wiping his hands on an apron with brown spots and burnt-out holes.

'Well, Sir, you know that I is Rahim's moomah.'

'She is my Dadie,' Jamini shouted.

'Oh y'ace; Mr Khan's mother—the jeweller. Y'ace.' He nodded slowly. He stared at the old woman and the boy from above his spectacles which hung half-way down his thin round head, round as a ball, which shone all over except at the sides where a few stubbles of hair grew. His face was splashed with two different colours, as carelessly arranged as the patches on the clothes of the old men of Woodford Square.

'Well, Suh! better read this note from Rahim. See if that explain what I want,' Binti gave him the piece of paper.

Jamini stared intently at a statue of an old man in the store.

'That's God,' he thought.

He was white, and made of plaster of Paris. He had a shaggy beard, and his hair grew into it, his eyes were large and blank, and his lips curled in severity beneath his heavy growth of beard. In the corner of Mr Innis' Drug Store, from the shelf with many jars of green and pink and yellow coloured liquids he stared, dust evenly smoothed out like shadows in the folds of his face. He saw everything. He was everywhere, Miss Lambert at his school around the corner had said.

'Mr Innis! That is God up there?' he said to the old man.

Mr Innis looked up at the shelf, then at the boy and his grandmother.

He was a man of great knowledge, Jamini thought, as the old man looked at them. With all these bottles on the shelf; it was he who made the sun and the moon and the rain; he was the only man in the Port of Spain who had God in his store; and if he didn't have a hand in making people, then nobody did.

Binti nodded to Mr Innis. He smiled. The boy had said it with such conviction.

'That's right, m'boy . . . every word of it . . . every word of it.'

Jamini stared at the statue, filled with awe, and Mr Innis re-read the note.

'Y'ace, y'ace, y'ace, I think we can arrange it, but don't let it get around to anyone, not a word of it now, not a word of it.'

'I thank you too too much, Sir,' Binti said. 'I done gone an' pay that rascal Bissoon ten dollars for this recipe to make vinegar.'

'You paid—oh, you should have come to me, I would have given it to you for nothing.'

'Ai-hai,' Binti sighed . . . 'well, anyway, I thank you too too much, Sir.'

She took Jamini by the hand, his head still turned in the direction of the statues on the shelf. Mr Innis held the door open for them.

'Thank you, Sir. thank you.'

'That's a-a-a-a-all right,' the druggist lifted his head all the way up, then bowed, his chin touching his chest as he closed the door behind them.

Outside the drug store Prince Street lay quiet. The Sunday shoppers at the Eastern Market had already gone home. The market was open only until 9 a.m. on Sundays. The vendors who edged into the entrances of closed buildings along the streets that led to the market had also left with their large round baskets of chickens, tied six together by their feet, squawking and croaking. They had left behind a smell of decay, little splashes of excreta, that stained the sidewalks white and grey.

The coconut vendor at the corner had gone home, too. The street looked strange without his donkey cart at the corner, piled four feet high with large glistening nuts, people standing at the sides of the cart, their bodies arched backwards holding the nuts to their lips, pouring its liquid down their throats. And the coconut man, standing above all the nuts, swinging his sharp cutlass, flashing like a mirror in the sun, its edges slicing through the thick green husks. All that was left behind were the deep ruts the cart wheel had cut into the soft asphalt road time and time again, bits of coconut shells and stems, and the hissing of hundreds of flies.

Binti hurried, her slippers slip-slapping, her measuring cup and small tin funnel jingling, as she hurried on to Quarry Street. Suddenly, she stopped hearing Jamini's footsteps behind her and looked around. He was standing half a block away, talking to someone in a balcony across the street.

'Lakshmi!' Jamini called, and a little girl came to the window.

'Jam,' she said, 'where are you going? Miss Lambert's School closed today—it's Sunday.'

'I know that, I'm going to spend the day with my Dadie, up Quarry Street.'

'Can I go too?' she asked.

'Boy, ay boy,' Binti's shrill voice sped along the quiet street. With a sigh of distress she put down her two gallon cans and sat at the edge of the sidewalk, wiping the coconut oil from her hands.

'Yes, coming,' Jamini shouted to her. 'Ask your father,' he said to Lakshmi. She shouted to someone inside the house, then shook her head, her two pigtails swung from left to right; one of them curled about her neck and down in front of her.

'I can't go.' She sounded disappointed, almost sad.

'See you at Miss Lambert's school tomorrow then.' He started running towards Binti.

'Suppose you lose you way? Suppose bicycle knock you down? What you poopah and moomah go say?—that I careless with you? That old man go just have so much, so much excuse to make him grumble.'

'I was only talking to Lakshmi, Dadie. She is my school friend.' He knew that she was peeved from the way she spoke. He tried to sound apologetic. Her hands were dry, but along the palms were two deep red canals, creases put there by the handles of the gallon cans.

He felt sorry for making her angry, he stood by looking sheepishly at her, her head bent, her eyes on her hands, trying to rub out the marks pressed into them by the weight of the can. The more he looked at her, the more he thought how the old woman was soft, and gentle; he saw her tiny feet, her small hands that had become hardened and that bore the rough marks of labour. They weren't large hands that gripped the hoe and swung the cutlass on the sugar-cane plantations, that had come to look like the earth itself. That were broken and mended again—not as beautifully, not at all as shapely, but twice as strong. Binti's little hands, the breaks, the welts, the mending . . . he saw these hands again and again, on the street, in the coal shop all week long; he saw them resting on her lips and blackened with the coal dust, haggling and arguing with the coal men who came to her shop.

'Come on now, Salun must be waiting since one whole hour with the coals, you playin' so much, ah hope he ain't gone away,' she said angrily, grasping the handles of the oil cans.

They could see the donkey-cart outside the coal shop as they approached, its bulk of coal sacks swelling out at its sides. Binti didn't like having to make the coal men wait, she knew how hard they worked. They felled great trees in the forest, then put them into large pits and left them to smoulder. The pits were watched and tended ever so carefully, dousing them with water to prevent the wood from going to ash when the pit became too hot. Several days later the charcoal left by the smothered fires in the pits was dug up, placed in old black sugar sacks, their tops tied together by criss-crossing thin green jungle vines. From the forests the coal men came on their donkey-carts, with hurricane lanterns through the night clop-clopping to the city, where they went to the many coal shops. Every week on Quarry Street Binti haggled with them.

Before the coal man had a chance to comment on her tardiness she became sullen, and adopted a tone of harshness.

'Open up the bag, open up the bag, man.'

'Yes, Didi, right away, Didi,' the coal man said, as he tumbled a bag to the ground and opened it.

'It lookin' so nice and full, I hope you don't have any of those cut-away bags they take in the seams—make you believe that you gettin' a whole bag when you look at it from the outside, everyt'ing lookin' so plump and fat and nice, and when done, all you have is a half-bag.'

She took up a piece of coal from the opened sack, turning it in her hands, tossing it two or three inches high in the air, catching it, feeling the weight of it as it fell.

'You puttin' all the hard coal on top. Take care when you empty the bags I find Balsa coal below. You full-up them bag by yourself and carry them right back where you got them from.'

'But is good coal, Didi. Feel the coal, man, for your own self. But how could you say a t'ing like that? You know how long we doin' business together, you think is fool I go try to fool you! You is a business woman. I is a business man . . . we is business people together, man. Now tell me, what right in the world I have to fool you?'

'You know how that Balsa coal does burn up quick-quick-quick . . . people hard up these days . . . when they buy three cents coal, they expect to cook tea, breakfast and dinner out 'er it. Three times a day they have to light the coal pot with it.

I don' want no row in my place, otherwise I go lose all my customers and then the two 'er we go stand to suffer.' In a dejected, uninterested tone of voice, she grumbled:

'Yuh askin' a li'l too much . . . 'specially since I don't know if is heavy the coal heavy, or if is wet you wet it with water befo' you bring it here . . . but anyway, put a dozen bag in there.'

She pointed to the bin which occupied a full half of the coal shop. It had been made by an old grey-haired Negro carpenter who passed by Quarry Street every day on his way to the city dump to collect odds and ends of wood, crates, and nails which he pulled from boxes too rotten for his trade.

She had never been able to forgive herself for the sin she had committed when she made *that* bargain with the carpenter, who raised a few hogs in the depths of Rose Hill, and did little odd jobs for people. He promised to do all her carpentering if she would let him have the remnants of ground provisions as they became dried out after several days of sitting in the sun, and would not be bought by anyone. Each day, as he passed by, he stopped to show her the choice pieces of lumber he had salvaged for her coal-bin, lecturing on the 'novice work' that was being done by 'boys' these days.

'What is all this talk I hearin' 'bout that old woman raisin' hog . . . she go do anyt'ing to make money . . . now she sellin' hog in the coal shop . . . boy . . . boy . . . boy,' Kale Khan called to Rahim along the stairway. 'What the Imam (priest) in the Mosque will say? The last thing in the world a Muslim shouldn't do, that worthless old woman doin'. Is all you children who will have to suffer when she spoil-up we name.'

Binti was surprised by the speed with which Kale Khan knew of her efforts.

'Well yes, is for the hogs I want the provisions, Ma Binti, I didn't know that your Prophet hate those animals so,' the carpenter said when she questioned him about the use of the old eddoes, dasheen, and potatoes. Their bargaining wavered in the balance. The carpenter started to take the lumber away bit by bit each day, disappointed with the news.

But after Rahim told her that the old man said she was actually selling pork in the coal shop, she stopped the carpenter one day.

'You build that bin, you hear me, and build it well, and you can have all the ground provisions you want; I don't care what you do with it . . . hog or no hog . . . that worthless old man go learn his lesson,' she muttered under her breath . . . 'he ears go drop off one er these days . . . he listenin' to my business like radio,' she told Rahim.

At the front of the bin was a small foot-square hole with a trap-door, which she kept closed when coal was poured in, and with an L-shaped rake made from a two-foot section of barrel-hoop she hauled out the coals, stooping close to the ground with her skirt ends tucked in at the backs of her knees. To measure out the coal she sold, she had a scoop, made from a large can of Blue Nose Butter, which, in spite of the constant rubbing and wearing of coal on its edge, still had part of Blue Nose lettering on it, with the words, 'Made in Australia' circled around the rubbed worn picture of a cow's face.

On one of the tiered wooden shelves along the front of the coal shop were hands of bananas, green and ripe, oranges, tangerines, lemons and hot peppers. On another shelf were ground provisions, dasheens, eddoes, yams, cassavas and sweet potatoes. On mornings these bits of produce along with the more perishable green leafy vegetables, watercress and lettuce, stood in the shade of Quarry Street, catching the eye of the Rose Hill residents who came down to the city on their way to work. Binti sat in the doorway of her coal shop watching the mornings pass on. Most of her sales would come in the evenings, unless someone wanted to be sure to get something and stopped off on their way to work.

'Ma Binti, put aside a handful of them long-stem callalloo bush for me, ah don't want to run the chance of all 'er them sellin' out by the time ah get back from work.'

She wasn't the type of woman who whined and complained, nor was she fretful, but she was exacting, and it was this that made her coal shop one of the best around the Dry River district. Some envied her the 'spot' she had, but those who were honest had to admit that she was a 'real business woman' so that when she was asked to put aside some item for a hurried worker on his way to the town, they did not feel hard put when she said to them:

'Look here . . . I ain't runnin' a business like a church, you know . . . if you want somet'ing, pay somet'ing. Suppose ah put aside them sweet potatoes for you and you ain't come and they dry up . . . eh! tell me that, is who go pay?'

'Ah rushed this mornin', man, ah too rushed, Didi . . . ease me up a little.'

'You so rush-up you can't put your hand in you pocket?'

'Here, here, here, Ma Binti, but you too precise, man . . . you too precise . . . you should have one of them big stores on Frederick Street. Ah bet you could run it better than all them collar an' tie people . . .'

'Don't bother with all this sweet chat . . . just pay me my four cents an' go you way,' she would chide them.

The sun rose directly overhead, at two o'clock. In the streets the air vibrated above the sidewalks, distorting the buildings beyond. She took Jamini into the yard, where they got two long bamboo poles which she used to suspend a few old coal sacks and set up a makeshift canopy to keep the stinging heat off the 'goods' as she called them. As she did every evening, long before closing time, she and Jamini gathered up all the heaps of produce and placed them together in a large mound at the back of her shop. With a bucket of water drawn from the pipe in the yard she sprinkled the 'goods', her small fingers drawn together to form a cup. In quick sharp flicks she pitched the water from her fingers in hundreds of scattered droplets, making a full abundant spray that looked like rain.

She had tried to teach the knack to Jamini, holding his hand in hers. She laughed heartily at the way the water fell in handfuls, running down his elbows, long before he could flex his fingers and send the spray pitching against the muddy ground provisions which she tried to keep as trim and fresh-looking as newly dug-up products, damp and moist, and smelling of the earth.

The afternoon meandered, the shouts and cries of boys playing cricket floated up from the deep gorge of the Dry River, the sun lay idle in the west. The sidewalks now gave off the heat they stored up all day long, and Binti set two plates upon the three-legged table.

The boy knew that it was getting time to leave. They spoke little now as they ate, and the quiet of her life fell upon him, the two visions he would always have of her—at the table, eating banana fritters, and standing on the Dry River Bridge, waving out to him, her palm across her forehead above her thick-lensed spectacles, shading her eyes from the sun; knowing that she waved to a shadow of him only, a blur on the bridge of the darkening evening. Then she stepped inside her doorway and the boy walked on down Prince Street to his home.

At the rear of the coal-shop was her home, her narrow cot, a bucket of water drawn from the pipe in the yard, covered with a dampened piece of muslin to keep the coal dust out, and a small earthenware bowl, with a cloth wick, filled with coconut oil for her lamp when evening came. Her cooking utensils she kept in the yard, sheltered by one of the bamboo-and-coal-sack canopies during the rainy season.

What dreams she dreamt, what tears she shed. They were only for the silent night, for the constant beating of the raindrops seeping through the loose slate shingles of her home.

Kale Khan: Hindustan: the day her young husband built a barricaded walk between her kitchen and the wall where she fetched water in Princes Town long, long ago when they first came to Trinidad, because he was jealous, wanted to keep her to himself, and did not want the eyes of other men cast upon her face. Was it true, she wondered? Was it all a dream? A young girl's dream. A young girl who had disobeyed her parents and run away one night to keep an appointment with a young Pathan of Her Majesty's Regiments . . . and never saw her parents again.

Oh! but life was young then. Young and free and forever. Not filled with dying and measuring out the lengths that made a mile, counting out the seconds in an hour; the open world was the house next door, and Trinidad was across the street; and all created for one night, the night they ran away together, losing themselves from the world. They wandered to the distant towns, and she ran with Kale Khan. She helped him laugh when he went in search of a strange mysterious ghost that called him in the night, that whispered madness in his brain, and she was happy when he came to her and said:

'Binti, one day I shall make you a necklace of filigree, so fine, that the spider in all its mystery and its fragile web will look upon and hold its breath . . . with these two hands . . . you'll see . . . You'll see . . .'

Was it really true? Was this all a dream on Quarry Street? An old woman who sat and looked at the world go past at eight o'clock; who smiled and let the dream unfold and said play on, dream on, for when it's done, I shall awake in Hindustan with jasmins in my hair; and she heard her voice so full of laughter saying to her mother:

'Oh, but mummie, mummie, tell me about the man I shall marry? Will he wear a saffron turban with a blood-red scalloped edge? Tell me, mummie, is he tall and are his eyebrows thick and black as coals? Does he have deep-set eyes that forever seem to hide their dreams? Oh mummie, mummie, won' you tell me? Please,' and she circled her mother, twining her sari about her, spinning her round and round. In the darkened coal shop with the rain-drops dripping from the loosened slate, from the quiet corners of the wooden bin where the thunder-clap had started sudden little avalanches creeping in the silent bin, she could hear her mother's voice ringing clear and bell-like, laughter flowing from her throat, gurgling out at Binti . . .

'But these are old hands, dry hands with fingernails cracked and split and filled with dust,' she thought, as she lit the flicker of a wick in the earthen cup with coconut oil, looking at her hands, and at her loose braid of thinned grey hair. She looked at her hands in the lamplight, her lean hands touched the bin, took up a piece of coal, then put it close against her cheek. She held it there, she rubbed its soft black dust into her skin, she felt its finely-powdered dust falling lightly on her neck, and then she knew which one was dream, which was true.

She cried that night; not like the rain, not like the wind-sweeping, spear-pelting rain, that gushed from the depths of Rose Hill, tumbling past on its way down to the Dry River, edging over the sidewalks of Quarry Street, lapping at her front door steps, but she wept without a tear, without a sigh, without a rise and fall of her bosom.

Hers was a time for crying, for the tightening of the throat that swallows hard, but not a time for tears.

4

Miss Lambert's Private School was at the corner of Prince and Henry Streets, above a rum-shop called the Empire Bar, its name spelled out in syllables on three wall spaces which contained the two doors: EMP-a door . . . IRE-a door . . . and BAR; then the corner wall. Its name was similarly spelled out on the walls of the Henry Street side. When its doors were open, some half-doors that swung in and out were placed on hinges set into the walls. Although adults could not see who was in the bar, the children on their way to Miss Lambert's school could see clearly from underneath the swinging half-doors, the feet of the early morning customers, a few wooden halves of kegs which were used as spittoons, and the trampled sawdust around the aged kegs whose hoops had rusted, swelled and broken away, leaving the slats quite alone, held firmly together by the encrusted layers of substances that had settled in them through their lifetime at the Empire Bar.

As the morning sun beat down on the street, flooding into the bar, soaking into its ancient kegs of rum, it dried out the aged odours of woodwork, the heavy mahogany counter, the far-away blackened shelves; and the smell of rum, fresh limes, and Angostura Bitters came floating up to Miss Lambert's schoolroom, so that by afternoon, either the heat of the day, or the aroma that crept up through the floorboards, left the whole school of fifteen pupils lolling gently, or fast asleep, with their heads nestled on folded arms on the edges of their desks.

Miss Lambert's eyes faced outside the door, her profile intensifying her large red nose. Whether it was naturally red, or became reddened from the constant wipings of the handkerchief she yawned into as well, it was hard to say, but her nose was more of a man's nose, or the kind of false noses that one sees during the Carnival season, incongruously, ridiculously stuck on to the face of a child. She had thin lips with a greying fuzz of a moustache that grew out of small wrinkles on her upper lip, and in the deep creases of her neck there were always lines of black dirt which sometimes absentmindedly caked into her thick fingernails after the children had had their assignments and went to work busily, leaving her all to her self to daydream.

If Miss Lambert ever looked back upon her activities for any day; if she ever asked herself how she spent most of her time, she would find that it was keeping the students awake. For of sins as punishable as falling asleep, there was gazing into space, day-dreaming, and finally yawning, the most sinful of all, which Miss Lambert herself found difficult to repress or hide from the pupils, although she used a handkerchief to cover up her mouth, and clenched her false teeth tightly together, when the devil himself had come upon those hot afternoons to tempt the greatest of saints with sleep so deep that it drowned out the seconds from Henry Street, the loud arguments of 'rum-suckers' downstairs, and some student's voice, monotonous and winding as a long curving empty road that ended in the clouds, as it recited out loud addition tables in dead-beat rhythms:

One and one are two
Two and two are three
Three and three are four
Four and four are five . . .

Taking the tables on the merit of rhythm alone, continuous sing-song poetry, the voice would sometimes go as far as 'six and six are seven' before the strap sliced through the air with a *swoosh*, and its loud slap awoke the others who were soundly asleep, bringing a sudden kind of busying to all the gazers, day-dreamers and sleepers in the room.

Jamini could get to school without having to cross the street; it was chiefly this reason that made Kale Khan agree when Meena and Rahim decided to send the boy there. The old man did not approve of Miss Lambert; without ever having met her he complained:

'Woman, woman, woman, this boy only have woman 'round him. Not good for Pathan child, mus' grow up to be man.'

But the frenzied cyclists who held the streets of Port of Spain, especially Frederick Street, were enough to make even Kale Khan compromise.

Down the steps Jamini went each morning, on his way to school, stopping at the old man's room for a penny and a final inspection of his dress.

'All right, boy, learn'am good in school, and don't play in road. 'An' look out for bicycle—damn worthless rascals does jump the pavement and knock people down.'

Down Frederick Street he walked, cutting through Mr Innis' drug-store, which was more frequently used than the street outside. The old chemist never minded; it gave the short-cutters a chance to see the thousands of medicines wrapped to their necks in newsprint so fine that they were barely readable; the old card-board boxes with stained and shop-worn labels that lined the shelves of the store, and the bargain box that contained remedies for all ailments, placed there because no one would ask for them by name, and so they had lingered on the shelves too long, collecting dust, their contents dried out, leaving only half-filled bottles of liniments and lotions.

'Morning, Mr Innis,' he called, as he strolled through the drug-store.

The old chemist who was never in sight, heard him, and called back, 'G-o-o-d m-o-r-n-i-n-g' in his usual way, stretching out the words as he replied from where he rattled his tubes and bottles and phials, forever mixing powders, herbs and coloured liquids, his reply was always the same although he never knew who was wishing him good morning.

He ran back to the drug-store, poked his head inside, and took off his cap.

'Morning, God,' he whispered to the bust on the shelf; pulled back his head and then went on his way.

Across the street was Dr Wilkinson's office; he was just getting out of his 'Baby Ford'.

'Morning, Doctor,' he called, and waited for Lakshmi, Dr Wilkinson's daughter, who also went to Miss Lambert's. She looked along both sides of the street to see if any cars or bicycles were coming, then ran over, and they walked along together past the rum-shop and around the corner to the narrow stairway on Henry Street which went up two long flights with a platform in the middle.

Jamini and Lakshmi sat at a large wooden desk, worn and ink-stained, which creaked with each movement. It was farthest away from Miss Lambert's table, around which sat the 'devils' as she called them, close, under her eyes, and within reach of the pelt of her curled-up leather strap; directly in front of her sat Tommy. It was Tommy who caused her to change from a cane to a strap. The day that he put a few screws on her cane by cutting deep rings around it with his penknife he won the choice seat in school, directly in front of Miss Lambert. When she used the cane that day it fell off in six-inch pieces with each blow amid roars of laughter in the classroom: she finished up the punishment with a foot rule, and went out of the class. She cried that day, but when she came back into the room Tommy was given the choice seat, and his punishment waited until the new strap came.

'I'll let you have the honour of christening it, sir, yes-sir-you-sir. Come, keep me company, get your books and sit there where I can see you.'

The mornings started with reading, each child read silently until Miss Lambert called him up to read by her side. Ding . . . ding . . . ding . . . the little bell went. Miss Lambert struck it with her outstretched palm for silence.

The sun coming in through the jalousies on Henry Street shot through the air like solid beams of marble, cutting out rectangles on the floor, on the desks, and as the morning traffic from the street below slowed, the voices from the Empire Bar floated upstairs.

It was easier to talk now, for Miss Lambert could never tell whether it came from the bar or from students who sat as far away as Lakshmi and Jamini.

'You don't have to be afraid, my mother won't bite you. She's nice and soft, and I'll tell her that you don't have a mother and wanted to come here with me to see her. Do you want to ask your father if it's all right, or don't you want to go—which?' Jamini asked her.

'I just want you to tell me first. Your mother must be pretty, all mothers are pretty, my mother was pretty, my father said so . . .'

'If you want to see what a mother is like . . .'

'I'm afraid, Jamini.'

'Look, we don't have to tell her that you came to look at her, but you can just come to our house and say that you came to play, and you can look at her all you want . . . she won't even know that you are there . . . maybe your father can get married again, and then you will have a mother, your own mother, and then you won't have to ask me all these questions.'

'Well . . . only a little one though.' The voice came up again from downstairs.

He was beginning to lose his patience with her again. She was always afraid, something was always going to happen. She was that way from the first day that she started coming to Miss Lambert's school. It seemed like years had gone by since she first wanted to go to his home, to see his mother, to see what a mother looks like, feels like.

Jamini always wanted to please her—it was a kind of pity—a kind of feeling that the whole world had left her out. Dr Wilkinson, her father, was busy all day, her mother had disappeared one day when she was just a child, people said that she had left the doctor and the child in India, and the doctor had come to Trinidad to get away from the memories he had in that country.

The girl lived in a little world by herself, waiting in her father's office until he had seen the last patient; sometimes it got to be quite late before they went home, and then the next day was the same all over again, except for school.

'You must never ill-treat a motherless child. The Prophet was a motherless child, and the Koran warn that you should always be good to people who ain't have no mother, Jam.' He could hear Meena saying these words to him; and he tried to get some feeling of what was going on inside her mind.

As he tried again, he realised that he only saw her face, her two long braids tied tight above her head, a thin path running from the centre of her forehead to the back of her neck; yet there was something, someone else, like himself hidden deep within her. Someone that felt, that laughed, that was afraid and timid.

It was something that he never thought about; it wasn't just her eyes, the laughter in her throat, the shoe she wore with a missing buckle; it was when he thought of her this way that it was hard to lose patience with her, not when he looked at the almost yellow hazel of her eyes.

'When I grow up, I'm going to India, to look for my mother,' she said.

'Me too, only I'm going back with my grandfather. He says that that is where we all belong.'

'You don't have to go to India, your mother and father and everyone of your family are here.'

'Yes, but we don't like it here, and we have some of our family in India still,' he said, wondering about the story he had heard of Kale Khan giving away his daughter at the Cawnpore Railway Station.

He had never been sure of just what had happened; at any rate he had an aunt somewhere, given away or left with a friend of his grandfather's. He was talking now just to carry on the conversation, one that she was interested in, just to keep her from sitting silently for the rest of the day all drawn in with that something inside of her.

He had asked Rahim if there was not something like that in everyone, something else, other than the image in the mirror.

'Boy, you growin' up now. Is good you learn these t'ings.'

When did he start growing up? Yesterday? Today? When he was nine years old? Now he was twelve. Where did it begin? How? It still baffled him; Meena, Rahim, Kale Khan, and now Lakshmi. They weren't just clothes and shoes and the sound of their voices, they were something else; but there were these rare moments, these sudden jolts, that told him of a vast mysterious world hidden far behind the eyes of Lakshmi that made her feel and speak and want to touch his mother's hand, and yet be so afraid. He couldn't tell her that there was no need, because she was another person in another world that hid itself from his grasp. Perhaps she was not as grown up as he was, she was only ten.

These moments told him that her hands, her hair, her face, her eyes, these were in the world he knew; the world in which they talked . . . but the other he could never reach.

'You growin' up boy, an' you have a lot to learn,' Rahim had said, and he knew that learning was not the kind in Miss Lambert's school. It was a different kind. He was learning that he was alone, locked up within himself; that everyone was locked up within themselves and quite alone. You saw their outer surfaces only. In the shops and stores, in the Square on Frederick Street, they saw each other's faces, but never got to know that great sea in all its darkness, from a deep and silent mystery that never surfaced, that dwelt alone, and perhaps would stay that way forever, and so would Lakshmi—she would always be outside of the grasp of his mind.

Miss Lambert sat at a table in the centre of the room picking her ear with a yellow pencil, with her head cocked to one side. The pupils cuffed each other, pinched, and Tommy was scratching a piece of chalk underneath the table with as innocent a face as he could hold, so that the boy who sat next to him would soil his serge trousers later on. His hand, the white chalk in it, moved slowly, curving round and round with the same motion that the yellow pencil made, as Miss Lambert twisted it round and round, her face pained, grimaced, and from time to time bore an expression of ecstatic pleasure. But the pupils knew her sudden glances, the instant stare of her large and flared-out eyes that caught them. One second she was looking out into space, and they dared to yawn, or whisper, then there were Miss Lambert's eyes. As if by instinct they knew that when she picked her ears with a sharpened pencil they were free from the quick and sudden jerks of her head that let her eyes catch them in some kind of mischief.

One of the boys at her table was showing an obscene drawing of a man to his neighbour, a little girl. She did not know what it was about. He looked even more annoyed at her as he scrawled larger and larger genitals on the drawing.

'Look, look at what she doing again,' Jamini whispered to Lakshmi, who had crawled into herself again, writing well-formed letters, slowly, painfully in an exercise book.

She looked up, and seeing Miss Lambert, stared at Jamini rather coldly.

'You don't have to point out things like that to people, you know.'

'I only . . . she's . . . she's the one who . . . besides she's only . . . . all right then.'

He jerked himself just an inch away, sat down firmly on the bench, and opened the lid of the desk, looking for something, nothing, then closed the desk with a gesture of finality.

'You don't have to point out things like that, you know.' The 'you know' . . . he had heard it before, it wasn't what she said—it had suddenly put him again into that void by himself. She was by herself in the smug satisfaction of putting him down below her. He had thought of her as her mother, as a woman like his mother, kind, gentle, soft. And now it was as if he had heard someone else's voice in anger. Whose was it? Her mother's, her father's? In her ways, her movements, there was a lightness, but sometimes as her words, her choice of them, had the ring of something that was cold and struck harder than the palm of a hand. It was as if someone had taken up a stone in their hand before hitting, and the blow was heavy, and hard, and cold.

She had heard them, Miss Lambert had heard the complaining voices in the street. If they were inside the bar she would take the broom-handle and start thumping the floor. It had happened before, and the noise, the laughter and loud talking had stopped as the broom-handle made small sunken indentations beside her chair from constant knocking on that spot. But the voices in the street had died down, and she still heard whisperings coming from the corner. She carefully rolled the strap into the palm of her hand, and she tip-toed towards the corner; her large flat spread-out heels slipped in and out, in and out of the twisted old shoes she wore, the careless wrinkles that formed in her loose old stockings swelled and tightened as her old flesh moved silently, tip-toeing, and the hem of her dress jogged, its uneven length wobbling with her movements.

Those who had seen her get up followed her in silence with their eyes, looking to see where the strap would fall.

'All right then, don't talk to me,' Lakshmi had said, turning her head to the wall, and as she did the strap landed *slap* . . . flat, stinging; it lay flat across her back, and she wrenched her body, uttered a sharp bitter cry, then held her head and started to weep.

Miss Lambert stood towering above her, speaking between her clenched false teeth.

'Stop it, stop it, there's lots more where that came from,' and her whimpering muffled into quick sharp jerks like her coughing. Miss Lambert only glared at Jamini, her bulging eyes filled with hate and disgust.

'I'm going to separate you two, I'm going to put an end to this little whispering romance in the corner. You, yes, you, Miss, bring your books and come and keep me company.'

She went to Miss Lambert's table; it was like a prison sentence, a curse, a mark for all to see . . . those who sat at Miss Lambert's table.

And Jamini felt alone; alone and curiously empty, the little whispering, the little romance—Miss Lambert had told him something about himself that he had not known; and he looked across the table that morning wondering if the girl too had not felt the feeling of his entrails, the emptiness of a dug-out hole spreading through his stomach.

The days became long with waiting, waiting, dreaming, waiting to get away from school, so that they could walk home together; now he knew that he wanted to be with her, just the nearness, nothing like the romance as Miss Lambert called it. And from that evening on he knew that she too was glad when the day was over; they pretended to each other that they had not noticed, but a strange pain with joy filled the days that followed, the the pain of waiting, the joy of meeting . . . and walking to the doctor's office after school; and he told Meena one day.

'*Mai*, I know who I will marry when I grow up.'

Meena laughed and said, 'Well now, who is it?'

And he teased her, and said:

'I won't tell you . . . you have to find out.'

And Meena laughed again.

'All right,' she said, 'I'll wait an' see if you won't tell me.'

And then they laughed together.

5

SOUNDS of hammering raced across the Square, struck against the walls of the Trinity Church, and came back. Two groups of carpenters and electricians were bent on their knees, working under the Town Hall, when Jamini and Lakshmi came to the corner on Frederick Street that Friday evening after school.

'Look,' he pointed to the Town Hall, 'they putting up the lights for Empire Day. Wait till it gets dark and the lights go on, our gallery is the best in town to see the 'lighting-up'.'

'I hope my father doesn't come till late late late tonight to pick me up,' she said, looking away from him as she spoke, her eyes in the direction of the workmen who hammered on thin long strips of board, mounting wires, sockets and red, white and blue bulbs on them. Already they had put the large letters, all in white bulbs that read '*God Save The King*,' along the balcony of the Town Hall, which had been repainted for the occasion.

It was an old wooden building with an overhanging gallery that extended out over the sidewalk. It was supported by large, square, heavy, concrete pillars, so thick with continuous layers of whitewash that their edges were blunted; and where the paint had peeled off and broken away there were left deep wedges, for the wash broke off, not in thin layers but thick masses of solid wall which had accumulated over the years of building up, layer upon layer.

The splashing of rain, the urinating of urchins and dogs, the rubbing of old men's itchy backs, as they hugged the stoops at night . . . blemished, stained, spotted and wore down the discoloured pillars. Law, tradition, necessity . . . some unfathomable need to keep Government buildings old, white, dark and filled with smells of sharp disinfectants oozing from their wooden pores worked constantly against the old men, urchins, dogs and the calls of nature that wrote their needs in yellow upon these pillars. Each morning the steps and the pungent sidewalk between the pillars of the Town Hall were scrubbed by a man with a pail filled with milky-white disinfectant to remove the grease stains and odours left there by the old men who made it a hostel at night. The central location of the Town Hall gave them ready access to the flowing fountain at Sir Woodford's feet, where they soaked their beards, looked at their shimmering reflections on the surface, filled their throats with water, hung their heads backwards making the most wonderful gurgling sounds, then pitched the rinse from their mouths directly at the figure of Sir Woodford After the morning wash they were ready for the little portering jobs, or the George Street coffee-stand. Tonight, however, they would have to find another place to sleep.

'I hope that they finish up before it gets dark,' Jamini said. A sudden fear of the lights not going on ran through him. He wasn't as much afraid of the lights not going on as he was afraid that the evening might be ruined. He looked at Lakshmi's hair falling past her neck, and he wanted to touch her, he thought he might like to kiss her the way he had seen Rahim kiss Meena, to hold her in his arms. He even thought that it might make him very happy if she should cry in his arms. As she was about to go past the entrance to Mr Innis' Drug-store he took her hand, leading her through the short cut, walking the third side of a triangle that the path through the drug-store made with Prince and Henry Streets.

He held her hand as they walked through the store, it was soft: through holding it alone he knew that she didn't mind, that she too liked the feeling of her hand in his, the light, soft, relaxed way she let her hand remain, not showing any feeling to him.

'Evening, Mr Innis,' he called; and the old chemist replied 'G-o-o-d evening,' but didn't come out.

There was something new in the drug-store. The picture of the place had settled in the boy's mind such a long time ago that it acquired a permanence which the smallest alteration would affect.

Across the statue up on the shelf was hung a string of Christmas-tree lights, but instead of its many coloured bulbs there were only three colours, red, white and blue. They flashed and flickered off and on in an irregular rhythm, sometimes only flickering, then going out when they should have stayed on, and the reflections of the lights made the bust take on strange and frightening expressions.

Jamini and Lakshmi walked up Frederick Street as the crowd dispersed, then into the wide gateway that led to the old man's rooms, and the stairway to Jamini's home.

At the far end of the gateway the old man stooped in front of a charcoal pot, a short bamboo tube between his lips, blowing into the red embers of a bed of hot coals. There was a smoky, charred pot on the fire, its lid half askew, from which thin droplets of liquid crawled, sizzling into dried scales around the outside of the pot, and the most tantalising odours crept along the passageway, curling up to their nostrils.

'That is my grandfather,' Jamini said proudly, 'you know how many people he killed at the Princes Town Hussay? . . . six . . . shot them down.'

She remained silent, she could see the profile of the old man squatting before the coal-pot, muttering to himself; then the long-shadows of the two children cast by the sun fell across the coal-pot. The old man put his hand to his eyes, the sunlight half-falling upon his face, shooting silver flecks into his hair.

'Boy, who that? That you, boy?'

'Yes, Dada.'

'And who is that with you? Come . . . come this side.'

He looked into the pot, stirring, as they approached. Before he could see them clearly he asked:

'You hungry . . . and your school-friend . . . he . . . he . . .' then looking up at them, 'Boy, you school-friend is a girl school-friend? Come.' He beckoned to Lakshmi to come closer.

She stood slightly above his head, her two large eyes looking into the old man's face, timidly, yet not afraid.

'Boy, go inside house . . . bring *pir-ha*.' (a small bench about four inches high).

He held the girl's face gently between his thumb and index finger, below her chin, slowly turning her face as if looking at it from every angle that the falling rays of the sun cut out before his eyes. He nodded once, smiling at her, nodded again, then let go of her face, still smiling, as he stirred the pot.

'So—and you is a good girl? . . . learn good lesson in Lambert School.'

'Yes, Dada, Jam and I learn good in school.'

'Good girl . . . good girl,' the old man laughed, holding her small hand, pressing it in his, shaking her arm as he laughed.

'That side boy, not too close to fire. Good man. Good man. Put books one side and sit down. Have 'um good something for you.'

They sat on the small bench, watching him stir the rice in the pot, his eyes pressed into frowning as he looked over the heat of the coal-pot into the milky-white water in which the rice bubbled. Steam mushroomed out as he took the lid off, dipped out five or six grains in the spoon and blew on them to get them cool.

'Boy, go upstairs an' get two cup. Come back *jaldi jaldi*,' he said, as he squeezed the cooled grains between his fingers, testing them to make sure that they were cooked.

'You come to see lightin' up with Jam, uh?'

'Yes, and they have put it up already, soon as it gets dark, *all* the lights will go on.'

'You livin' far from here?'

The boy came down with two enamel cups, one with spotted white on blue, the other white with long chips from rim to bottom.

'The doctor, 'round the corner on Prince Street is her poopah, Dada.'

'Oh—oh—so, an' why you didn't tell me that this is Doctor Sahib's child, boy? So, so, so,' he muttered, shaking his head as he drained the rice-water into a pan. He put the pot on the ground.

The embers on the coals became whitened with ash as they burned without the old man blowing into them, then he started sprinkling water over the fire to save the coals for another time. He jerked his head away swiftly from the tossed-up steam and bits of ash that shot from the coal-pot as the water made a harsh slapping sound against the coals, glowing a pale orange-red beneath the yellow-grey ash.

'Boy, look inside on counter. Bring spoon, salt, and mango pickle.'

Jamini swallowed his saliva. The waiting, the smells of the old man's cooking, and now the mango pickle! The muscles somewhere at the back of his jaws tightened with anticipation.

Kale Khan poured some of the rice-water into the cups. Slowly he measured a heaping tablespoonful of rice in each, one in the pan from which he would have his. When the boy came back he took the salt and sprinkled it in slow grinding pinches between his fingers on the surface of the thick veil that formed over the rice-water, and threw a morsel of mango pickle in, which broke the surface and sank very slowly to the bottom.

'Mix up, mix up . . . and drink,' he told them, as he started stirring in his pan, the spoon clinking on the side, quickly at first, then more slowly. He held his head up, poured the contents bit by bit into his mouth, his throat moving up and down, up and down, as he swallowed; then he put down the pan and cleared his throat with great relish.

'Ahhhhhhhhh.'

'Better make haste before your moomah begin to bawl behind you, boy,' he said, wiping his mouth with the back of his wrist. 'When you finish bring *pir-ha* inside and carry your school-friend upstairs. But take time, take time, take time,' he said, as he walked into his room, dragging his feet close to the ground, one hand pressing on his waist, squeezing a spot that must have become cramped from squatting so long before the fire. In his other hand the iron rod walking-stick dragged behind.

The stairway was always in darkness, no matter how bright and blatant the sunlight flooding on the yard and the street outside. Jamini again took Lakshmi by the hand as she walked uncertainly in the half-darkness, unsure of the number of steps and their height.

At the top of the stairway, light from the window in the kitchen where Meena sat made the steps more visible. She looked up as she heard the sound of footsteps.

'So you stop first at your Dada with you' friend, eh?' Meena said, peeling some pigeon peas in a white basin. She drew Lakshmi towards her, passing her hand behind the girl's head, unfolding the collar which had worked its way inside the neck of her dress.

'And what is your name?' Meena asked.

'Lakshmi,' she answered.

'That is a nice name for a pretty girl like you,' she said, patting her on the shoulder. Then, to Jamini:

'I hope you ain't carry this chile too, and eat so much at you' Dada that you can't eat dinner tonight, boy.'

"It was only a little bit,' he said, anxious to get away so that they could go to the gallery and look out toward the Town Hall.

'All right, go on now, inside, two of you, I have cooking to do.'

As they left Meena heard Rahim talking to the old man downstairs:

'Everyt'ing all right, *Barp*?'

'Yes, boy, everyt'ing all right . . . you see boy bring he schoolfriend home?'

'No, not yet. I just close-up the shop.'

'Well, go on upstairs.'

'You ain't goin' out to see the lightin' up tonight, *Barp*?'

'Lightin' up . . . what lightin' up? . . . they tryin' to fool these damn fool people two time, three time in the year with all kind of nonsense. No, boy, I too old for all these tricks, they can't fool me with Empire Day and King Birthday and Queen Birthday.'

'The Government spend plenty money to put up all them lights for we to see,' Rahim said.

'Yes, yes, Government *too* sweet, *too* nice. G'wan upstairs, boy; an' tell that boy to treat that chile good good good . . . you hear, Rahim.'

'All right, *Barp*,' he said, as he walked up the steps.

'The children in the gallery,' Meena said. 'Go see you son bring home daughter-in-law for you . . . nice girl.'

Rahim blushed. 'What kind of nonsense you talkin' now, Meena? You just puttin' foolish ideas in the children head.'

'Well, the boy tellin' me since last year he know who he goin' to get married with.'

Rahim sat drinking the cup of tea Meena had ready for him every evening. He peered into the black liquid, turning it around and around in the cup, looking at his reflection on its surface . . . thinking. Then he spoke.

'But Meena, look how t'ings does change, eh?'

'Which way you mean?'

'Ah mean when we two get married, we ain't even see one another till the day of the wedding. Who would'er t'ink that in we own children lifetime t'ings would'er change so?'

'You mean you would'er want you son to get married the way you get married? Wake up, Rahim, time change.'

'Well—sometimes ah does wonder, wonder if t'ings wasn't good in before times. Sometimes ah does t'ink the old man have he reason . . . ah mean, well, is hard to explain but sometimes ah really doesn't know what good and what ain't good for we. An' it look like if t'ings does happen while you ain't even noticin' them, like if all we fall down in a river and we ain't have no way to get out; an' when t'ings happen we just have to obey them . . . like if we have a master.'

'Rahim, you does worry too much . . . t'ings changin' every day . . .'

'Yes, but what goin' to happen to us? We ain't belong to Hindustan, we ain't belong to England, we ain't belong to Trinidad, and day by day . . . '

Rahim did not like it. Meena was right. Things were changing every day. He saw it in his trade; many young people were no longer interested in jewellery and the fine handwork from the best artisans. They preferred costume jewellery, coarse, gaudy, and flashy. True, there were those who sought him out because he was one of the best, but many other tradesmen suffered. When they complained to him, he tried to bolster them up.

'Is only the young people who don't know 'bout these t'ings. Wait till they get older, and get a little sense . . . they have two eye to see good jewel from machine-made jewel.'

But he knew the truth to himself, he lied to the others, and secretly he wondered what he and all the others would do. They had come a long way from the sugar-cane plantations, they had sacrificed a few years in apprenticeship; the young men who came to him because of his reputation, and Kale Khan's reputation since the days in Princes Town, he taught them diligently, painstakingly . . .

'Boy, melt down that ear-ring, it ain't fit for donkey to wear. Look, come here.' *Snap*. He broke the delicate filigree before the apprentice's eyes. 'Now start over again. When something come out of this shop, people does respect it. You hear? If you ain't have the patience and the love for this work tell you' moomah and poopah to send you to work in hot sun in the cane field. You have to make filigree fine, fine, fine . . . and strong, strong, strong . . . fine like spider-web, and strong like iron. That is why you moomah and poopah send you here, to learn.'

Was he telling them a lie? Was he building up a world that would run away from these boys when they grow up? Would anyone care for the work they could do?

'Man, they have machine up in England an' America that go do all these t'ings . . . then it go be easy for we,' he overheard one of his apprentices saying. It bothered him, it annoyed him, as he listened.

'In all them big, big, country they have machines that does sell food and chewing gum . . . you put in a money and snap you photo; put in a money an' you hear you voice on record. A fella who does sweep up at the airport went up there. He save up he holidays and he get so much miles by plane . . . Man, he say them Yankees smart for so . . . they have machine tractor runnin' an' runnin', an' a man sittin' down in a house pressin' button. That tractor ploughin' up land fo' so . . .'

'Is so . . . man, what you sayin' at all?' the other apprentice queried.

'Is true true t'ing . . . you t'ink is make up ah makin' up all this talk . . . you don't go to movie-house or what? Boy, next t'ing you know they go make people who go live forever with one of them machine.'

'That is the life, boy . . . that go be the day.'

'Get out . . . get out,' Rahim shouted. 'You damn rogue.'

'But Khan Sahib . . .'

'Go on home, get to hell out-a' here. Tell you moomah and poopah *I* send yuh home because you want to sit 'pon you tail and let machine eat, drink and sleep for you.'

'But Khan Sahib, me poopah go kill me with blows.'

'Boy, I ain't care what he do to you . . . you deserve it, you is lazy scamp, you go do only bogus work in this trade. Machine eh . . . machine go eat good and you go feel your belly full, machine go make chile and you go sit 'pon your backside, and then what you go do—watch? You go watch, eh!' He chucked the boy out of his shop, hurrying him on with a cuff on his head.

'You want your son to get married the way you did?' he heard Meena saying.

He looked at the tea, saw his reflection in it, a small growth of beard spreading from his skin, a few of the hairs grey-black. He watched the shape of his nose, Kale Khan's mole on his cheek, the fine lines etched out in the corners of his eyes as he peered into the cup.

He thought of the days before he got married. The little carat hut in Princes Town and the people who came. First an old man with a sharp, pointed face, who recited prayers from the Koran. Rahim looked at his eyelids trembling, his eyes palpitating beneath them, then the old man drew both of his hands to his face, recited for a few seconds, kissed the palms of his hands, opened his eyes and went away.

An old barefoot woman, her toes pointed into the earth as if they tried to bore holes in the ground, came to wash his feet and anoint them with the oils she brought in an enamel cup without a handle.

As the day of the wedding grew near a man came to massage him each day with oils, spices and perfumes, preparing his body for marriage, and on the last evening he bathed behind the carat hut, a piece of white cotton about his loins, standing in a pair of wooden-soled slippers. He dipped rain-water from a large rusted metal drum with a calabash, and the water coursed over his limbs and body, cold at first in the light wind of the evening, then cool and refreshing.

The following morning the barber came, seated him on a condensed-milk box in the yard within the arch of an arbour of peas in half light, half shade. The barber took twice as long to cut his hair that day. Afterwards Kale Khan rubbed his body with oils that smelled of saffron.

From a canister in the corner of the hut, his father took out a piece of bright saffron silk, which would be used for Rahim's wedding turban. The silk had a blood-red scalloped edge that would trail down his back; it was the same piece of silk the old man wore when he and Binti were married. He stared at it without speaking. Rahim heard his words again, 'You goin' to you own house now, boy.'

In between the emotions that welled up in him, his bride, the name of Meena, he felt a sharp pang of sadness strike at his chest, pressing hard; he felt alone, lost. A mysterious air drifted into the hut as the old man held the turban cloth. Rahim felt the gnawing loneliness of his father's life, but he did not speak.

'Come, sit down, time to get ready,' the old man said, and he started to wind the turban about Rahim's head.

Rahim wished that his father's hands would touch him, he wished that he would hold his face in his hands, look into his eyes, and speak to him, say anything; but the old man went on tying the turban around and around, drawing the silk tightly about his head.

'Too tight?' he asked firmly.

'No,' Rahim answered.

His fingers brushed against Rahim's ear before the bands of the cloth covered them over under the turban. The feel of his father's hands touched something like sorrow and pain deep within him. And still Kale Khan did not speak to him.

They went on foot to the bride's home, and Rahim saw her face for the first time; and when he took her home they spent days, weeks, shyly telling each other about themselves, looking at each other . . . he knew that love would have been old, and tired, if they had known each other beforehand, he knew that the excitement which swelled in his bosom like pain with the wanting was right . . .

He turned toward the gallery where his son and the girl were standing at the window. Jamini's eyes were on Lakshmi as she looked out to the Town Hall; watching her, unnoticed. She turned around, saw Jamini's eyes, looked into them, then shyly looked away, and Jamini placed his hand on hers along the window-sill.

Rahim felt that there was something wrong with the world that was slowly swallowing him up. He wondered too if love, love such as he and Meena knew, was not also dead.

A burst of light flooded into the house from outside, Rahim looked startled to the window. The boy and the girl were shouting:

'The lights are on . . . come and *see* the lights.'

Rahim went to the window, followed by Meena, wiping her hands on her apron.

People in the streets rushed toward the Town Hall. From all directions they were converging to that one spot. Some were running across the lawns of the Square to get there more quickly, and children were walking ahead of their parents, as if to hurry them on. Tommy ran out of the gateway shouting:

'Miss Dee, Miss Dee . . . look at all the lights.'

His mother came out of the gateway and shouted at him:

'Behave yourself, you little vagabond. Why you bawlin' like that? You t'ink I can't see?'

Meena said, 'Rahim, why you don't take the children for a little walk downstairs to watch the lightin' up? Dinner ain't go be ready for a little while yet.'

'You want to go downstairs?' Rahim asked the children.

'Yes, yes, oh yes,' they said excitedly. Lakshmi seemed very happy. Jamini was glad, he knew that it was the lights, the Empire Day, yet he felt that it was his doing, that he had made her as happy and excited as she was.

'All right,' Rahim said, as they both surrounded him, bursting with laughter. 'All right, all right,' he said laughing; then he placed his hands on their heads, remembering how he yearned for the touch of Kale Khan's hands that day. He stood silently for a moment, looking at their faces, their silent, puzzled questioning faces.

'Yes,' he said, looking at them, '*I* goin' to take you to see the lightin' up. Come on now,' he laughed, 'who goin' to reach downstairs first?'

The Town Hall and the streets were floods of red and white and blue. No one would suggest tearing it down tonight, not the balconies nor the pillars, not the stained steps. Not tonight, with its thousands of lights mounted on wooden frames along the cornices and balconies with 'GOD SAVE THE KING' . . . 'LONG LIVE THE KING' spelled out in large dazzling letters made up of white bulbs mounted on wooden frames, ornamented with crowns, orbs and sceptres, criss-crossing each other. The building itself was lit up by pale-blue floodlights; in the streets were people who came to the city once a year, from all the hidden hills and hamlets of the island, to promenade and watch the lighting-up.

The floodlights spread a magic on the walls, the pillars, hiding all the cracks, blisters; the yellow stains and uneven blotches that marred the building by the callous light of day. The old, frayed Union Jack which usually hung like a mouse-torn rag from its flagpole was replaced by a silken one, so light and shiny it was, waving in the night air, looking all the more colourful as the floodlights played into its shadows and creases when it furled and swayed, dancing in slow-motion dignity to the strains of *Rule Britannia*, which the Orphanage Band played.

Those who had scoffed at the Town Hall, those who had said that it should be torn down and a Public Comfort Station placed there, because so many had become accustomed to relieving themselves there, those who wanted it torn down to have a Hostel built for the homeless dregs of sugar plantation vagrants, did not feel this way tonight. They suddenly became aware of its lines, its projecting gallery, its flagpole, its windows and jalousies; for so the talk spun out among the crowds:

'You can't believe that it is the same Town Hall, man . . . look at we flag flyin', man . . . look at we colours, but just look at we colours, man . . . an' we got get a cable from the King he-self . . . we is subject of the Empire, man . . . let we make merry, man . . . today is we celebration, even the King he-self have to send an' tell we that he remember we . . . We is children of the Empire, Papa . . . children of the Empire, man!'

'Jam,' Tommy called out.

Miss Dee slapped him across his mouth. 'Control yourself, you little vagabond . . . you want everybody to t'ink that I raise you like a animal? Evening', Rahim,' Miss Dee said.

In the Square an old porter by the name of Sookiah who pushed a hand-cart about the city was balancing a bottle of rum on his head singing *Rule Britannia* in an off-key Hindustani tune. People laughed.

'Come on an' fire one with Sookiah, everybody,' he invited, adding, 'today is we bachannal . . . today is we fête.'

The milling crowds were on all sides of the Square. Rahim, Lakshmi, and Jamini went to the west side of the Square to see the Red House. It was the largest, the tallest, and one of the most beautiful buildings in Port of Spain, painted a dull brick-red, weathered with time and rain and sun. As they approached they could see the strange warm colour the building basked in; it too was flood-lit, by red lights.

Jamini ran a stick along the bars of the railing around Woodford Square. He stopped at the corner, looking for one particular rail, one that had a deep bullet indentation in it. Kale Khan had showed it to him one day, told him how it was put there during one of the early riots when the Indian peasants went to seek conference with the Governor and the police opened fire on them, crippling them in the warm morning sunlight amid the stench of gunpowder and the shrieks of wounded women, running bleeding through the Square.

They walked into the public passage of the Red House, which everyone used as a short cut.

They walked past the closed office where all illegitimate children had their names written down in red ink. They went past the two grey cannons left over from the Great War which were sent from the U.K., one on either side of the fountain in the middle, with a statue of a woman whom Jamini thought to be the Mother of the Empire. The mother in the song that Miss Lambert taught them:

Land of Hope and Glory,
Mother of the Free.

It was a statue of a woman with a pair of huge wings, pointing an arrow from a tense bow aimed straight at the Police Station across the way on St Vincent Street.

Rahim stood at the fountain, one foot perched on its rim; the children were playing by the cannons. He spat into the fountain water, then looked around to see if anyone had seen.

Lakshmi, with her head tilted all the way back, peered up through the open roof to the dome of the building; the three little lights in the dome seemed miles away from her.

Jamini was piercing his fingernail into the soft dribbles of paint that hung from the ends of the cannons. They had been freshly painted for Empire Day. The paint clung thickly in ugly wrinkles and ripples over them. The boy found it difficult to believe that they had once been objects of action, that their wheels once sped over battlefields, that the small part like steering wheels with long screws, the metal seat, shaped in a curvature of the human posterior, also with long screws, had actually been moved about, or adjusted for action at all. The paint smothered the entire feeling of action, leaving the cannons more like two old lumps of paint. So too were the cannon balls, piled up on either side, welded together into solid pyramid-like masses by the continuous layers of paint, from one public holiday to another.

The Indians were particularly fond of the Red House. It reminded them of a Hussay, the papier-mâché replicas of their heroes' tombs which they pulled through the streets at festive times of the year amid great ceremony, drum-beating and promenading. They said that it was red because *they* liked the colour.

The joke told about the illiterate Indians who came to festivals in the city proved their point. At the many handcarts which sold soft drinks during the festivals they would stand, debating which of the sparkling drinks they would choose to quench their thirst. Invariably, when asked which flavour they wanted they would say, 'Gimme *Red Red* Soda.'

And so it was that they loved the Red House. Some say that the design was stolen—from Hindustan—but there were others who knew differently.

The Red House meant that they were all illegitimate children, that there were no legal records of their births housed in that building . . . they knew that the small plot of land their forefathers worked and toiled for was registered there . . . they knew that they would never be able to inherit that land, for in the musty parchments that the Red House kept, they did not exist, and if they were questioned, they were bastards in the eyes of the law, for there were no records of their parents' marriages either.

Yes, in the Red House where names of illegitimate children were written in red ink for their lifetime, for posterity!

The Red House and its bright red ink stained them at their roots.

No, the myths and the legends would last, they would not forget the riots, nor the smell of gunpowder, nor the uniformed men in white helmets and brass buttons. The Red House was red, with *their* colour, with *their* blood, their bright red blood, blood that stained the sidewalks. Red with the colour of the ink in which their births were registered, it was theirs, with the Union Jack and English judges, theirs to go to so that they could have justice done, theirs truly in many many ways.

They swept the floors, they shone the brass on sunny mornings. They kept the hedges and the lawns. And in the hallway they polished the plaques on the stilled cannons with Brasso so that all would know that the Red House did indeed belong to the Indians of Trinidad—yes, *and* the Union Jack, *and* the Mother of the Empire was their mother. Yes, and so was Empire Day.

6

IT HAD started swelling in the bowels of the thick grey clouds, straining in its wild convulsions to tear the heavens loose.

The rain had come to the mountains of Trinidad, to the parched peaks that dug their searching fingers deep into the clouds, probing for the damp, drenching flow of life when August came.

The wind was high in the sky yet the trees in Woodford Square stood motionless on the face of a strange and darkened earth that seemed to have lost its orbit.

A workman crossed the Square, walking home alone. He stepped uncertainly, glancing up at the sky. He seemed to feel the distance, the shell of the sky broken open, and all the devils of the dark coming down to taunt him with the great distance between him and no other land.

But the clouds would stop their running, would soon come walking down. The shell of the sky would enfold the night, and thin mists walk the mountainsides.

These were the nights of the steamboat whistles, and fog-horns in the dark. These were the nights that came nestling closely, wrapping themselves in the pillow sacks, waiting for the raindrops to come tap-tap-tapping on the window for the quiet voices of lovers lying abed in houses of the hamlets dotting the hills, their single eyes of pale yellow light going off . . . going off to sleep. Such were the nights when the rainy season came.

The wind came down ruffling the trees, it swept up the branches of the Calabash tree, its old dead leaves went skating up into the air as the wind dived in and out again. The lightning broke the sky with a searing cutting of cloth, the galvanised roofs rattled, the loose nails ran along their corrugated canals and then they settled into the black night.

The boy lay in bed, listening to the first large drops ringing on the roof. The smell of the Square drifted into his window as the cracked, dry earth swallowed the rain, as the old, dry leaves lay flat against the walk; ending their restless crawling in the night wind, and no one slept until late in the morning when the rain sang in monotone, and the water from the spouts dug holes in the earth.

No one slept till late in the morning on the first day of the rainy season . . . they listened. The old men from the Town Hall statue knew that mornings after nights like these would be full of new hopes, new dreams. They hustled to Kale Khan's room at six o'clock. They brought hot coffee and tea and they sat and listened to the raindrops playing hide-and-seek in the wind outside.

After they were settled with their condensed-milk tin cups reflecting the pale yellow light of the cup flame, Mongroo spoke.

'Khan Sahib,' he said, 'let we get a few head together and write the Governor a letter . . . tell 'im we want to go back home to Hindustan . . . even if we have to die after we get there, man.'

Then silence fell, and wisps of steam curled up from the milk tins in their hands.

'Hai-hai,' Pooran, another of the old men, sighed, sucking his teeth, moving his head dejectedly, from left to right.

New fires scorched at the dead nerve ends, new blood pounded in the worn down cells, the mixing of their old bones with the half-remembered clay of Hindustan, the pressing of their feet, their wandering cracked soles on old wet earth that they remembered when the rainy season came, the smell of coriander cooking, soaking into the wet air, wafting its way with the breezes through the rain, sifting through the steam of rain-soaked earth. It coiled up to their nostrils, scratching out an old, old yearning buried there.

'Ah does always remember Hindustan when the rainy season comes man . . . ah don't know why . . . it does grieve me to know how far we is from we home and we people,' another old man rambled on.

'Is true what all you boys sayin', you know, I t'ink is more than time for we to do something,' Kale Khan said. He sat on the edge of his bed, a white towel over his head, its ends hanging loosely over his shoulders. In the early light of the rainy season's dark dawn, he looked like one of the judges of the High Court at the Red House, dressed in a flowing wig, taking his place once again as a leader to these men who still remembered him from the Princes Town Hussay. He ground his teeth slowly, meditatively, his jaws palpitating in and out, in and out, the faint light from the cup flame falling on one side of his face.

'I goin' back home one day . . . one day God go find a way for me man . . . ah miss my people too bad . . . don't care what you say, you own is you own . . . nobody could deny that,' Kareem said; he held his milk tin by its lid, using it as a handle, his eyes focused at a point somewhat in mid-space.

'Sshhh,' Kale Khan said, motioning with his finger to his lips. He cocked his ear, listening.

'Who . . . who that walkin' outside?' he called out to the darkness.

'Me, is me, Dada, Jam,' the small voice said quickly, then he came into full view and stood at the doorway. The old men looked up at him.

'But look at how these children an' them growin' up right befo' you eyes, Khan Sahib . . . is them too we have to t'ink about.'

'Why you ain't sleeping', boy, rain wake you up too? Come this side, sit down.'

One of the old men poured some hot tea. He gave it to the boy, and Kale Khan seated him at his side, placing his arm around him. Jamini huddled into the old man's embrace as if coiling away from the dampness of the air.

'Ah hope you ain't wake up nobody in the house,' the old man said.

'No, Dada, they still sleepin'. I walked quiet, quiet, quiet.'

'Good man,' Kale Khan laughed.

The old men smiled. There were about five of them sitting in a semi-circle on the floor. One of the chickens from outside came in, cluck-clucking; a grating, complaining sound gurgled out of its throat; its feathers were damp and it frizzled itself from the dampness and the rain. Kareem threw an empty match-box at it. 'Shoo,' he said. The chicken jumped. It squawked angrily as it half-flew, half-ran out of the old man's room in search of a warm corner to roost before daylight. Kale Khan started coughing as he laughed at the way the angry bird left the room, complaining and fretting.

'You know I did leave my good wife an' chile an' come Trinidad when they tell me how rich, rich, rich I could get over here. From the time we leave port in Hindustan they treat we like if we was worse than dog in them ship. Is only then I say to misself "But boy, what damn fool t'ing you gone an' do?" By that time all o' we was so sick we didn't care if we live or die, and you t'ink anybody give we a glass o'water—women an' children too. Hai! Hai! An' when we get here ah say, "But look at how ah never hold cutlass in me whole whole life, that is the riches?" Ah does wonder if me family livin' o' dead o' what, man,' Mongroo complained, his voice breaking towards the end.

'They play the same trick on all o' we, now look at we,' another complained angrily. 'First I was shame, how I go look at my family an' them in their face when I ain't have a black cent. I say better stop here, what the use goin' back, but now I does feel that even if I dead when I go back, ah still want to go, just to see what happen to that wife an' chile o' mine.'

The morning light was slow in breaking out on the horizon, and the smell of the old men's pipes, the sooty taste of burnt coconut oil that the smoke from the cup-flame ribboned out hovered about the room. It hugged the walls and touched the faces of the old men sitting on the floor, it wove itself into their patched-up clothing. The smell too liked the warm dry room, and would not venture out to wash itself away in the rain outside.

Jamini sat on the block of wood of Kale Khan's pillow, his head cupped into his hands. It was a good feeling. The mornings came later than usual during the rainy season, there was still no sound of movement coming from upstairs, he could stay with his grandfather and talk longer than usual.

'Dada, how soon before we get to go to Hindustan?'

Kale Khan looked at the boy. What had Mongroo said? That these children would suffer; that they should go back; that it was the fault of the older folk.

'Khan Sahib, you see, you seein' with you own eye an' hearin' with you own two ears what kind of mind these children an' them have. We can't forget them, you know, is we fault, is *we* who make the mistake, man.'

Kale Khan got up and poured a little coconut oil from a green bottle into his lamp. The lamp flickered, his large shadow was cast across the wall, larger than the giant's picture on the wallpaper, then he turned to the men, his shoulders stooped, his head jutting forward from his stoop.

'Don't t'ink I forget my days, ah does remember well, and don't t'ink we country forget we. Last week papers say that a man comin' here from Hindustan. I done write a letter already. We country goin' to be free one 'er these days, an' already they sendin' a man here to hear we grievances. Wait, just wait an' we go see how much he go have to hear 'bout how they treat we, don't worry,' Kale Khan chortled, 'wait, boys, wait an' see.'

'But Baba, you is a straightforward man! It ain't joke you jokin' wid we ah hope, is dream we dreamin' o' what?'

'It ain't joke I jokin' o' dream yuh dreamin'—we time comin.' Yuh hear what these Sahib an' them does say:

Tit for tat
Butter fer fat,
You kill mi dog
And ah kill you cat.

You remember dat?'

The men looked at him.

'Well is that self: When this man come here they go try to sweeten we up, but I go see to it that all the t'ings that happen to we reach back to we country, and besides that, they have to make arrangement to send all of these people back, at *their own* expense. We work an' sweat for that, don't worry all you head, the time comin' soon soon soon. . . . . It does take two hand to clap, you know, well, now is we chance,' Kale Khan assured them.

The talk wove in and out. They chanted in their broken, raspy voices about the coming of the rain, and a quiet happiness stole across their hearts, a quiet consolation, a feeling that all that was not as it seemed, and they believed it, for as the rainy season came, and the rain came falling full days and nights, the mango ripened, the Keskeedee sang, the season of weddings followed, offerings to the poor for the good year came around. They could already smell the odours of curry cooking in large yard-wide cauldrons, nestled in holes dug into the ground, blazing orange-red with fires that made the milky rice-water bubble, that sent smells of coriander, cumin, saffron and the magic spices of Hindustan tracing through the wet air of evenings. They would meet and talk and tell tales of long ago, they would see the children of their children marry in the month of the rainy season and the ripening of the mango, and their doubts were fired once again with new hopes, pulling the loose ends of their incomplete circles together.

The morning light came up from behind the hills of Laventille, thin mists walked along the mountainside, and the road-sweepers whistled at their mule-carts in the street outside. The old men left in a fine drizzle that made their beards soft, and soaked itself into their dried-out pores, it made their complexions soft, their hearts young and light, for tomorrow would not be tomorrow, would not be filled with fears of the old old old tomorrows, now that the rains had come to Trinidad.

'Dada,' Jamini said, after the old men left, 'you know what Miss Lambert said to do if you want something?'

Kale Khan stood at the counter, pouring out some juice from his hollowed-out radish from which the mustard seeds sprouted. He sipped it from an enamel cup, making a face, then passed it to Jamini, clearing his throat, 'Ahhhhhhh.' The boy took the cup by its handle.

'Now, what you say Lambert teach you in school?'

'Dada, she said that if you want something . . . to ask God for it.'

'Y-e-s,' Kale Khan said, sweetly, cunningly, 'and what else she say?'

'Ask and it shall be given you, and next time I go to Mr Innis' Drug-store, you know what, Dada, I will ask God if we can't get a ship and go to Hindus . . .'

'What is that you say?' the old man shouted angrily.

'Dada, Miss Lam . . .'

'Shut up!' he shouted. He knocked the cup away from the boy's hands, it pitched towards the door. The cup rattled as it rolled across the room and struck against the door in the quiet of the morning. In the stillness that fell across the room fine clinking sounds came from the cup as its enamel splintered off the dents.

'You is a *damn-fool* o' what?' he shouted.

Silence. The boy looked away from his stare.

'*Eh . . . answer up*!' he shouted again. 'You lose that tongue o' yours o' what?'

Jamini knitted his fingers in his lap, looking down at them.

'Ask Lambert if she ever see God. Tell she I say to show you He face.'

Still knitting his fingers in his lap, looking down at them, he answered meekly.

'But Dada, I see him in Mr Innis' Drug-store. He looks like . . .'

'O-ho . . . an' you see 'im put he hand in he pocket an' give anybody a shilling? Answer me that.'

'No,' Jamini said, sitting quietly. He wanted to say that it was He who made the rain. He and Mr Innis. It was they who made smoke and fire, the smell of burning leaves—from all the bottles on the Drug-store shelves they planted seeds, it was they who made people well when they were ill; with powders wrapped in three-cent and five-cent packs, and Bay Rum when their heads ached, and iodine, black iodine that burned, but dried up cuts and sores; yes, it was they who . . .

'God dead!' the old man shouted, his eyes glared out, his arms hung down to his sides, pushed back behind him as he stood, arched above Jamini. 'Listen to what you Dada say. He dead an' gone long time gone. Is that old woman, your Dadie, an' that old witch Lambert 'pon Henry Street what puttin' stupid idea in your head o' what?'

The boy could hardly speak now, the pain at the base of his throat tightened, and he kept swallowing. It tasted salty. It seemed that the tears that were wont to rush to his eyes had somehow forced their way to his throat, now they pressed hard, tightening up his neck.

'No,' his voice forced out feebly, although he was sure that he could speak, 'I don't know who told me so, I saw Him in Mr Innis' Drug-store one day and I knew it was God.'

'So,' the old man grinned cynically, 'is you who is the fool, you ain't ask nobody *one* word, an' you t'ink that that is God?'

'But Mr Innis said so, and Dadie . . .'

'O-oh . . . so now it comin' out, now you rememberin' who an' who tell you all this nonsense. God is a stupidness, is a Nancy story, you hear. Do you work, an' do good job, make good lesson in school, that is all. Don't bother with all this nonsense talk, you gettin' to be big boy, you must learn sense. It have God for foolish, foolish people who ain't want to do they work. They prayin' an' prayin' an' they t'ink that God go throw rice in they lap. You is Pathan chile, an' Pathan make to work, an' work good good, good. Nobody ain't go give you nuttin' in this world, you have to make everyt'ing you-self and that t'ing you see in Innis Drug-store is a statue, is a stone, and Pathan mustn't make stone he God. That is what different different people have in them church too; they go with long face and say "God, gimme motor-car, God, gimme bicycle, God, gimme boy-chile, God, gimme this an' that, God, don't let police lock me up".'

Kale Khan screwed up his face in the most ugly way as he spoke these words, saying them in a sing-song tune, a sort of pleading and begging which even the boy thought ridiculous.

'It ain't have nuttin' like that, so you better break you mind from all this kind t'ing.'

But Jamini wondered. Suddenly the skies fell down and the world died.

The rain fell outside like water poured from the roof-tops by playful children. The days and the nights would be colourless chaos. If the world was not made of strange and mysterious perfume locked up in the jars of Mr Innis' Drug-store, then it was dry and rotten. Why were flowers beautiful? Why were some flowers of the poui yellow, others mauve? Why were their petals twisted and coloured in such delicate hues? Who was the master of all this? Where did the rivers then flow, and why? And who killed God, he wondered, but he was afraid to ask, to talk, afraid that the old man would again begin shouting, and he sat in silence.

A sudden emptiness fluttered in his stomach. What would become of the old woman on Quarry Street? Everything was going to be all right because she prayed to God. And Miss Lambert, Aunt Matil, he would be afraid to look up at the stone tomorrow the statue. for he wondered if he might not find out that God was indeed made of stone, of cold white plaster, armless, bodiless, silent, dead, staring from his hollowed-out eyes, seeing nothing, hearing no one who came pleading to him for help.

'Dada,' he said meekly, 'I think I'd better go upstairs now.'

He felt tired, he felt as though he had been running and running, for miles and miles, now he had stopped, and his body ached, it felt weakened and drained.

'Wait,' Kale Khan commanded angrily, 'Wait! I want you to remember this lesson well. God dead, you hear me? They wrap 'im up in white cotton, an' stuff two camphor ball in he nose. They tie he two big toe together with white, white string, an' sprinkle 'im with red hibiscus petal, then they put 'im in the ground an' cover 'im up with he two hand crossin' 'pon he belly. That is where God is . . . below the ground.

'It ain't have God for Pathan, you hear! Pathan is he own God. You is Pathan son, Pathan grandson, don't let people fool you with this Nancy story. These damn fool lookin' inside book for God, is there you t'ink you go find He? An' He go do nice t'ings for you? You have to do everyt'ing with your own two foot an' hand, an' when it break-up an' spoil-up, is you who have to make it over—by yourself—that why Pathan God dead; that why Pathan is he own God. Now g'wan, g'wan upstairs.'

The rain fell, it poured. In its uncertain wandering paths and ways it cut canals. It cut out devious wedges of the land as it went searching for the open mouth of the sea. In the morning it made the charcoal wet, and the children teased their parents who struggled to make breakfast fires, and the coal-pots emitted wet grey smoke and would not kindle. The children hid below their beds; from below their dry bed-sheets they jeered:

House full, kitchen full
Can't catch a thimble-full
Guess what it is?

Through the monotony of the endless rain they sang, their small hands stretched out of windows, catching raindrops.

Rain, rain go to Spain,
Never come back to Port of Spain.

But Jamini did not sing with them, he knew that singing would not stop the rain. It had come to shut him up like all the other children who could not go out to play, to wander, to catch the falling flowers of the poui in Woodford Square. Next door, he could hear Tommy pleading with his mother to let him go out.

'Is all right for we to go to school when rain come, but is not all right for we to spin top or pitch marbles. I can't see the sense in that,' Tommy grumbled, winding a string around his top.

His mother was fixing dinner in the kitchen, after she had spent a long time to get the fire going.

'All right, young man, you talkin' too big for you size, now go inside and take off those pants er yours. We go see who is boss in this house.'

Tommy started pouting his lips, still winding the top, sitting on the floor with a sullen look on his face, a slow whining in his voice.

'If we go out to play we go catch cold, but if we go to school we ain't go catch cold—it don't make sense to me,' he said sullenly.

Miss Dee kept right on breaking up some callalloo bush into long pieces, throwing them into a pot in which some crabs had become bright red from cooking.

These were the last words of the conversation Jamini heard. He too was tired of the cooped-up way they had to spend these days. In his room on the gallery he wound a toy which his grandfather had made for him with a bobbin, an elastic band, and a stick from a frozen icecream. He wound it slowly, bored with it too. The bobbin crawled lazily along the floor, came up to the wall; it turned and ground against the upright wall, then stopped.

'Jam . . . Jam . . .,' a voice called from the street below. He went to the window. Across the street and the grey air, and the spears of rain, and the children from a house up the street singing 'Rain, rain, go to Spain, never come back to Port of Spain.' stood Tommy, looking up to the gallery, his hand over his eyes to keep the rain from splashing into them.

'Tommy, what's up, what are you doing in the rain?'

'Come on down and let us play, man.'

'Play what?' Jamini asked. 'The top nails will sizzle in the mud, the marbles will stick in the ground . . .'

'Shhhhhh . . . not so loud . . . let we play "jockey," let we play racing boat, man.'

Jamini looked around. Meena was safely in the kitchen.

'I thought your mother lock up you pants in the bureau, Tom . . .'

'Shhhhhh . . . you comin' or ain't comin'?' Tommy asked, keeping his voice low.

'Okay, okay. Wait in the gateway,' Jamini said, then disappeared from the window.

He tip-toed down the steps, crawled on his hands and knees past Kale Khan's window, then he and Tommy, filled with laughter at the way he sneaked past the old man's room, ran out of the gate way to the street.

Outside the canals that flowed down Frederick Street to the sea were swollen with bright-red muddy water, starting in the hills of St Ann's, rushing through the city on its way to join the Gulf of Paria.

Jamini started rubbing a matchstick with a piece of hard-candle that Tommy handed him after he was done with it. The hard impervious grease of the candle would make their craft go skimming along the water all the more rapidly.

Two boys who were singing 'Rain, rain, go to Spain,' saw Jamini rubbing his matchstick, and soon they too came splashing down the street to join the race.

'Ready, set,' Tommy blurted out, then, catching himself quickly, he looked back to see if anyone had heard his voice in the street. Now he whispered, 'Ready . . . set . . . go.'

They dropped their craft into the canal water, and off they went, slipping along the eddies and rapids of the Frederick Street canals . . . the lightning little matchsticks, folded paper boats, a bit of wood, a straight pin sticking out of it for a mast. They rode their boats and motioned, and whipped, their hands slapping hard at their sides as though they rode horses in a race. Now that they were far from home they shouted at the top of their voices:

'COME ON, MISS TRINIDAD . . . GET UP, MISS TOBAGO . . . DOWN THE ROAD, DOWN THE ROAD, MAMA, DOWN THE ROAD.'

The stores were already closed, they had Frederick Street to themselves. One of the boats got caught up in a tiny whirlpool, the boys roared, they helped it to free itself, and off it went.

'Aye-aye-ai,' the owner shouted, 'now you go see the fireworks,' he screamed as the little paper boat bounced out of the whirlpool with Tommy out in front, leading the crew, shouting 'Jam . . . where you hidin' that old Diesel, come on up, man, come on up.'

A cyclist came by from out of nowhere and out right in front of Tommy. It missed him by inches, the wheels of the bicycle cut two tall V's of water as it sawed through the canal. The cyclist raised his feet to the handlebars, coasting through the splash he made, leaving Jamini, who was following closely.

'Oh, Gawd,' Tommy burst out, as the water splashed him up to his face. His and Jamini's clothes were red with the mud of the canal water.

'Why you don't look where the arse you ridin', you big bitch?' Tommy shouted.

'They go put you in gaol for that nasty tongue 'er you's, you li'l bastard,' the cyclist turned around and yelled.

Tommy stood by angrily watching him ride on. With his fingers he scraped the water off his forehead, shaking his hand, then wiping again, curling his fingers and sweeping the water as it dripped down his face forming drops at the point of his chin.

'Wait till I get big, see if I ain't bust you arse for you.'

'Why you don't go home an' tell you mother to get a tooth brush with soap for that stinkin' li'l mouth you have?'

'My mouth stink, but yours stinker, you big bitch . . . just because you big you t'ink I 'fraid you.'

'All right, you li'l vagabond,' the cyclist answered, and turned around sharply, coming back to the boys. As he did, the front wheel skidded and he went sprawling. His chest slapped the road as he pitched forward from the bicycle. The boys ran a few yards, then stopped. He got up, and started rubbing his hands. The front of his jacket and trousers were muddy.

'Now we go see who is man,' he said, coming after the boys again.

In their bare feet they started running down Frederick Street, the cyclist after them. As he got to the large expanse of water flowing down the street he stopped dead, looking at his shoes, afraid to try a jump across the width of the swollen canal.

'Ah know you face, you know. Don't let me see you walkin' in the road, otherwise ah go bounce you an' send you to hospital,' he called out, shaking his finger at the boys as he spoke.

They laughed at him. 'Come an' catch we nuh . . . you say you is man.'

'Haul you arse, big bitch . . . you hear me . . . haul you arse,' Tommy shouted, as he and the boys ran all the way down Frederick Street and caught up with the boats.

'Hey: Look where we is—we at Marine Square,' one of the boys shouted. The others looked up suddenly; they hadn't realised that they had come that far from home. Everyone plunged his hand into the water, took out his boat, and started running for home.

As Jamini started crawling past his grandfather's window, he felt a painful twist on his ear. The twist pulled at his ear lifting him up until he stood face to face with Kale Khan.

'So . . .' was all the old man said, glaring at the boy.

He let go of his ear. 'Come on this side,' he motioned to the door, with his right hand, his eyes piercing the boy.

'Meena go kill you with blows, you ain't have no sense o' what? Take off that wet clothes, and here, put on this.' The old man took a merino and pair of trousers from the line which Meena had hung across the front of his room. 'Better leave this wet clothes here. G'wan upstairs now, before anybody know that you run away to play in rain.'

Meena was still in the kitchen. She hadn't missed him. He heard Miss Dee's voice next door saying:

'Ah wants you to repeat the last words I hear you say before you leave the house this evenin'.'

Silence.

'That tongue o' yours waggin' whole day, now it dry up in you skull. Tell me that you want me to come an' pull it out with a pliers.'

'Ah say that if we go out to play we catch cold . . . but if we go to school we ain't catch cold,' Tommy said.

'And . . .?' Miss Dee questioned angrily.

'And that it don't make sense to me, mother,' Tommy added, his head hung low, avoiding her piercing stare, as she towered above him, one hand on her hip, the other motioning with her pot spoon.

Pock . . . pock, the pot spoon sounded on his head.

'Call me Miss *Dee*, you li'l vagabond. You tryin' to sweeten me up callin' me *mother*.' *Pock* went the pot spoon on his jaw.

'Oh Gawd . . . Oh Gawd . . . . Oh Gawd . . .' He screamed, bringing the neighbours to their windows.

'Thou shalt not take the name of the Lord in vain, sinner,' Miss Dee said, her teeth clenched. He started to sidle away, but she grasped a hook-handle walking-stick, caught him around the neck with it, and started tugging hard, pulling him back towards her. The veins on his neck stood up as he screamed, pressing against the crooked handle of the stick. Miss Dee swung the pot spoon left and right, trying to find an opening to hit him on his head again, but he flailed his arms on his face, his eyes, his mouth.

'Miss Dee, don't hit the chile on he head, man . . . you might fracture something,' Meena called from her window. The other neighbours shook their heads and sucked their teeth in disgust.

'Is only woman does beat a chile like that,' Kale Khan shouted.

It was always the same when Tommy got a licking, everybody knew that no pleading from the neighbours, nothing could save him, for Miss Dee's temper only seemed to increase as she continued to beat him until he was reduced to a curled-up ball of snivelling and hiccoughing.

'Murder . . . Murder . . . Oh Gawd . . . My hand break,' Tommy bawled.

'Ah is goin' to take that devil outer you today—today,' *pock . . . pock . . . pock*. The pot spoon landed on his hand. 'An' God alone in His true senses will thank me for it.'

He held on to the walking-stick, trying to catch the pot spoon as it waved back and forth, landing on his head, his jaw. Miss Dee tugged hard, jerking at his neck. His head tossed backwards and his eyes rolled.

'You goin' to listen to me . . . you goin' to hear?' *Pock* . . . 'Those who can't hear must feel, sinner.'

'Oh Gawd Oh . . . Yes, Miss Dee . . . yes, Miss Dee,' he whispered. She moved the walking-stick from his neck. He crawled into a corner, whimpering.

Miss Dee went to her pot, sticking the spoon on the rim. 'Come here an' fan this fire before it go out,' she commanded Tommy.

They were sweet words, words that fell like honey, words that told him her anger had passed its worst.

Jamini prayed to God that night to let the old man die. He prayed to the God on the shelf in Mr Innis' Drug-store, because he was afraid, afraid for the old man, afraid that God would crush him, would snap the thin long bones of his legs in two, pop open his skull like a tennis ball under a tram.

'You have no fear of God, you little vagabond. . . .' How many times had he heard Miss Lambert say these words? Looking over to the Trinity Church he clasped his hands and prayed the way Miss Lambert had taught him, praying as he looked to Miss Lambert's Church which she said was the House of God, praying for the old man who did not fear God.

He fell asleep and dreamt Kale Khan was dead and woke up sobbing in his pillow. Meena was at the side of his bed. She sat close to him and began running her fingers through his hair, softly, slowly, saying, saying, 'Go to sleep, go to sleep,' whispering in his ear, 'Is only a dream . . . go to sleep now.'

He listened to the rain falling outside, telling him from its sound on the galvanised roof that it was just a dream, and he felt Meena's fingertips touching lightly on his forehead, the warmth of her body.

He heard the raindrops striking on the leaves of the trees in Woodford Square, and he fell asleep again, glad that the old man had not died, glad that he had only been dreaming.

But back in his room Kale Khan did not sleep. Each time he clashed with his kin, his mind went back into the past, re-counting all that had led him to his beliefs, his insistence on returning home to Hindustan. His thoughts went as far back as the days before the trams and the pitch roads, before the radio, before Indians wore suits and rode bicycles to work in the offices of Port of Spain; to when they came to Princes Town that night with hurricane lanterns to the celebration of the Hussay, the religious festival of great floats drawn through the streets to the din of drummers, dancers, musicians and stick fighters.

That year the festival was to take place under police protection. Its road was marked out. 'You hear the news . . . we can't cross the train-line this year.' The news rang out from Princes Town into the hills. Mounted police and armed officers were assigned along the strip which the Hussay traversed as the crowds gathered from early evening.

'But where is we stickman tonight?' people asked as the evening grew and Kale Khan did not appear. A muffled gasp shot up through the crowd when at the far end of the strip a tall, turreted, church-like Hussay launched out onto the road. The horses jogged and neighed as if they too sensed the sudden charge that shot through the crowd. As the Hussays approached, the stick fighters could be seen as well as heard. They sidestepped and swiped at each other in jest, then waved their *lathis* high in the air. And then there was the sound of a stick as it struck the ground three times. The players fell back to the sides, the continuous rhythm of the drums faltered. Eyes searched for the man who had struck the ground for it meant a *real* stick fight, a broken head and a fight till blood. All eyes focused upon a thin young man with dark circles around his cold, white, deep-set eyes. His shoulders were bony and wide, but he was small from hips down, thin at the waist and legs. A black handkerchief was tied about his forehead, its two points hung down behind his head like braids of hair. He searched about for a pair of eyes that would meet his. His body tensed, his shoulders arched in waiting like a snake, the better to strike.

Out of the crowds and in front of the Hussay darted a figure dressed in white flannel trousers, narrow at the bottom, like riding breeches. His feet were bare, and across his chest he wore two leather cartridge belts lined with bullets; a revolver was tucked in at either side. In an instant he was on the strip with a *crack*, *crack*, *crack*, of his *lathi*. 'Look . . . is Kale Khan,' a man in the crowd shouted. And they edged up as close as they could. 'Let me see if is true . . . Kale Khan does wear a *Tabeej* on his arm when he come to play stick fight.' As the figure turned round to let someone remove his belts, they saw the *Tabeej*, a religious charm placed in a small silver box which was tied with a fine black string around his arm, another paradox of his Pathan blood. 'Well, at last we stickman come! At last we have somebody to fight with that pissin' tail boy tonight!' they said to each other, boastfully.

The mounted police stood up in their stirrups to get a better look at the figure who had roused the crowd. They watched him jutting his *lathi* in the air. The drummers started beating their drums with a new zeal, a new pride, which would lead up to the frenzy of the stick fight. Kale Khan held his *lathi* at both ends, swaying left and right in front of the Hussay as the drums beat for him, not glancing once at the dark boy who challenged the stickman of Princes Town. The boy stood to the side now, waiting, more sullen now as Kale Khan preened and paraded before the Hussay, his head thrown back, letting the cymbal clashes peck and pull at his chest-muscles, letting the drum-beat summon up the fighting passion in him. The crowd watched his body begin to quiver, his arms shaking his *lathi* from the wrist, pointing it at the dark boy.

Pat-pat-pat, the sticks went as they cracked each other, once hitting the ground, then they walked away, turned, and came to face each other again. The dark boy smiled at Kale Khan, whose bones were clenched within his jaw. *Crack-crack-crack*, the sticks met again and the dark boy swept his *lathi* fast at Kale Khan's feet.

Kale Khan jumped into the air and the crowd sighed 'ah.' The dark boy looked at him through glass-white eyes, warning him. The two men traced a circle about each other, each more cautious now of the flashing sticks, the copper wire wound about their surfaces glinted in the yellow flambeau light.

Crack-crack, *crack-crack-crack* the sticks met again as they touched the ground, and Kale Khan's came up first . . . then came crashing down straight to the dark boy's forehead. The boy fell to his knees, threw up his hand, and broke the blow with his left-hand pad. He bared his white teeth in a smile of pride.

And the crowd said, 'Break open he head . . . Where these pissin' tail boys come from at all? . . . They go learn they lesson when they get they head break open . . . That damn boy go remember Kale Khan so long he live.'

Pat-pat-pat, the sticks went quickly, and the boy's stick slashed

Kale Khan's arm . . . 'Aye-aye-aye,' the crowd whispered, but the *lathis* went on *Crack-crack*, *crick-crick* waiting for an opening. Kale Khan hit the ground and the dark boy broke the blow with his *lathi*, his white eyes stood still for a second looking at the *lathis* end, and Kale Khan in that split second came crashing down upon his shoulder. Kale Khan hit him on his buttocks and he twisted like a dried-out stump, arched his body like a bow.

'That boy is a fool or what? Kale Khan was only playin' with he . . . He done gone and beg for trouble tonight . . . Kale Khan should'er break open he foolish head for 'im, let them know how bad we Princes Town stickmen is.' The crowd jeered as the dark boy's *chelars* ran to him and got him out of the way of the on-coming Hussay.

'Aye, your backside burning . . . you lucky,' a man jeered as the *chelars* squeezed past the tight crowd at the strip's edge.

Ahead, the shining white steel girders of the railroad tracks could be seen in the pale moonlight with two large 'X' shaped crosses bolted on the top of poles on either side of the road, marked 'Rail Road' on one arm of the 'X', 'Crossing' on the other. Immediately behind the shining tracks were the two hundred mounted policemen. Kale Khan was at the head of the procession now. He jutted his *lathi* into the air in rhythm with the drums. His body was like new silk in the moonlight, his chest and shoulders glistened with the warmth of a delicious sweat as he waved his *lathi* at the pressing crowd. Then he made a complete turn about, slashed his *lathi* beneath his feet and jumped in the air. And then, suddenly, there was a '*crick-crack-crick*' on the ground. The drumbeat faltered again. Kale Khan swung sharply around and there in front of him was a little boy of about five waving a *lathi* at him. He felt his heart pound, and then, seeing the child, his face broke into a sea of laughter. The child's mother came running out of the crowd, but Kale Khan motioned her back as he parried and faked with the child. Then the little boy started back to his mother who shook her finger threateningly. He lurched away from her grasp, and ran zig-zag down the strip, where he stopped dead in front of the horses. Now he turned and raced down the tracks, his mother close behind. One of the mounted police reared his horse, its front legs high in the air, then with a loud smack on the horse's flank he lunged down the tracks, and with a sweep of the long clubs used to break up crowds he swept the woman off the ground with a blow that landed in the small of her back. There was no cry from her, only a pained grimace as she arched backwards as though the main support of her body had collapsed with her. The child turned to see how close she was, and saw her falling. As he ran towards her the momentum of the horse and rider which had not yet halted came tumbling down upon them, with a dull sound, and the childs' entrails lay exposed on the earth. In an instant the crowd had surged towards the police lines, the mounted troops drew back fifty yards behind the tracks and there was a great volley of noise and smoke as they opened fire on the crowd, felling men, women and children; then they came galloping through, swinging their clubs left and right as they rode. Two of the Hussays were on fire, fine sparks shot up in the air from their splintered bamboo skeletons. Some of the peasants had jumped at the horses and pulled off a few riders, and there were small knots of men fighting on the ground. Some, who had carried their cutlasses had them drawn, and women were wailing as they dragged the bodies of their men off to the sides.

'Kareem . . . Mustapha . . . Kurban,' Kale Khan called.

'Oh God . . . look what they are doing,' one of the men said as he came running to Kale Khan, for in the distance, the brigade mustered itself and prepared to come riding down again.

'Khan Sahib, it look as if they mean to kill every man here tonight,' another man said to Kale Khan as he came running up with his gun and holsters. 'Let we show them . . . just this one time,' said another, for this was not the first scene of this kind.

'All right,' said Kale Khan. 'Is fight they want, let we give them a fight they go remember when they write the history of Trinidad. Break up, break up now in two, two, three,' he ordered the men who gathered about him like flies now. 'All you boys who have two gun, give one to somebody else.'

And as the hoofs came pounding down upon them, they spread out like ants, shooting, hacking, and letting their *lathis* fly, felling several of the mounted police. 'Pick out one man,' shouted Kale Khan, drawing out each of the four syllables as he was accustomed to do in his army days in Hindustan. 'One man. One man.'

And as the brigade came riding down again, he felt something hit his thigh. His leg was as cold as ice. He looked at the punched hole in his flesh and, torn between anger and the numbness in his leg, he pounded his thigh as though it were the cause of the evening's madness. The horses were bearing down upon them, and his hand was empty. He had his man picked out, an officer with a bright red moustache. Wild with anger he looked out for his gun. But there was his *lathi*. He snatched it up, and as the brigade came closer and closer he began swirling it about him, loving the sound the heavy wirebound stick made as it sliced through the air, then he let fly. It struck the officer across the mouth with a loud crack, the horse tumbled and its rider fell, and Kale Khan saw the bright red blood burst out of his mouth like a fountain of deep red wine. The crowd fell upon him and a dozen *lathis* came crashing down as was happening in several other spots.

In the distance a bugle was sounding retreat. It was like music in Kale Khan's ear. He heard horses running wild without their riders, he heard sobbing and crying in the fields, and he saw the early morning moon going down. 'To Hindustan,' he thought. And then he felt a sharp pain in his thigh.

'Khan Sahib, you get hit,' one of the men said excitedly as he saw Kale Khan leaning back on his elbows looking across the chaos in the fields. And then, looking at the dead officer at his feet, 'You shoot me one time only . . . but I kill six of you first boy. Is all right. Is all right.'

7

THE evening came to Port of Spain with the sun splashing over the Hills of Laventille, spreading a strange, pale, orange light that made the buildings seem to vibrate before the yellow disc of the sun sewed itself into the waters of the Gulf of Paria. Thin, long, stretched-out shadows of overhanging galleries projecting from the houses along the city streets flung themselves across the road like silent sleeping dogs that stretched from time to time.

The trees and the houses, the faces of the wandering men, the children screaming in the deep and solemn backyards, the tired-out smell of tar; these were the things that felt the evening coming; and if it had not happened this way before, one might have thought some monstrous disaster was in store before nightfall. As it was, the night had come with murmurings like this before, and nothing had happened. It was an infinity of life that came with evening, always promising a tomorrow, a tomorrow that always came; and if some playful god had clipped a few days from the calendar, it would have been the same, no one would ever have known, because the days flowed on with a sameness, and the late-from-work who wended their way home to callalloo made from the blue-crab, and cascadee from the Caroni swamps, they knew that the world was always there; that no sudden storm would sweep over Trinidad to make it new, or confusing, came the morrow.

In the setting of the sun, the fire-red skies, and the thin wisps of idle clouds, those who had read great books and crossed the seas had come to Trinidad; they said that in these skies at evening there was beauty; but the workman wended his way home across Woodford Square, with a nip of Black Cat Rum tucked under his arm. He walked in the shadows of this evening, and it was enough to expect the sun on the morrow, coming up dripping from its ocean depths, wet with the dew from the mountains of the East, it was enough to *expect* it, no one had to *know* of tomorrow. The end of today promises, as love promises love, fidelity, infinity, and a feeling that life would go on forever. Today was ending with a tiredness in the bone that promised sleep and rest, and growing and mending of the run-down cells.

In the dark of that night Christopher Columbus, Lord Harris, Sir Ralph Woodford, Sir Walter Raleigh, Drake, Hawkins, Sir Ralph Abercromby, and Don Chacen, who sank his ships with Spanish gold off Chagauramas Bay—they would walk the streets in heavy armour of steel and brass, mirror-bright to catch the light of the moon; and the cemeteries of the dead who fought for this island, this Trinidad—this kind of night was theirs, this falling down of evening would touch upon the white, forgotten crosses of their tombs in the graveyards that lay level, over-run with jungle that fears not death, nor axe, nor scythe of man; they would walk the streets and strike the bushes with their long, long staffs. They would cross their swords by the lighthouse down on Frederick Street, and touch their torches to the flared-nosed cannons; they would fire pistols into ancient kegs of rum and drink the golden yellow liquor; they would feast on wild meat like the Manicou, and dance down Frederick Street with women who had gypsy-fire in their eyes, who tip-toed on the cobble-stones, holding their petticoats high.

The streets should not be lit with haloes round the light bulbs; a single voice should wander down Chacon Street crying 'eight o'clock and all is well,' while Raleigh's men were crawling up the mountainside to seize the town for England far away.

Along the wharves and docks of Port of Spain where lumber lay that smelled of forest still, and the old soaked wooden planks hanging with the lash of the sea, the air on nights like these had a taste of the nights of old, with galleons lying out at sea, winking their starboard lights at Port of Spain, the waters of the Caribbean washing on their sides as they rode and swayed at anchor in the dark beyond the jetty.

They had not died, these scents and odours, these men of long ago; they were kneeling in Columbus Square, receiving His blessing, and saying thanks to God this night.

You could hear their voices echoing with the discovery of the New World. And in Woodford Square, Sir Ralph Woodford was looking out to the Trinity Church beyond; he'd laid its foundation stone—how long ago?

Lord Harris spoke from his pedestal up on Knox Street, to the emptiness in Lord Harris Square.

Sir Ralph Abercromby marched up and down Abercromby Street, looking for the Spaniards.

And Drake, Hawkins and their lusty men; their masts were straining out beyond the Boca swelling with Caribbean wind.

The land was old and filled with mysteries hiding in the broken-down forts and outposts overgrown with weeds and hibiscus going to sleep. These were the mysteries of the night, of men who lived long, long ago.

But of those whose footsteps fell on Port of Spain today, none would have mourning for these dead . . . the streets would never echo with the workman hammering on iron spikes to keep the tram-lines straight, hammering in a sleeveless black merino, his glistening skin exposed to the sun.

The clerks who bicycled down Frederick Street to its shops and stores, and the men in collar and tie, who sold the postage stamps—their ghosts would never wander through the streets of Port of Spain two hundred years from now. The stained steps of the Town Hall, rubbed black with greasy dirt from the bodies of the old, old men, these were the shortcut echoes of their lives; they would be white-washed clean and leave no mysteries in the land; they would not hold debates on rainy nights within the archways of the buttressed balcony that overhung the Town Hall. It was so when evening had fallen, it was quiet with only the silent voices of the past, for the city knew that it had no dreams to give them, no memories of its men of today, and it hid its face in the darkness of the evening with only the bells of Trinity Church telling—counting out nine o'clock.

And Rahim said:

'Boy, is time for you to sleep. I don't know why you all time watchin' out, watchin' out in that Square. If you keep on lookin' an' watchin' in the dark, one day you will see somethin' that will frighten you.'

The boy turned to his cot, lying north and south along Frederick Street. He heard the old men's coughing from the steps of the Town Hall across the Square, and he wondered if he had not already seen that frightening thing that lurked in the dark, through his window looking out to the Square.

In the corner of their living-room was a gilt picture of Saint Anne playing an organ, looking out into nothingness. A dozen small cherubs strewing flowers, with wings and halos, soared above her head. Rahim had bought it at an auction sale. Below it was the table where the kerosene lamp burned, and Meena sat on a rocking-chair with a copy of the Koran, chanting, reading, letting her voice play between song and recitation, bringing into the room a silence and reverence such as lingered on the Mosque on Queen Street after all the attendants had left.

The evening pulled tightly upon his sinews. To the west Raleigh's men, to the east Meena's haunting chants that filled his ear; the voices of the long-dead men asking him whither, asking him who he was. His voice beneath his breath caught the rhythm of Meena's chants. The words fell in a pattern that he knew, and his head tossed lightly from left to right as the chanting lowered and rose. But his eyes were empty, his thoughts as dry as crab shells tossed up on the shore, empty, waiting to be filled by the running of the tide, with the salt-water of the sea, and the substances that would fill the empty holes, the hidden corners, but would never raise the semblance of a single movement.

As Meena chanted on, stopping from time to time to clear her throat, he knew that his mind had lost the meaning of the words she read, and he wondered if perhaps God was not dead.

'Meena,' he said feebly; but she did not hear, and then he spoke to himself again, saying:

'Meena, tell me, Meena, what are the meanings of the words. Tell me so that I shall always remember, so that I shall remember them on judgment day when the Angel asks me to read a Suré, to speak the name of God. Eternity is a long time for my soul to wander, and I feel it falling off the ledge, falling down into a bottomless, soundless sea. What are the meanings of the words,

Meena? My mind wanders into a nothingness that has lost its closeness to these words pressing upon my mind.' He shook his head from left to right as if to shake off the sleep that dulled his senses, as if to speak lament; for his mind and his memory swelled only with sounds of things he had once known, they lingered close to his lips, at the tips of his senses, but would not scratch their stark impressions there.

'Is there a Suré in the book for the mind that wanders? A tonic, Meena? For the soul that weakens and drifts away? A verse for the tired who have come to the dark, not knowing why? To call them back?'

The wind came into the room where Meena and Rahim sat. It turned the page, and it blew Meena's veil from her head. The tongue of flame sputtered, the jalousies fluttered, and the lamp went out.

'What wrong?' Meena started. 'Something bad come into this room.'

'I can't find the matches in this dark,' Rahim said. 'Meena, feel on the table. See if it there.'

The wind died down as fast as it came.

Meena found the matches and re-lit the lamp.

She looked at her son, Jamini, lying fast asleep, his arm hanging off the edge of his cot.

And she thought she heard the wings of the Jumbie bird flapping, flying away from the Calabash tree.

She took the boy's arm, placed it on his cot, then she closed the window and came back to the chair, and said:

'I have to start all over again,' replacing the veil over her head.

Then they heard the old man striking the floor, his wooden slippers clot-clotting, his walking-stick knocking, as he walked to the pipe in the yard.

'Meena, I think I'll go downstairs and keep a l'il company with the old man, it look as if he still 'wake.'

'You don't want to stop 'till I finish?'

'You read, Meena, finish the Sure, my mind ain't too clear tonight.'

Meena read, and the tongue of flame stood still. It rested like a thin-tongued petal of the red hibiscus, sleeping in the hills on a windless night, as Rahim silently went downstairs to sit and talk with his father.

The old man coughed and knocked his stick on the floor when he heard Rahim's footsteps outside.

'Boy—that you, boy?' then he saw him, and said:

'Don't walk about like thief in the night, walk like you have two feet, and eye that ain't 'fraid in this dark. Sit down, sit down.' The old man paused, seated on his bed, looking down at the floor. He nodded. 'Night time too long, day time too short: old people never get sleep. What you doin' walkin' in this hour? An' that boy, he gone to sleep?'

'Long time, *Barp*, since nine o'clock ring.'

'You mind bother, boy, you gettin' face like old old man, same like mine, you is a boy. Mustn't get old befor' you time, mus' joy life, have plenty to do befo' you look old man like me; is you tired, o' what?'

Rahim sat silently, his hand on the arm of the rocking-chair.

'Is the boy,' he said at last, 'he ain't lookin' good, he ain't like school, he tell his mother God dead. I don't know what get into that boy . . . he was learnin' good, good, good, now it look as if he ain't care.'

'Is I who tell him God dead. He have some statue in Innis' Drug-store, an' he t'ink that is God, and that old woman givin' him more and more foolish, foolish idea,' the old man grumbled on.

Rahim sat lost in thought

'Ah wish I did know o' these t'ings, ah wish ah did know what to tell the boy when he start t'inking all o' these t'ings.'

'Pathan must never worry in he head which, which way, what, what t'ing good for he to do. Must act, act fast like a lightning. Mus' feel that fire in he Pathan blood that tell he what wrong and what right. Mus' do without t'inking and t'inking. Is that what confusin' you mind?'

The old man sat on the edge of the bed, still wearing the small white towel he had placed over his head to protect him from the dew outside. He held a large white radish, whose inside he had hollowed out. In the shell he had placed a few mustard grains, which sprouted in the water he poured into the radish each day. There was a black umbrella wire pierced through its top to make a handle. He drank some of the water from the radish, licked his lips, swallowed, uttered a sigh of satisfaction, then hung it on the wall.

As he believed in this medicine, so he believed in his blood, and the voices that spelled out his actions, the voices that whisper to every Pathan the right, the wrong, the good, the bad. Rahim had gone astray. They should never have come to Trinidad; it was a cruel land, cruel in the ways of a lover. It did not stab with one sudden blow, it did not stand to watch the incisions made; it gnawed at the entrails and spread a quiet venom that chased through all the veins and marrows. It had settled in Rahim's blood and dulled his Pathan senses; the old man had seen it in the land, he had fought it off. He had led the Princes Town Hussay, he knew what he had to do, he did not wait for it to seize his limbs and freeze his bones. He would have said to Rahim 'You are not my son,' but he saw in him the movement of his own body: the beginning of the stoop of his back. He had seen him smoke the old clay pipe in Woodford Square over a game of chess; he had seen him twisting the filigree wire; he had seen him as a boy; he had seen the mole upon his cheek, the double-haired mole. He knew that this was his son, but the disease had infested his brain. He wished that they were wrestling with the elements side by side with the hill tribes of Hindustan, dwelling in the mysterious valleys of the Pathans, the last outposts that prevailed against all the invaders who swept past the centuries in Hindustan.

'*Barp*, the boy should'er dream, and believe all kind of foolish nonsense and fin' out what he had to fin' out later on, it would be better that way.'

'Boy, what have reason, an' what ain't have? Do you work, and do it good, good good; don't bother this reason, reason, reason nonsense, you go do good job,' the old man said firmly.

'Yes *Barp*, that is true . . .'

'An' you want for me to tell you why I does do what I do? I don't know, I really don't know, *who* know? Great, great man don't know, is not for we to worry, Pathan only have to *do*, boy—to act!'

'Yes, but what is the . . .' Rahim's voice trailed off.

The old man shifted the towel from his head to his shoulders, he had no explanation to give, no argument to bear each action out and tie it up with other actions.

He became sullen as he thought of Rahim's strangeness, his energies draining away on things he could never know, while time was running on and he knew that Rahim would not act; would wait and be cut down as he fought within himself.

The Trinity Church clock was striking ten o'clock.

'Rahim, Rahim,' Meena called. She walked down the steps and stood in the doorway of the old man's room, hearing him saying:

'This place ain't make for me, for you, none er we. We have we country and we people don't mind what it is. You own is you own. Come, come, sit down,' he turned and said to Meena.

'*Barp*, where we have to go? We done born and live here, what we go do in Hindustan? We live in Trinidad all we days, even in the Koran it say that a person should help to build up the place where he get he bread from. That is not good to have bad-mind for that country and even that Government o' that Rajah that give him food and shelter, you can't kick a bowl of milk. . . .'

Then he stared, his voice loud in the night, 'You want to know who the Government is! Is the Englishman who have so much brains that he have to make a empire to share it with. You seein' how the Englishman does share he brains with the Empire. You does ever feel the blood crawlin' an' crawlin' when they play God Save the King? Land 'er hope and glory? An' you hearin' what the song sayin'? "God who make thee mighty, mighty, make thee mightier yet." God ain't make Trinidadian mighty you know; but he give them Englishman to teach them how to be mighty, to teach them how a daffodil does smell, what daisy look like. We have hibiscus in Trinidad you know, and poui, but they teachin' we how to smell a daisy. You t'ink they teach we how to do jewellery work? They teach we how to forget all that we learn and bring come with we from Hindustan. That is what Government make for. Government is a "Obeah," a stronger "Obeah" than anything that we have.

'Look at all we local boys, them who gone to England an' come back, an' right away they start talkin' like Englishman; people frighten to tell them their troubles, their heart shakin' an' shakin' like some dry leaf in the wind when they get in a li'l trouble an' have to face up wid them in Court House. That is the Government.

'Is a English Obeah that stronger than we Obeah? Ah have to say to misself that those boys spoil, they spoil-up an' come back Trinidad side; they laffin' and laffin' at they own poopah an' moomah; they t'ink is a shame to eat wid their hand, and they settin' up their face when they see India food. You know how they come so? These boys was good good boys when they go England side. They shame to tell people that they is Indian, that they come from Trinidad. They sayin' that they is from South America, from the Continent. Is a nasty shame, an' that is what we king doin' for me, that is it.

'Tell me, you ever see King? You lucky if you see he face on a half-shillin'. That money ain't yours, is Government money. You t'ink the King put he picture on cent an' penny for we to say he have good looks? You t'ink is pretty he pretty? An' that's why they put he face on dollar-note? You wrong—is the stamp; it mean that that have to go back to the owner one day, one day, an' you lucky if you could hold on to it long 'nough to see what the King face look like. What the hell Government ever do for me?

'Government is the Union Jack flyin' 'pon top the Town Hall. Is the fête with people dress-up in nice clothes walkin' 'bout with whisky an' soda in they hand below big, big electric light in Government House by St Clair's. You could only peep an' see from passin' in the tramcar . . . nuttin' mo' . . . nuttin' mo'.

'Government is the bicycle licence that you ain't have five shillin' to pay; is the police who come to lock you up. All the big job that rich people child does get, the soft job with collar an' tie, you never see we gettin' them. When we get Government job look well an' see what we doin'; we sellin' Postage Stamp in the Treasury, that is all the big we brains big . . . no mo'. Government ain't make for poor people like me an' you, is a somet'ing that big, big people make to keep thief from their garden, an' is the same poor people who have to build up the gaol—that is what we payin' for. Gaol-house, court-house, water-tax, licence.

'You know where all that money goin' up to? The Island ain't have money to put up a shelter over these people head; sugar cane workers over, slavery over, an' now they say that they give we freedom—freedom to tote load in Woodford Square? To sit there on old soap box and pick out louse from one another head? Them boys is dead, dead, dead, dead, they ain't have wife an' chile, they like a tree—worse then that Calabash tree—least the tree have hundred 'pon hundred of seed, an' it could see itself growin' after it dead an' gone. What the use of them boys' life? They is animal, they is stone. Why Government ain't charge them a licence like dog, why they ain't give them dog licence, eh?

'But yes man, is *we* Government, is true, is true, you could find we in court-house, in the police station an' in the royal gaol up Frederick Street. We is the Government all right. You could find we up by Quarry Street, breakin' stone to build the road for motor-car to run 'pon, an' tell me who have motor-car? Yes man, we is the King he-self, we could buy a nip'er Black Cat Rum, an' we bigger than Police he-self, an' when we drink we rum an' tumble down, when the fire in the rum explo' in that fire we have in we head, well, the Government go take care o' we.

'You know where? Up Frederick Street, to sleep on cold cold concrete. Food free too—ginger tea an' stale bread, leave-over bread from the bakeries in town. When you come out people say "Eh-eh . . . but look how fat an' nice he get man, look how we Government takin' care 'er he." It ain't fat you fat you know, is swell you swell-up from sleepin' on cold cold concrete. But anyway we have consolation, they say we lucky. If you drop dead an' you ain't have nobody, is Government who go bury you, you know where? In the Hangman graveyard. They go bury you next to the murderers an' breakneck hangman an' them. Government does pay, pay for everyt'ing, for the scissors tail evenin' suit an' the black top-hat the coachman have to wear to bury you in—as a respect. An' people go tip they hat when you passin' down Tragarite Road on you way to St James for you six feet hole; nobody to follow you funeral, you have to say praise God you ain't have to walk to you grave-yard. The Government givin' you free horse an' carriage ride to the Hangman cemetery in the back of St James . . . that is where we Government puttin' we fast as we go to sleep below the Town Hall and never wake up.

'They have a place for we. All those boys like Mongroo and Kareem an' them who sleepin' in the dew. You t'ink those boys does sleep easy when they dream that the coachman comin' in scissors tail an' top hat?

'When I dead an' gone I don' care, you know, you could feed my body to dog, but those boys does worry, worry, worry, worry, because God don't send them Angel Gabriel to Hangman buryin' place. Them is the leave-overs, the dregs that go get leave out when Judgement time come. Government—huh! Can't even bury these people in a decent way after all they do for this land.'

The old man curled up on his bed, his face to the wall, holding his hands between his legs. He took full, deep breaths of air, making a soft rasping sound as his chest swallowed in and out, in and out. He was tired, tired, tired, as though he had just accomplished some fantastic physical task. Meena and Rahim slipped away quietly.

8

A PALE yellow disc of the sun peeped up over the hills of Laventille.

At eight o'clock a soft mist rose from the grass, lingering over the earth like a scene in fairy tale books. All was quiet, the smell of wet grass and loneliness, and the sound of rustling leaves, and soft morning breezes in the tree tops.

At ten o'clock tiny balls of crystal dew-drops rolled off the grass, fell into the forks of the blades, and wet the earth.

At noon the sun climbed into the heavens and burst into a wild, white fire of silent silver heat that flooded the sidewalks making their images sizzle and dance, and the shadows of passers-by fell in small circles beneath their feet.

At one o'clock the streets were empty. The wheels of a lone donkey-cart sliced out deep ruts in the soft asphalt road, leaving a zig-zag trail of small horse-shoe imprints between the two long lines cut out along Frederick Street.

At two o'clock the larger shops rolled down canvas awnings as solid shafts of sunlight squeezed through the doorways along Frederick Street, pressing like tight corks into their bottle necks.

At three o'clock Mr Hardaker, came to Rahim's shop, fanning himself with his black felt hat. He took out a soiled handkerchief and wiped around the inside rim of his hat, then he dropped into one of the rickety chairs that Rahim kept for customers.

'But Kayan,' Mr Hardaker began. Rahim flinched at the way the old man always pronounced his name. 'What we need is a *shelter* in front of the establishment from this *terrible sun.*'

Mr Hardaker spoke with the rise and fall of speech-making politicians.

Rahim went on working with his lamp and blow-pipe, his face blackened with the soot of the lamp as he soldered broken jewellery that had come in for repairs. He heard Kale Khan coughing from his room which was just behind the shop.

'If you keep too much chair in shop, just encourage idlers to come an' sit 'pon backside. Talk . . . talk . . . talk . . . all kind nonsense talk, never have time to do work,' the old man had said.

But then there were times like the Hussay season, Carnival, Christmas. Many people came to the shop, and he had to offer them a seat. The truth was that he enjoyed a little chat to pass the time of day, especially now that there was so little work to do. He hated sitting there alone, looking out at the hot street, thinking, pondering so many things. Yes, he liked to listen to Mr Hardaker, his talk about England, the United States, what the people did in the great countries, so many things, and most of all their partnership, their plan to re-model the shop with electric lights, glass cases, perhaps an electric fan for the ceiling like the larger shops had down Frederick Street.

'And you, sir, you've been a good lad?' Mr Hardaker asked Jamini. It was a sort of game they played. As far back as Jamini could remember, Mr Hardaker had always asked him this question. He would always reply, as he replied now, 'Yes, sir, very good.' Then, from a lump of putty, which he always squeezed between his thumb and index finger, Mr Hardaker would break off a piece and give it to Jamini to squeeze between his fingers; then from a small paper bag he would take out two eucalyptus drops and give them to the boy.

Jamini remembered Mr Hardaker saying, a long time ago, that he did not like the sour taste in his mouth, and so he always carried eucalyptus candy about. It seemed like a strange kind of luxury to the boy. He remembered thinking that he too might do something like that when he grew up. But now the old man seemed ridiculous; there was something sickening about him, and the sour taste in his mouth. Jamini thought of him as an old fool, and disliked him even more as the years went by.

'Have you been a good lad, sir? . . . yes sir . . . there's a good lad now . . . there's a jolly good lad. Ha! Ha! Ha! I've something for you, lad. What do you think I've got in my pocket, lad? *Eu—ca—lyp—tus.*'

He wanted to scream, 'Eucalyptus drops. You old fool . . . what else?'

Jamini put the eucalyptus drops into his mouth. He saw himself as a man wearing long pants and still having to go through this same game with Mr Hardaker, a game which even now seemed silly.

He wondered, 'What would this old fool think if he knew that I have kissed a girl, that I love someone and she loves me? What would he think if he could hear some of the things I have said to Lakshmi? Would he ever believe that I could do such things, say such things, or would I have to play this game with him for ever?'

Mr Hardaker moved on the chair, searching in his pocket. The chair made a series of squeaking, crunching sounds. It was a large wicker basket affair which Rahim had bought at the auction along with the picture of St Anne.

Mr Hardaker was a thin little old man with hair growing at the back of his neck. When he grimaced, his two overlapping front teeth were bared, making a small triangle of the top of his mouth. His lower teeth were ground down, and stood in a yellow slanting row. It was hard to believe that his bright little mouse-grey eyes had stood the punishment of age and time, for although his body seemed tired, as if some cancer of life had gnawed away at him, his eyes were bright as new agates. It was hard to think that in a far-away England he was the product of love, of a consummation of lovers, that these lovers who bore him had known tenderness for this man, for this lone wanderer who seemed to have fallen out of the womb with creases at the back of his neck and large brown freckles on his bony, blue-veined hands and fingers. No! Mr Hardaker could never have been a child, nor a boy, nor a lover. No imagination could stretch itself into seeing him in any of these roles; if the clocks were turned back to his beginning he would not be there. No day in the past would reveal him in the spring of youth. He had come from a nowhere, a land of the aged, entered the world through its back door—old, bald, and squeezing a piece of putty between his fingers.

Rahim blew out the sooty blow-lamp; it made a grey twist of curling smoke that smelled of vile unburnt kerosene, and the cherry-red piece of filigree he was working on hissed as it hit some green acid in a bowl which he used for cooling and cleaning. He rubbed his eyes; they felt dry after working close to the heat of the lamp.

Jamini knew that now Mr Hardaker had come, he could slip away from his table where he worked evenings after school; for he was to learn the trade of his father, and his father's father. Rahim, and even Meena, agreed with the old man on this. The boy should have a trade, no matter what else he might want to do later on, he must learn his father's trade.

'Kayan,' Mr Hardaker said again.

Rahim flinched a little. It was the one thing that bothered him about Mr Hardaker. Couldn't he pronounce his name properly? It wasn't such a difficult name. It wasn't just the pronunciation; there was something else. It made him feel servile. But then, here was a man who went to parties and balls at the Governor's House; he painted portraits of the rich people in Queen's Park. How many of *them* would come and sit here, talking on equal terms?

'These boards need a little touching up, man. We'll do that first,' Mr Hardaker added, looking out to the two sign-boards which Rahim had drawn in front of the doorways to keep out the sun of the afternoon. It was he who had suggested the sign-boards to Rahim, and he who had painted them in his free time when he wasn't doing portraits of the rich people, he had thought out the design.

'You've got to advertise, man, advertise, like those blokes in America,' he had said, the day he came by with a small box, thick with the spillings of hundreds of colours dribbled over its sides, and a yard-long stick with a little cloth ball at its end. He was dressed in his old but sedate-looking black suit, smelling sweet of turpentine. On two boards about six by four he had painted the faces of clocks, one on each. The first one had spindly little arms and legs. Roman numerals encircling its face, and a large winding screw for its head. Its face was tied in a sling that passed under its chin, and ended in two large knots above its head. Its mouth hung downwards like an inverted 'U', and one eye was covered by a black patch as it hobbled along wearily on two matchstick-like crutches, one of its legs grossly wound over with bandages, was twisted to one side and dragged behind in its pained lumbering. No face was so filled with misery and distress, and Mr Hardaker had painted it a pale white, with two little black X's on its cheeks.

On the other board was a smiling, running, laughing clock! No crutches, no bandages. Its face beamed as it came running out of the board, flailing its little arms in the air, its legs free and agile. The eyes joined in the happy smile of its face and on its cheeks were two discs of pink rouge. The signs were labelled 'Before' and 'After'.

'When people see these signs and they go home . . . why, they will certainly remember to bring their broken clocks and jewellery to be repaired,' Mr Hardaker had said as he and Rahim looked over the wet sign-boards.

Rahim beamed, he crossed the street to get a better picture of the way they looked from a distance. Suddenly he saw that his business had a name, 'Trinidad Gold and Silversmith Co.' spelled out above the faces of the clocks. He felt important. In the streets he could already hear the passers by, 'Trinidad Gold and Silversmith Co. Rahim Khan Prop.'

But how long ago had that been? After the rain, after the sun, after the faces of the clocks had come to look alike, and now that business was going downhill, he used them as a pair of shelters which he drew in front of his doors to keep out the blatant sun.

Mr Hardaker still sat in the chair making notes in a small black book of the things they would do in the shop, looking at the walls, at the black darkened ceiling, peeling from the heat and the soot.

'And those showcases, we must get new glass for them.'

Rahim had stuck long, Y-shaped pieces of tape across the broken glass. He had replaced an entire pane with a square piece of cardboard. His work tables were black with burnt-out holes from the spilling and cooling of red-hot globules of metal on the wood. He could do with a new work table, bright white and smelling of pine, and wooden hammer handles, nicely-shaped hardwood that came from England instead of the knobby tree branches which fitted loosely into the hammerheads. (He had hurt his finger a while ago when a hammerhead slipped out of the makeshift wooden handle, pinning his finger to the anvil.) He could do with some plated tweezers, new files that were sharp and did not take hours of rubbing across the metal to shape it.

The thought of the shop lit up by electric lights, new tools; they created a new enthusiasm in him, but still he was downcast, saying to Mr Hardaker, 'This is a dead business,' shaking his head in doubt.

'Let me worry about that. There's no reason why those big shops down Frederick Street should get all the trade.'

Rahim's interest livened up again. 'Why not give it a try?' he thought. Mr Hardaker could pass the word around to his friends. There was no reason why he could not get some of the work that the big shops did. After all, they did not do any work themselves. They had nice offices, showcases with mirrors in them, electric lights, advertisements in the newspaper, but it was Rahim, and people like him who really did the work. The big shops only paid them a small fraction of what they charged for the goods. Didn't people realise that? Why didn't they go to the small shops like Rahim's? They would save themselves money, and people like him would not be so hard up. He couldn't understand it. His heart swelled with pride at the thought of the new shop, yet he still kept saying to Mr Hardaker, 'I don't see how this thing will work.'

'The eyes of the world are looking to Trinidad. We can't let them down, man. We've got to do things for ourselves, we can't let people come in from the outside and show us how to move ahead,' Mr Hardaker bellowed, fanning Rahim's enthusiasm each time it lagged.

Rahim wondered what Mr Hardaker meant by 'come from the outside.' Didn't *he* come from the outside himself? He had won the first prize in the Trinidad Turf Club sweep-stakes about ten years ago, bought a few houses with it, and had never gone back to England.

There were slow footsteps coming from the back of the shop, followed by the clink of Kale Khan's walking-stick.

'What you talkin' about, man?' Kale Khan demanded of Mr Hardaker. 'That is the same talk we hear when we come Trinidad—you know that? How much years 'pon years we hear that?

Now sugar dead and gone and *we* leave-over. Man, stop this nonsense talk, you hear? Who the hell we is that people want we to make a place for weself?'

'But *Barp*,' Rahim interrupted, 'Mr Hardaker was only saying . . .'

Kale Khan paid no attention to him, he started coughing. The rainy season had kept him confined to his room. He spoke his words with strain.

'You think even a schoolboy in England know where Trinidad is? Answer me that, Hardaker! *You* build up the Island, we people tired; they suck blood, and you know what they do with it? They sitting 'pon they backside in St Ann's and St Clair's, and they making law in they big house with ten sergeants waiting 'pon them hand and foot. They sitting 'pon they backsides up in England and puttin' Trinidad sugar in they cup of tea! Yes, it well sweeten'in them up, but you think when they put that sugar in they tea they does ask, "Where did sugar come from, man? What kind of ground it grown from, man? What kind of work it take to make this sugar grow, man?"

'Yes, but if . . .' Mr Hardaker swallowed, preparing to speak. His throat rose up and down as he did, showing a few stubbles of unshaven, dirty grey hair attached to the loose skin of his neck; his mouth fell into the little, listening 'O' as before, his eyes registering the intensity, the rise and fall of Kale Khan's angry voice.

'But if *what*? Man, don't talk stupidness; is all right for you to talk. You come Trinidad, you win sweepstakes, you put thousand, thousand dollar in property, what the hell you know, boy? Is *me*, and *people* like me what makes this land. With we blood, and now we tired and we want to go home. All you bitch up in Government House want to keep we stop here, they ain't suck enough blood from we already? They want more?

Mr Hardaker was quiet as Kale Khan spoke. The old man's words seemed to hit something inside him, varying his expression with each tirade. He started to answer Kale Khan again. 'Yes, but if—if . . .'

'If shit was sugar farmer wouldn't plant cane,' Kale Khan said disgustedly, as he handed Rahim a few small envelopes with jewellery that he repaired in his room when he felt well.

'If . . . if . . . if . . .' he half-coughed, half-muttered, as he walked away in disgust, dragging his iron rod walking-stick behind him.

Jamini had slipped out of the shop. He stuck his hands in his pockets and started up Frederick Street.

'This foolish old man,' he thought, 'with his putty and eucalyptus drops . . .' Why didn't he give him sixpence instead? Then he could go to the movies with Lakshmi.

They were all the same—Mr Hardaker, Rahim, Meena. It was always talk of money, money, money. Everyone talked about it, nobody had it. What did sixpence mean to them? To him it meant that he and Lakshmi could sit in the dark back rows of the Empire Theatre—there, where he had first touched her breasts.

They were small. He had thought that they felt like the wild oranges that grew between the cocoa trees, as his arched fingers wandered across her bosom, searching with an instinct that played a tune to the movement of his wandering hands across her warm body, finally coming to rest in a little valley between her breasts. He had suddenly become afraid that day. He had felt that she was a woman, and he still a boy. If Rahim and Meena had let him wear long pants he would be a man, he wouldn't feel that she was running away from him. He had become peeved at her that day. She kept looking straight at the screen while a strange feeling quickened his heart. Perhaps she was ashamed, perhaps she did not want to look into his face, to say to him, 'Yes, I know you're fondling my breasts,' perhaps it was easier to know and yet to pretend not to know. Was that what she thought? He remembered the long kisses, how quickly two hours sped by. The kisses were no longer fumbling. They had loved in all the movie houses of the city—the Empire, the Globe, the Royal and the De Luxe. They had *their* seats where he waited the most painful waiting, for he always got there first. He knew her silhouette in the dark if the show had started. It was a kind of cheating—cheating the world that lived in the light of day, stealing kisses that the streets forbade. He liked to touch her lips, gently, as the humming bird's grazed the hibiscus flower and then to hold her tightly, sighing close to her ear, telling her to love him, that he would always love her.

Yes, why didn't Mr Hardaker give him sixpence instead, then he could be happy for two hours and a whole week of nights, recounting, re-enacting, saving up the words he did not say, but would next time. And Kale Khan, why didn't he give him money any more? It was he who always gave him something when Meena and Rahim said no.

There was only Binti now. If only she did not live so far away on Quarry Street. Perhaps it would be better if she lived downstairs in the old man's room. Yes, if there was anyone who cared about him these days it was she. She, to whom sixpence meant infinitely more than it did to anyone like Mr. Hardaker or Rahim or Meena or Kale Khan.

When Mr Hardaker left the shop, Rahim looked around for Jamini.

'Humm,' he muttered to himself angrily. 'As if I didn't have enough troubles on my head already.'

He kept thinking how right Meena was about the old man, about the boy, there was a stubbornness in him like the old man. 'I really don't know what does get into that boy these days.' Those were Meena's words; now they were his. The boy only liked to idle about. He was gone for hours, and when he came back and his mother or father asked him where he had been he would sullenly reply, 'Nowhere.' What did he do? Where did he go? It seemed to have started that day when he came home and told Rahim that God was dead. From then on he hated school, he didn't want to learn the trade. He wasn't lazy, nor clumsy. He remembered the time the boy worked for days making a filigree brooch for Lakshmi. Rahim had helped with suggestions. 'This boy go be a good good jeweller one day,' he had thought, and then his interest waned. Rahim shook his head in despair.

'Rahim Khan,' a man called from the street. He was getting out of a car. 'It's good to see you, old man. Remember me?'

Was it . . . was it really . . . 'Gopal?' he asked uncertainly.

'Yes, indeed—Dr Gopal these days,' the man said, smiling. So it was he, Rahim's old friend from Princes Town days. They had grown up together, now Gopal had travelled all over the world and come back to little Trinidad, a big doctor.

'I've got a little job to be done, and I thought, well, why not . . .' Gopal's voice trailed off.

Rahim suddenly thought that he might smooth off things with the old man. Dr Gopal could examine him, help him knock out this cold that hung on, making him more and more disagreeable. He asked Dr Gopal whether he would sound the old man's chest, it might cheer him up a little to see one of the local boys who had become a great man now.

'Why, surely, only I thought the old rebel was dead and gone a long time ago,' Dr Gopal joked heartily.

'Yuh mustn't talk like that, man, ah mean Doctor. That is a bad joke,' Rahim said seriously.

'Come on, then,' Dr Gopal clapped his hand on Rahim's shoulder, 'Let's see what we can do.'

Rahim thought that he should perhaps ask the old man first. He remembered how indignant he was at mention of the word 'doctor'.

'Wot this doctor, doctor, doctor. Every time you have cold you want to run an' see doctor,' the old man had grumbled; but they were almost inside his room now.

'*Barp*,' Rahim called quietly. The old man lay on his bed, curled up on the old sign-board, facing the wall. '*Barp*,' Rahim called agin. 'Look who came to see you.'

The old man moved on the bed, facing them. He held his hand over his eyes against the light from the outside; still, he could not see them clearly. 'Who that, boy?'

'Is Gopal, *Barp*. Yuh remember Gopal from Princes Town who send his son to study doctor in England.'

'Oooooh,' Kale Khan said, clearing his throat as it slowly came to his mind who Gopal was. 'Gopal son, eh . . . that right, you is a big man now, boy. Let me see you face, you gone so far and learn doctor work.' The old man sat up in bed, looking Dr Gopal over carefully.

'Is the same Gopal who used to mind cow in Princes Town? Is he son who gone an' get big man now?' he asked Rahim.

'Ah-ha-ha-ha,' the doctor laughed nervously, then condescendingly blurted out, 'Hullo, Kale Khan, I certainly have heard a lot about you from father but then I don't expect that you remember me, I was just a tot when you reigned in old Princes Town.'

Kale Khan eyed him quizzically. His eyes narrowed, and his movements were slow as he got up from the bed.

'Sit down, boy,' he said coldly. 'What kind of talk this? That all the manners they teach you over there? I is you poopah friend, not you friend. Sit down there an' keep tail quiet. Let me see if you is Gopal son o' no.' The doctor sat down sheepishly in Kale Khan's rocking-chair as the old man inspected his face carefully.

'Yuh gone an' married Sahib lady over there an' bring come in yuh poopah house?'

Dr Gopal smiled nervously. He didn't answer the question. What business did this old man have asking him whether he was married to an Englishwoman or not? Everyone for that matter complained about the local boys becoming professionals, then marrying up in the United Kingdom. He didn't have to sit here and talk to this old man at all. The old man had no right to speak to him this way.

'Well, how do you feel today, *Barp*?' He addressed the old man respectfully. That would get him off to a good start. 'Any pains? Anything you can tell me will help. What seems to be the trouble? Let's—.'

'What the hell I payin' you for, boy? You tell *me* what wrong, don't ask me question, you is doctor, not me,' Kale Khan interrupted him.

'Yes, *Barp*, yes,' he laughed nervously again. Kale Khan gave him a cutting glance. 'But you'll have to give me some—er—clues, something to go on. You know what I mean. We'll have to narrow it down something only after you give me a little help. You help me a bit, I help you a bit, ah-he-he-ha-aha.'

'Get the hell outa here, boy. Damn vagabond; gone all the way to England an' ain't learn a damn thing,' Kale Khan shouted angrily.

'*Barp*, yuh mustn't. Dr Gopal . . .' Rahim, who was looking on quietly, started to stammer out.

'An' you keep you tail quiet, too,' Kale Khan shouted at Rahim, chilling him. 'Let me tell this pissin' tail boy *who he is* and *what he is*. *I* know you poopah when he was a grasscutter. You hear that, boy? You hear me? You listen good to what Kale Khan have to say. You tell 'im I say that he son ain't learn nothing an' come back here, you gone England and throw away he money. Where you gone an' learn doctor work, boy?'

This was really too much, Dr Gopal thought to himself, yet he caught himself almost defensively answering the question.

'Well,' he replied, 'I was in London, and Edinbur . . .'

'Aha,' Kale Khan said, cutting him short again, 'an' you lick Englishman boots over there, an' now you come back here an' you want to talk more big big English than Englishman he self, eh?'

'Well, now, really, Mr Khan,' Dr Gopal said, reaching for his little black satchel at the side of the rocking-chair.

'Keep you tail in that chair till Kale Khan done talk, you ain't have no *manners*, you rascal? You gone England, put on bow-tie an' collar an' come back here callin' me "Old Man"? That is what they teach you over there? You callin' you poopah "Old Man" too? An' what the hell you is pissin' tail son-wa-bitch, get the hell outside my door. Tell you poopah if he remember him *me, Kale Khan* thrash his backside with tamarind rod for thiefin' grass from my land. That is the money you gone an' learn doctor work with? You hearin' me, boy? Is Kale Khan talkin'. Ask you poopah about that,' the old man said, as Dr Gopal began to get up.

'You see this,' the old man pointed to the bullet scar on his thigh from the Princes Town Hussay, when he was wounded in the riot with the police. 'Sahib teach you good, good, good, but Kale Khan teach you better. They shoot me one time, but I shoot them, six er them. Now you want to come befo' my do' an' talk like you is Englishman. Boy boy, boy.' Kale Khan called to Rahim, 'Get rid 'er this rascal . . . Come on, *jaldi-jaldi*!'

'Damn worthless children in the world today. Gone England with he father money an' he ain't even learn manners,' the old man muttered as Rahim and Dr Gopal left the room. 'You would 'er have more manners if you did stoop right here in Trinidad an' learn to be grass cutter like you poopah, worthless scamp.' He stretched out full length on his bedboard, his face turned to the wall as if he did not want to see them leave.

9

THE rains had come and gone, the mango season was over. The hard seeds of the fruit took roots and stood in slender foot-high stalks in the shade of the mother tree. The season of the weddings was past, and the racing of the tiny paper boats along Frederick Street canal.

All these were gone with the rain and the smell of fresh-cut grass that clung to the wet blade of the watchman's scythe in Woodford Square.

Silent brooding mornings hushed in grey that wept warm tears along the streets, the smell of damp bark from the Calabash tree —gone, all gone into the nowhere of time past. The friendly darkness of the rainy season had run away from Kale Khan's room, the taste of his pipe was dry, gashing the walls of his throat like razor grass, and his steady coughing could be heard in the quiet of the night as he swore, then cursed, 'son-o-'wa-bitch,' and his body arched and bent, his large eyes widened as if they pushed out of their sockets when he choked; then he cursed again, cursing the cold and the cough that did not leave with the rain, cursing the restlessness that grew in him as he waited for word from Hindustan.

'Rain come an' gone, boy. This cold stop,' he complained to Rahim.

'You must try to rest, *Barp*,' Rahim pleaded. 'Everybody sayin' that you doin' too much. Let we take care of your cooking. Let Meena get a washerwoman to do up your clothes.'

Kale Khan sat on his bed, his frail legs tucked under his rump, half listening, his eyes closed, his head turned to one side, away from Rahim. Just like Rahim, the old man thought . . . woman to do Pathan cooking, woman to do Pathan clothes. Rahim should know better. Even if he didn't mind those things for himself, the least he could do would be to remember how Kale Khan felt about having people hovering about his room—to cook for him!

'And how things going at the shop these days, boy?' he asked Rahim cunningly.

'So-so,' Rahim sing-songed, trying to sound indifferent.

'And you send that worthless scamp home for making bogus-bogus work,' Kale Khan asked.

Now Rahim knew that he had heard everything. Rahim *had* fired one of his apprentices, but Mr Hardaker had told him to stay on.

Mr Hardaker told Rahim that after all he too had a say in the hiring and firing—he was a partner, he had his own *investment* to think about. American tourists were buying up everything. What if the filigree did break up two days after they bought it? Their ships would be hundreds of miles at sea.

'Can't you see that things have changed, man, *changed*! We are not working for those broken-down pennies from the sugar plantation workers. They're dead, finished. Those days are over, man!'

What really angered Rahim though, was that the apprentice stood about with a sullen smirk on his face all day. He took his orders from Mr Hardaker now. If he had to ask anything of Rahim it was done through Mr Hardaker.

Had he been blind when Mr Hardaker suggested this partnership? He had just joined in with the old fool to pick up some extra work that the tourists brought in. He'd done his best, at least he had tried, but what a blind fool he was. The shop was swept right out from under his feet. He had never thought of it that way, now it was clear.

More and more new regulations, more and more papers, licence—now you had to have a licence to operate a jewellery shop. Book-keeping, each job, each article, each purchase or sale had to be recorded in ledgers, otherwise no licence. Books, books, books, writing, writing, writing. All of this book business he had left to Hardaker. The whole illiterate gang of tradesmen fled to the country where they worked in peace for the big shops. Some of the old jewellers worked in the back of these shops. They were like a little zoo. When the tourists came in, they were ushered to the back of the shops to watch the workmen in their cages—all enclosed to make sure that they didn't make off with a piece of gold.

The more he thought about it, the more clearly he saw that he was just another workman in Hardaker's employ. Oh, yes, the signboards were his—or were they? Hardaker had repainted them. Some old tools were his. He could pull out with that. The man owned the whole place, what would Rahim do with it anyway? Those ledgers, he could barely write his own name, and those worthless scamps whose parents had entrusted them to Rahim, they flinched from his instruction now. They didn't want to learn anything, they wanted to learn enough to make a 'Yankee Dollar', that was all. He was too demanding, he made them work. Hardaker would pass off anything they made. They knew how to get around Rahim. It was the *big* boss, Hardaker was the big boss now. An Indian like themselves? Never! It had to be the Englishman; those worthless scamps! To hell with the whole blasted thing. Meena was right, things had changed; yes, and Kale Khan, and Hardaker. Things had changed, only *he* was left out of the new scheme.

Now, talking to his father, he could only tell him that Hardaker had decided to keep the apprentice now.

Kale Khan grinned caustically. Rahim knew that the old man was laughing at him.

'So!' Kale Khan grinned, pulling out his legs from under his rump. 'Is so things turn out, eh? Is now only things turn around upside-down. Is who working for who anyway?' he asked Rahim, and still there was no answer.

'Well,' Kale Khan concluded. It was none of his business; this was the beginning, or was it the end? He was out of it, and he was glad to be out of it. Hadn't he warned Rahim? What was the matter with this boy? Did he really think that he could stay here for ever, in Trinidad, and make a fortune, build a big shop, new counters, glass cases, so much breaking down and building up, painting and cleaning, electric lights? Well, he was his own man now, he had to do things his way. Perhaps this was good for him after all, perhaps he would be able to see the only path that was open to his father, yes, to rouse up the Indians in Trinidad and leave for India.

Already the residents of Woodford Square had heard of the letters the old man was writing, the coming of a representative from India who would see all the degradation they had suffered, who would right them, compensate all these wretched souls, take them back to their homeland—Hindustan. Word had reached the market place, and an occasional vendor came to the old man's room to hear with his own ears: Was it true? were they really going home?

With the help of Jagu, his right-hand man, who did everything from papering his walls to lighting his fires on the mornings of the rainy season, and Jamini, who had come back again into the old man's life, he sent out messages about the meeting he was going to hold in Woodford Square. The boys shuttled about from one end of the city to the next, asking people to tell others. Wait . . . just wait and see. This time it wasn't going to be like the Princes Town Hussay. They weren't going to riot and get themselves shot down for nothing. This time they were going home. One hundred and eighty thousand Indians going back home to build up their own country.

As the days went by, Meena was more and more aware of Rahim's worrying. 'Why we don't take the whole thing to court house, Rahim? We ain't rob nobody, we only tryin' to get back what is we own,' she suggested simply.

'But Meena, you-self too,' he started, 'You think one Englishman go cut another Englishman throat? Is just a waste of money to get a lawyer an' make a case.' He paused for a moment. 'They will throw it out of court before I even get a chance to open my mouth.'

Well, that was true. She had to admit he was right, but she wasn't dismayed. 'Rahim, why you don't get a Indian lawyer? They know how things is! They study just as good as them English lawyer, and they know how these things does happen. They could fight your case better for you.'

He brightened up at the thought. Why hadn't he thought of it himself? Then, he became afraid that nothing would come of it in the end, anyway.

'You know how these boys is.' he told her. 'Is true that they read from the same book like a English lawyer, but when they come back, they ain't have the *power* that English lawyer have in the court. When they come face to face with a English judge, they frighten to talk up. You know that for yourself, Meena. These boys frighten that they go lose they profession if they talk back too hard to the judge, an' you know how Hardaker always have them big big high-class people for his friends. What chance people like we have? Court house ain't make for poor people.'

'Is true thing what you sayin', Rahim, but try it. You could never tell. Talk to a few people here an' there, an' see what they have to say. Perhaps we have somebody who could argue for we in the court. After all, we only tryin' to get back what belong to we by right, an' fair is fair. Somebody have to listen to me.' Meena pleaded with him, reasoned with him.

Time passed, two days, three, four. Meena wasn't going to push him into seeing a lawyer. It had to come to him slowly, as if he were preparing himself for a leap into the sea from a great height, and she knew him, knew how he worked things out in his own way.

So the next morning then, Rahim got dressed in his black serge suit, a white shirt and his green tie. Green was a lucky colour for Muslims to wear.

'Meena,' he said, 'only a cup of black tea this mornin', my stomach feel so full, I don't think that I could take anything. Don't worry though, is a good feeling. I mean . . .'

'All right, Rahim, all right, I know what you mean.' She had hoped that he would have something, but she wasn't going to press him. She had roasted some small cherry-red tomatoes in the embers of the fireplace, crushed them with raw onions and a clove of garlic and sprinkled a little salt. The *roti*, flat roasted discs of bread, were still being turned from one side to the other, small bubbles swelled out in the flour, turning a golden brown as she kept rotating them to get an even heat. All this could wait.

She let him drink his cup of tea, and then she watched him enter the Square from the window.

One of the city's urchins stood polishing a brass plaque as Rahim turned into St Vincent Street. He tried to read the letters on the plaque, but the greyish polish and the movement of the boy's hand back and forth obscured the letters. He held the boy's hand still for a moment, spelling out the words on the plaque.

SAMUEL SALWAN . . . Barrister at Law. When Rahim went in, Mr Salwan was sitting in a swivel chair, behind a desk, on which there were hundreds of papers. Behind him, and around, were shelves of great thick books, dusty, torn and aged with disuse.

'Sit, sit,' the lawyer said, looking up fleetingly as he went on filling in some forms which he folded one over the other as they were completed.

So this was the great Indian lawyer. It made Rahim feel proud to think that an Indian like himself was such a big man, a man who could get up before English judges and tell them a thing or two. He had heard how Mr Salwan defended Indians in the court and got them off lightly. Rahim sat on the chair the lawyer indicated, looking at the fat little man with a balloon of a face. Mr Salwan's stomach seemed like another balloon which strained at the buttons of his tightly fitted waistcoat each time he drew his breath. Sensing that Rahim was impatient, perhaps a little bit uncomfortable, he said, 'I'll be with you in just one moment, Ranjit.' He sounded as if he were talking to an impatient child who had to be patted and coaxed; and then, did he say 'Rahim' or 'Ranjit?' Had he heard him correctly, Rahim wondered. Finally the forms were all filled in, and Mr Salwan put them into a drawer.

'Well, Ranjit,' he said rubbing his palms together, leaning back in his swivel chair. Rahim looked at him a little puzzled. Why was he calling him Ranjit? The man didn't even know him. Now that he was through rubbing his palms together, Mr Salwan began cracking his fingers, *crick*, *crick*, *crack*, *crick*. It made a disgusting sound in the dead office. Then Rahim watched him try to cross his legs clumsily, and when his fat little thighs could not be manoeuvred one over the other, he lifted it over with his hands, groaned a sigh of relaxation, and started again.

'Well, I see you've made up your mind to take my advice and plead guilty. Well, now.' *Crick*, *crick*, *crack*. He started on the knuckles of his other hand. Rahim flinched with each little crack, staring at the thick, short fingers.

'Well, my good man, I can assure you we know what's best,' he continued. 'Y'ace, we know what's best. Always better not to court trouble, Ranjit. Always better. I'm going to do great things for you, y'ace, we are going to do great things together, Ranjit, and lucky thing you came to me. I'm on very good terms with Judge MacIntyre. Y'ace, I believe we can . . .'

'What the hell is this madman raving about?' Rahim wondered. Judge MacIntyre, plead guilty, don't court trouble? Who was going to do great things?

'Man, you must be mistake me for a different one of your customers,' Rahim put in coldly.

'What, whazzat you say?'

Slowly, deliberately, enunciating each word icily, Rahim said:

'I sayin' that my name ain't Ranjit, an' you never see me before in you whole whole life. I just come in today this first time. I is a new customer!'

Mr Salwan leaned forward on his swivel chair, almost toppling forward. He uncrossed his legs with some effort and laughed foolishly.

'Aha . . . ha ha, so . . .' His black teeth showed as he laughed.

'Well, then, aha ha . . . what can we do for you today, Mr . . .?'

'Rahim Khan,' Rahim completed the sentence for him.

'Y'ace . . . Y'ace, of course. You are the son of that grand old man who led the Princes Town Hussay.'

'Yes, man,' Rahim added quickly, thinking that he didn't come here to discuss his father.

'Well, your father is making lots of trouble for the authorities, you know. We must learn, we must learn not to court trouble, we Indians.'

'Well, suh,' Rahim started feebly, 'this is the way things stand . . .' He went on to tell all the details of his shop—Mr Hardaker, the boys who worked for him, the way the laws had come upon him with all their requirements for book-keeping, and how he was almost being put out into the streets, as it were.

Mr Salwan leaned back in his swivel chair, rocking back and forth, listening to Rahim's story. With each rock the chair gave a little creak, with which the lawyer's steady nodding kept time. Rahim's story droned on and on, and as he looked at the nodding of the lawyer's head, he felt that it implied a mood of sympathy, one of understanding. He could almost hear Mr Salwan saying, 'Yes, it is a pity. You've been taken advantage of. Oh, yes, I know. We Indians have paid with our blood to live and breathe.

You've been tricked all right. We'll have to put this Mr Hardaker in his place. You don't have to go any further, you don't have to tell me. I'm an Indian myself, I know how it is.'

But presently, Mr Salwan stopped nodding, and his head started a left-to-right motion. Now he put his fingers to his chin and wagged his head from left to right as if something pained him. Rahim's hopes fell at this instant. He had the feeling of futility he had warned Meena about. Then Mr Salwan spoke.

'Well,' he said, 'I don't know, I just don't know,' he added gravely. 'It's really Mr. Hardaker's place now, isn't it? I mean technically, that is, until we can prove rightful ownership, Ranjit.'

'Man, my name is *Rahim*. And you mean to say that it ain't have one law in all them big, big book that you could read out in the court house?' Rahim waved his hand at the rows of unused books on the shelves.

'Well,' Mr Salwan started, 'you brought some money with you, of course. There'll be . . .'

'Yes, yes, yes, man,' Rahim offered, anxiously reaching into his breast pocket.

'Good, good, very good. Now let's see. First of all, who pays rent?, he asked Rahim.

'Is I who—er, well, is he—man, is the two o' we who pay the rent, half an' half everything, that was we agreement.'

'Then do you have any of the rent receipts with you, anything like that with your signature on it that we can use as an exhibit in the court?'

'No, man, I ain't have nuttin' like . . .'

'Well, never mind.' He cut Rahim off. 'I'll call the agent of the place. We can find out from them easily enough.'

Rahim gave him the agent's name, and he found the number and started dialling on the telephone.

'Hallo . . . Hallo there . . . Salwan here, 'S' as in sugar, A, L, . . . Yes, I want to get some information I have a client here who says that you are his agent, and I wonder if . . .'

Rahim kept looking at the piles of old newspapers stacked up around the room. Dust had gathered along the canals cut into the bundles by the string that tied them. Two people came in. They entered the office quietly, on tiptoe. Mr Salwan indicated two chairs to them, smiling broadly. They lowered themselves slowly as if to avoid the slightest creak the old chairs might make. Then they began talking in whispers, holding their hands to their mouths. Mr Salwan nodded to them as he waited on the telephone, his head cocked to one side. Then he looked up at the ceiling, his arm stretched out along the desk, his fingers moving, tapping on the desk.

'Hallo . . . Hallo? Yes, I'm here,' he answered the person on the telephone. Rahim started. He began feeling uncomfortable now, his stomach was grinding about, knotting itself into tight lumps. He wished these people weren't here, listening to all of his private business. What a fool they would think he was.

'Oh, I see,' Mr Salwan said on the telephone again. 'Yes, yes, I understand.' There was a tone of disappointment in the lawyer's voice. It speared into Rahim like a shaft of heat. His whole body was sweating now. He took out his handkerchief and inserted it under his shirt, mopping his chest and armpits with it as he waited for the lawyer to say something.

'You are quite sure, are you?' Mr Salwan was saying, when there was a click which left him staring into the mouth-piece with a stupid look of surprise on his face. At least three seconds went by before he awoke from this trance.

'Ah, now, let's see.' He stared addressing Rahim. 'You see, Mr . . .' The fat fool was rubbing his fingers again as if searching for Rahim's name in their friction.

'Man, don't bother to talk,' Rahim said, disgusted and annoyed. He pulled out his handkerchief from between his neck and collar and walked out into the street.

He felt exhausted as he walked slowly back to the Square and sat down, oblivious to all the passers-by, at the edge of the fountain. He dampened his handkerchief in the basin of water, and held it still, looking at the statue of Sir Woodford, wondering why *he* couldn't be someone great in the world so that people would build a statue to his memory.

10

In the days that followed, Rahim found himself restless, without the routine he was accustomed to, he found time slipping past. Morning slipped into afternoon, afternoon into evening. Night had drawn its coal-black sheet of sleep across the town, bringing with it a darkness that had lost its friendliness, and now only the sounds of men who lived in the night came through the window. The last tramcar rattled along to the depot, its lights flashing across the ceiling. He could see the purple sparks that the wheels splashed out as it hurtled along the quiet streets of sleeping Port of Spain, then silence again.

And now an old man was coughing from across the way—or was it crying? Yes, it was crying. It was Sookiah, the town fool who wept at night under the Town Hall steps. Crying because he had lost his name, lost a word in the infinite vocabulary of the word, one word in all the millions of sounds that are uttered in the air. The old man sobbing on the steps had lost some hinge on which life swung along the marked paths of his destiny, and now he wandered, feeling nothing but a vast distance between himself and the world. What was there in a name? When he was born the vast constellation of the universe was set in one unique pattern, all the stars taken into a great cloth, shuffled, and thrown across the heavens, never to arrange themselves that way again. In that moment, when he drew his first breath, his name was chosen; a sound that would forever be in harmony with the pelting planets, the suns, the many moons and stars, so that he might be one with them.

An old man with a yellow beard sitting at his silence in far-away Hindustan had given him his name . . . but now it was lost—lost in the old records of the Red House. Everyone called him Sookiah, and now, late at night, with the golden rum from the sugar-cane he had come to plant, he searched his addled brain, for the breath of air that caught fire in his throat. As the wild brown liquor idled through the burnt-out nerve threads of his brain, as it pushed and coursed along the weblike bundle of his nerves, he could almost hear his name coming back to him, and he would shout out amid deep sobs from beneath the Town Hall, 'Sookiah! . . . Sookiah! . . .' Then his voice became a scream as he held his head and pounded it against the stout pillars of the Town Hall crying out, 'Oh God . . . ah lose my name! . . . ah lose my name! How I ever goin' to go back to Hindustan without a name?

The following day, Rahim went to the railroad station early in the morning when the trains arrived, bringing all the clerks and peasants to the city. As each train arrived, the station bustled with activity. Here a man was unloading chickens tied six together by the feet, then another was arguing with a truck-driver about the price to take his goods to the market-place, and then the whole trainload of passengers was gone, leaving only a frightening silence in the station.

The railroad station was not very large. It was not its size that frightened Rahim, but its darkness, its high ceilings with a few dim light bulbs hung from far up. He had thought that he might spread out a few items on a cloth on the ground so that the passengers might stop and perhaps buy something, but the time went fast. He had hardly settled on what he would do before the bustle was over and the crowd was out and lost in the streets of the city.

He left the station and went to a bar across the street. As he pushed open the swinging half-doors of the Britannia Bar, a gust of air swept past his face, air that had lingered upon the old wooden casks of rum, air that had hung about the spittoons filled with milky-white disinfectant, air that wove about with early morning sawdust smells. He ordered a drink and the bar-tender left him the bottle from which he poured some clear white rum into a glass, then added water to it. As the water mixed with the rum, it heated the glass and a thin wisp of pale-blue smoke curled about inside it. Rahim held the glass tightly, feeling its warmth on the palm of his hand, then he drank quickly.

He was standing at the far end of the long mahogany counter, his eyes opened wide, but fixed in space. There were only two other customers at the other end of the bar. He could hardly hear what they were saying, but he guessed that they were fairly drunk already; he could tell by the slur and drawl of their voices. Above the two large kegs which dominated the backdrop of the bar were two small dusty Union Jacks arranged like the letter X and below them was the bar's slogan 'Rule Britannia.'

He spat into the spittoon, breaking a thin film of black oily disinfectant which gave way to a milky-white substance beneath its surface, then the black oil slowly closed the broken surface again.

Suddenly a great rush of blood surged through him. His body felt warm, his head cleared, and he was swallowed up by a strange mood that took a firm hold of him. He thought of all the people who must be wearing some fragment of his filigree close to their person—that perhaps they must reflect for a moment upon the hands that had wrought it.

At the far end of the long counter the two men were calling out to someone in the street.

'Hop! Hey, Hoppy, come up and chop a liquor with we,' they called.

Rahim looked up.

'Hop-and-Drop, you old rascal.' The older of the two idlers laughed, slapping a little deformed man who came limping into the bar. One of his legs was shorter than the other, and as he limped across to the counter, high on the left foot, low on the other, up on the left foot, down on the right, Rahim realised how he had come by his name.

'Boy, I broken . . . broken, broken, broken,' the man said in a raspy grating voice.

'An what the hell you doin' here in the Britannia if you broken, Hop?' the older idler said. 'You must have money to pay the Britannia when you come in here.' A wicked grin swept across his face as he nudged the other man with him.

'Man, you invite me in the Britannia and I come—besides I have a bad bad thirst, and I is not one to turn my back on friends when they call me,' the cripple said.

'Hop, you old scamp—I bet you had a thirst since the day you moomah drop you.'

'You thirsty enough to give we a dance, Hoppy?'

'Man, my throat scratching like if I swallow a branch of nettle.'

'Come on, Hop, give we a dance, man,' one of the idlers laughed, and both started clapping their hands, singing:

'Hop Hop Hop
You hop and you drop
Give 'im one drop
The man can't hop
Give 'im two drop
And he hop like a top
Hoppity hop hoppity drop
Hoppity hop
Drop drop drop.'

The little cripple bounced, hopped, grinned, and with his head thrown back, bobbed up and down as his comrades clapped and helped him along by poking him from time to time, to add a little more frenzy to his dance. As his head flapped back and forth on the loose hinge of his neck in the eerie dance, Rahim caught sight of a few ground-down stumps of black teeth set in the blue-black gums of his mouth. Then he felt dizzy from watching the little cripple dance. He had his drink and left as the two idlers took hold of the ears of the sweating little cripple, and drew him over to the counter to join them in the nip of Black Cat Rum they had standing on the counter.

Rahim walked slowly up Frederick Street, and each time he came to one of the large shops, he paused to look at the huge display of jewellery in the windows. He thought of what pains he had gone to to make a single brooch, how much it meant to him to have each of its minute dots of metal shaped into perfect spheres, each sphere soldered on to a frame so that in the end, the intricate mass held together with the strength of a single bar of solid metal. He wished he could see the jewellery more closely so that he could enumerate the flaws in it, but there was so much in each window that he was left with a feeling of incompetence, of utter uselessness. At forty-one, he was old. He knew now that he would never be the jeweller he dreamed of, he knew that he had no great moment in his life like Kale Khan did when he led the Princes Town Hussay in his youth, he knew that in the minds of his father and mother, in Meena's eyes, perhaps Jamini's too, he was a definite kind of person, one in whom the seed of self-destruction was sown, one who had a marked-out path, an unswerving destiny. He remembered the first time he had worn a pair of long pants—Kale Khan had brought them home. 'Boy, look on the bed, it have something for you,' the old man had said. And when Rahim saw them, when he put them on, he took a small piece of broken mirror that the old man used for shaving. Rahim held the mirror in his hand, moved it up and down, examining himself from waist to feet. He would never know such exhilaration again. He remembered the first time he made a necklace, and sold it for money. The customers looked at him and said, 'Boy—you goin' to be a jeweller just like Kale Khan.' And as the days, the weeks went by, he knew that he would have to say something to Meena who was patient and never pushed him nor asked questions. But the day came finally when Rahim went home with the new mask that dejection had cast on his face. The lines of his mouth arched downwards, his smile, when he did smile, was a wry one, and all of Meena's consolations were swept aside. She felt an importance that she had never known before with this new person Rahim had become, and that day, as if he knew that some explanation of his plans would have to be discussed with her, he had an extra shot of the water-white rum at the Britannia, and he took on an air of indolence before facing her.

'I don't know, Meena. Since I lose the shop it look as if I can't do anything,' he started off.

'Don't worry, Rahim, everything does take time. You still have two hand and feet; it ain't as if you cripple. You know how much people know your work. You have to take courage. Is courage you have to take,' Meena said to him.

But why was everyone so free with advice? Why couldn't they see what was so simple—that he was a fool, that he couldn't read his own name, that he couldn't see what was happening under his very eyes when Hardaker first asked him to go into partnership, then that fat fool Salwan and his shelves of law books, afraid of an English judge.

'Take what courage?' he screamed at Meena. 'Courage does bring food and put it in the pot? Courage does teach you how to go back to the time when you was young and let you start out again without making the same foolish mistakes? Courage does cut loose the millstone you have round your neck when you have wife and child and it too late to go back and do things right?'

'So that is what responsible for everything—your wife and child? That is the big mistake you make? Well, Rahim, it ain't too late,' Meena said. She had made up her mind that day that she was going home to her parents. For the first time she lost her patience and told him all that she had thought long ago. It had not happened with the loss of the shop; it had started happening long long ago.

'You ain't only lose the shop, Rahim, you lose yourself. You lose your religion, you lose your God, you lose your belief in everything, and it ain't have no right and wrong in this world for you. You is your own God and Master, you take away that power from somebody else hands and you have to make up your own rule and regulation. You think that you can do that? Great great people turn their back on God, and he leave them all alone. You think you could do that and have any peace? Rahim, you lose yourself, that is what you lose, is not the shop, or your wife and child that have you livin' like a fish out water, is *you, you yourself.*'

'All right, so I lose myself,' Rahim screamed at her as he got up to leave the house.

'Rahim, if you leave this house and keep comin' home two-three o'clock in the mornin' I goin' home. Nobody can say that I didn't try my best.'

He know that Meena meant it, that she would go home to her parents, but he still had his pride. 'Lost everything, includin' myself, but I still have shame, I ain't lost that yet.' He wished he had it in him to tell her to go away, to leave him alone, but he felt in a vague, amorphous way that there was some hazy truth in what she said. He got up defiantly and left the house without looking back at her, afraid that he might ask her to explain to him, to tell him what was the unseen thing that drove him night and day into a restless world that made him feel like running, moving until he was tired, but afraid to sleep, afraid of lying in bed at night tormented by the questions that hid in the darkness.

He was standing at the long mahogany counter of the Britannia Bar again. Why? He could not tell. There were no sales to be made from the little broken suitcase he now carried about with him, the remainder of his stock in it. In the beginning it pleased Meena to see him leave the house with it. She felt that he was out in the city somewhere trying to start a new kind of trade. Later on, however, even Rahim had to admit to himself each time he took up the suitcase that it was simply a good excuse for the time he spent away from home.

'What you havin'?' the bartender asked.

'White puncheon rum, with water,' Rahim said.

'One fire-water,' the bartender said as he went to fetch the bottle.

On a large panel behind the cash register was a picture of a seated woman in profile dressed in flowing draperies. The effect was to accentuate her large, well-formed bust, and the sheer draping led one to speculate whether or not one could see the darker shades of the nipples. On her head she wore a helmet that reached far down her neck at the back. At the top of the helmet there was a sweep of red feathers. It was quite similar to the helmet worn by the Governor on pompous occasions. In her left hand she held a tall trident, and in her right, a great shield with the design of the Union Jack painted on it. In the background was the blue sea, its great waves tipped by little white caps.

This was Rule Britannia: This was what 'Britannia rule the waves' meant to Rahim. The dampness, the rain, the pungent aromas of rums from Caroni, Esperanza, Sobo, Usine St Madeline—all the elements had worked upon the wall on which Miss Britannia was painted, and around the middle of her body, the plaster swelled out slowly.

'Hoppy, you li'l bitch! What you gone an' do to Miss Britannia that her belly swellin' up so?' the customers had chided the little cripple as they warmed themselves with rum in the rainy-season darkness of the Britannia.

It drizzled zig-zag drops, it rained, it soaked into the mahogany counter. Each day someone asked the bartender without fail:

'Man, it look like if Miss Britannia makin' baby. When she drop the chile is free drinks for everybody on the house.'

But it all happened so slowly, and then one day the customers came in and found that the plaster had broken away and was repaired, leaving only a gaping white patch in Miss Britannia's stomach.

'It look like if they sew she up, man,' one customer commented.

'The old Britannia weak in she belly, boy, she can't take it no mo'. Things really bad when the old Britannia can't take on a Hop-and-Drop,' another commented.

There were no free drinks on the house, but it was still remembered by many that it was the cripple who put Miss Britannia 'in the family way,' and the little cripple would smile with a strange sense of delight and secret accomplishment whenever some idler brought him a drink and toasted his virility, and Miss Britannia's eventual collapse as a result of it.

'I must run . . . I must run . . . I must run,' Rahim kept muttering to himself, not knowing why. And hearing a deep resonating ship's whistle humming in his grain as he muttered these words, he thought that he might try to hawk his jewellery at the docks where the great ships tied up alongside. The thought of this new possibility lightened his heart, and he was glad that Meena was not here, glad that he could take full credit for his resourcefulness.

After this he spent most of his time on the docks. One night, returning home, he was suddenly aware that he was alone in the house. Meena had gone, Kale Khan and Jamini were away somewhere stirring up more trouble, urging the people to go back to India.

The Calabash tree across the way was in darkness. All the colour had vanished from the sky now and the leaves of the tree made a latticework of black and white against the sky. He heard the flapping of large wings across the way, then the still latticework shivered and fluttered as a bird alighted on one of its branches. Then, no sooner had the tree stood still again than the bird began crying from within its darkness . . . '*Twee twee twee.*' Three times the bird called, three times the Jumbie bird called, and he knew that someone was going to die. He foraged clumsily through his shirt, placing his hand on his chest where he thought his heart must be, but his heart sang on. Still straining with anxiety, he thought that the bird had come calling for him. Suppose his heart should beat like that again, then explode within, then stop forever? He did not want to die, he did not want to die alone like this. There should be someone to bring him his last glass of water, someone to caress his brow, to hear his last cry. He wished that Meena had not gone away; he wished he could go to her and tell her how he felt. He was sure that that was all it would take to bring her back home, yet that pride, that Pathan brow, could not bend.

'*Twee twee twee*,' the Jumbie bird called again from the Calabash tree. He wanted to hurl something into its branches, but then he remembered the tales of those who stoned the Jumbie and were found dead soon after.

'*Twee twee twee*,' the Jumbie bird called for the third time, and he knew that death was only across the street, hiding in the Calabash tree. And now, in the stillness of the house, he heard the eerie *clot*, *clot*, a soft padding sound coming from the back of the house. His heart pounded, then fluttered like an arched leaf caught in a current of air. His hand dived into his bosom and he pressed upon his chest trying to quiet its strange murmuring so that he could listen again. The house was in complete darkness now as he listened, tense, petrified. He heard the soft padding again *clot*, *clot*, *clot* then, 'Rahim, ay, Rahim,' a tiny voice called, and as if out of nowhere, out of the darkness and shadows Binti stepped into sight.

'*Mai*?' he called questioningly, as if he were still not certain.

'Boy, why you have the house in darkness?' the old woman asked.

Rahim got up quickly and lit the lamp. Its chimney was so sooted that it gave off a dim pale brown light.

'So when last you eat?' the old woman asked, taking the sooty chimney off the lamp. She got a piece of old newspaper and inserted it with her tiny hand into the chimney, turning it around and around.

'I eat something down by the docks 'bout four o'clock this evening,' he answered.

Binti replaced the glistening chimney on the lamp and looked about her with a certain sense of relief. She shook her head wearily as she went to the kitchen to warm some food she had brought.

'Come on here, sit down and eat. Since Meena gone you ain't yourself.' She paused to push up the bridge on her spectacles. 'You going to bring she back o' no?'

Rahim continued eating quietly. He did not answer her question.

'You have that same Pathan blood Meena have in she, and that is the whole trouble. You won't go that side and get she, she won't come this side,' the old woman said.

'*Mai* . . .' Rahim started, but then he said nothing as the old woman waited expectantly.

'What you doin' for money these days?' she asked.

'Don't worry 'bout me, *mai*, I have money,' he said sullenly.

'Well, I was only askin'.'

She took off her spectacles and began squeezing the bridge of her nose. Then, *Twee twee twee*, the Jumbie bird called. Binti pulled on her glasses quickly and her eyes caught Rahim's looking at her sheepishly. The expression on his face was like that on Jamini's when the old woman had caught the boy in some bit of mischief at the coal shop.

'What that bird callin' for?' she demanded sulkily.

Rahim shrugged his shoulders. The old woman got up angrily and went to the window. 'Hey, you, you son o' wa bitch, you come for me, eh? You come to tell me 'bout nice nice place you want to carry me to, you nasty bird. Well, I ain't ready yet. Go round Port of Spain two three mo' time 'fore you come to call me.'

'*Mai*,' Rahim called, 'come back from the window an' leave the bird alone. You know what people say 'bout . . .'

The old woman flared up in a rage. Her anger at the bird now turned to Rahim. 'Why?' she shouted at him. 'Why I should leave the bird alone? You ready! You ready to give up everything. You ain't eating, you ain't lighting lamp in your own own house, you ain't want to go and bring Meena home, you ain't know where that boy Jamini gone, you ain't care how the old man poisoning the boy mind from day to day, day, but what wrong with you? You ain't care 'bout nothing o' nobody? Is ready you ready to go with that Jumbie bird? Is 'fraid you 'fraid that Jumbie bird or what? *I* ain't 'fraid, you know. But you, it look like if you give up. It look like you want to invite that bird to come in this dark dark house and eat from the same plate with you. That what you want?

'Boy, I don't know how you grow up this way. Different different thing happening to people every day, every day in this world. They still have to live, but it look as if you only waiting for some bad bad thing to happen to you. I used to say that is the old man fault the way you bring up, but now I don't know. It look as if you have some kind of bad spirit in you. You *want* to destroy yourself. You *want* to sit down in this dark house. You *like* to listen to that bird. You *want* to make he come an' call you.

'What thing you do with your life that make you so ready to give up? Answer me that! What hardship you see that you ready to shut your eye? You think the world go come with a silver spoon an' put food in your mouth? You think that life is a merry-go-round that you must ride 'pon, an' when it stop you must get off and say that the ride over and is time to shut my eyes now and wait 'till Jumbie bird come to call for me? That is what you think? Now your ride over and you waiting. You ain't care 'bout nobody else. You ain't care 'bout Meena, 'bout your own own child . . .'

Her voice ended on an upswing, as though she could have said much more, but her breath was spent, and she had become more and more agitated physically as she spoke, building up a momentum of words that left language insufficient. She stormed to the window. 'Hey you, you black bitch, you hiding in the Calabash tree. Tell me,' she called out into the darkness, 'tell me what you want.' But there was only the soft silence of Woodford Square, and the splintered spray of the fountain beyond, water falling upon water. 'Why you ain't come out an' show your face, 'fraid me or what?' And still there was only the sound of the dancing splintered spray of water falling into the cauldron beyond.

'Jumbie bird, ay, Jumbie bird!' Her tiny voice strained cutting throught the night air.

'*Mai*,' Rahim pleaded, 'come 'way from . . .' but no sooner had Rahim started than there was a flapping, fluttering sound as the branches of the Calabash tree quivered, the dried-out seeds in the large brown pods rattled, and the bird flew away from the tree.

She turned to Rahim now, all anger gone from her. She knew this child that she had yielded up to walk below uncertain skies. She knew this angry blood of a Pathan as she knew the thunder and the rain of Quarry Street.

'Boy, I ain't vex with you, I only have to make peace with my own mind sometime and that is why I have to tell you all these hard words. I have to go home now. Mornin' does break soon soon these days an' I have 'nuff 'nuff work to do in the coal shop.' She pulled her veil over her head. 'You going to come to see me soon?'

The next day he was in the Britannia Bar, when he saw a grotesque mask of a face stuck between the leaves of the door. The ugly head turned and twisted slowly around, its marble-white eyes turned upside down in the sockets, and a broad grin on its face. The bartender took one of the wooden spittoons and threw its contents at the face between the doors.

'Hop-and-Drop, you li'l bitch—get away from there.'

The little man had ducked as quickly as the bartender had reached for the spittoon.

'Get out from here, you short-cut bitch. Is a freeness you looking for,' the bartender shouted, putting back the empty spittoon.

'Man, how you know that I ain't have money?' the cripple called from outside in his raspy voice.

'How I know that you ain't have money! People with two hand and foot can't work in Trinidad—and you with your blasted hop and drop! Where the hell you get money from? I break off other foot for you if you put it inside here. Then they go call you Hop-and-Hop, you damn rascal.'

The bartender was so amused by his own words, he began laughing. The cripple still remained outside, and then hearing the gurgle in the bartender's voice he pleaded again.

'Man, my throat dry like stale biscuit. I got to have something to wash it down with,' he called putting an added rasp in his voice.

'Hey,' Rahim called out to the bartender. He was going to buy the cripple a drink. The water-clear rum of the Britannia strained the tiny web-like nerves of his brain—turmoil stretched them like an eager lover—he wanted to see the cripple dance again. But presently, as his eyes fell to counting the change he had lying on the counter, the cripple came flying into the bar and tumbled on the sawdust floor followed by two men, the same two idlers who frequented the bar, both of them rollicking with laughter. They had evidently stolen up on the cripple as he peered between the slit of the swinging doors, and surprised him with the push that sent him sprawling on the Britannia floor. The cripple tried to scramble to his feet, but one of the men pounced on him and began fishing about his crotch.

'Where you hiding it?' he laughed. 'Come on, come on!'

The cripple giggled, gurgled, rolled and kicked. The other man arched backwards in laughter as his companion searched for the cripple's genitals.

'Come on, Hop—we hear you have two lolo's—a hop one and a drop one—we have to find out if is true, *today*, *today*.'

But the cripple, out of breath on the floor, still tossed about with an odd and irregular rhythm as the other man tried to hold his feet still.

'Boy, the hop foot here have more strength in it than the drop foot. What you find, man, what you find . . . he have a hop and lolo or no?' one of the idlers asked excitedly.

The cripple pressed his legs together and tried to draw them up into his stomach, but the two men had him pinned down—and then:

'The li'l bitch have a lolo like everybody else—one lolo,' he said, releasing the panting cripple. Quick grating, rasping breaths came from his throat as he sat on the floor, buttoning up his pants. The two men towered above him with fake anger.

'Hop, yuh ain't shame? You have a lolo like everybody else. What woman go want you?'

The cripple, still on the floor, was trying to brush down his old rags that were covered in sawdust from the bar-room floor. He too seemed disappointed that the men did not find what they were searching for.

'Man, I hear it have a dwarf up in Arouca village Hop does do it with—he ain't hard up like you think.'

The bartender stood with his arms stretched out along the counter, his head hung down laughing silently as it swayed from left to right.

'Barman,' one of the idlers called, 'you know how to fix up a hop and drop liquor?'

Still convulsed with laughter, the bartender shook his head.

'Bring two glasses then—a tall tall one and a short short one, and is Black Cat we drinkin'.'

One man then filled the tall glass, the other the small one, and they lifted the cripple off the floor, and each taking one of the glasses in turn said,

'This is for the hop—let he hop long long long!'

The other toasted, 'This is for the drop—let he drop long long long!' and so saying they tilted the cripple's head back and poured each drink down his throat. No sooner had the liquor passed his throat than one of the men reached for his genitals again.

'And now you have to give we a dance . . .'

Rahim felt as if one of the forced fibres in his brain had broken —there was a bright flash, deep behind the sockets of his eyes accompanied by a loud noise in his ears as if something had indeed exploded in his brain. He ran out of the Britannia Bar, and as he entered the street, the sunlight of the afternoon blinded him momentarily. He staggered against the wall and pressed his eyes until they hurt. 'Oh God,' he muttered to himself as his vision returned slowly, and with it the slow anguish that seethed in his mind, the depths of loneliness. He had seen himself as the cripple, and the hopelessness of his life threatened him now as it had never done before. He saw himself as the friendless cripple, the unwanted rascal who would be made to dance for a drink in the Britannia in the long damp days of rainy-season darkness.

As he ambled along, he shuffled, picking up one foot before the other like the cripple did, and all the ventures, schemes, failures began to gnaw at his bones. No shop, no trade, no home, no wife, no family. He walked straight down to the lighthouse, and on the railing of the pier he held his head over the water, taking deep breaths.

11

NOW WHETHER it started when Kale Khan told Jamini that God was dead, or whether it was because Rahim thought him a fool and told him so many times, it is hard to say, but there was not only a slow drifting away from the people closest to him, but a following of strange impulses that did not themselves mean much beyond a kind of activity to chase away the boredom he now felt.

Lakshmi's father also thought that the boy was becoming a rascal, and forbade her to see him. She continued to be Miss Lambert's pet, and he felt it most when she asked him why he ran away from school, when she said she was ashamed to walk with him because of the way he dressed. She had become more beautiful each day, and the breasts that he had first touched in the dark of the theatre had bloomed in womanhood, yet she was cold and evasive. She hurried home after they met secretly in Woodford Square. There were no more kisses under the trees. At first he thought that her parents were becoming strict or because she was growing up to be a woman, but later on the girl's father came to Rahim's shop and complained.

'I want you to keep that vagabond away from my daughter, Mr Khan. That boy only loafin' about the town and he will give the girl a bad name. I know they grow up together, but is a shame the way things turn out.'

Jamini wished that his father would throw a barrage of insults upon the man. Instead Rahim only nodded agreement. 'You hear, you hearin' what troubles you bringin' on my head? You ain't shame? I have 'nuff, 'nuff troubles as it is. Leave decent people children alone, boy!'

Although they had met a few times after her father came to Rahim's shop, he knew that something infinitely gentle, infinitely fragile was slowly dying inside of him; like the dew drops balancing on the lace-work of spider-webs that spread across the morning grass. One spearing of a dry leaf falling, one shout, one clamour, and the fine web that held the crystals of the dew would break. That day had finally come when he knew that she tolerated him because it was easier than refusing to see him. He could tell it in the taste of her mouth, the flavour of passion in her mouth was gone, there was only fear now, fear that someone would see them and tell her parents. Rahim had stopped giving him any pocket money, and many times when Lakshmi went to the cinema he was left waiting outside so that he could walk home with her through the Square, and their meeting was over in a few short minutes.

Jamini sat waiting one day on a concrete runner in which the railings of the Square were set, when he spotted a large dead rat on the grass. Suddenly he was rich. He had simply to take the rat across the street to the Sanitation Department in the Town Hall and they could pay between sixpence and a shilling for it. It was the largest rat he had ever seen, in good condition too. The Town Hall did not pay well (or at all) for rats which were frizzled by cats. How suddenly his luck had changed. It was like picking up money in the street.

With a leaf between his fingers he picked up the rat by its tail and examined it more thoroughly. The dead rat laughed with a foolish grin on its face as it stared through wide-open eyes at the upside-down world.

'But suppose Rahim finds out, or Meena, or Kale Khan? Then what?'

He thought of all the things he could buy with the money. He could still get to the Globe Theatre, even if the show had started, he could find her. He knew where she would sit. He would wait in the darkened movie-house, sit in any seat till his eyes became accustomed to the dark, then he would move over when he saw her. His hands trembled. He felt a wild anxiety, a strange thrill, delighting, and at the same time shaking him a little.

The clerk was seated at his desk in the Sanitation Department as Jamini crossed the street. He was writing large well-formed letters in sweeping circles into a ledger which covered the entire top of the desk. From one book to another, to still another, and then into the ledgers. That was all they did. When the government paid out a shilling for a rat, it had to be recorded and re-recorded. Your name would be going down in the history of Trinidad, perhaps the records were sent to the Red House, where they were copied again by another clerk.

'Well, what have you got, boy?' the clerk asked lazily, without looking up from his ledger. His cork hat lay on a chair beside him. He was dressed in the same official uniform as the police, complete in every detail, except that it was all in khaki, whereas the police wore black and white.

'A rat, a big rat, sir,' Jamini said.

'Fill in the form. I'll be with you in a minute,' the clerk called to him again, but still they had not looked each other in the face. Just then the telephone rang. Jamini began filling in the form. It was a bill of sale which the owners of dead rats, bats, mongoose, etc. had to sign. The last lines of small print said something about 'hereby surrender all rights to the city of Port of Spain.' The clerk was still on the telephone. His voice was more friendly now more like the real meaning of 'civil servant'. How strange it was, if you were rich and had a telephone, you simply had to call to get service. He had the forms filled in, now, with a false address.

'Thank *you* for calling, sir. Goodbye,' the clerk said and finally hung up.

'He is sweet and nice to the telephone people because they don't bother to collect for the rats found in their homes . . . he probably pockets all those shillings,' thought Jamini.

'Well?' the clerk said, coming over to him. He held up the rat. The clerk looked at it carefully.

'Good shape? . . . No holes? How long ago did you catch it, boy?'

At last he thought, the clerk was tearing out the form from the receipt book and going over to a little black canister.

'This morning, sir. Big, eh?' Jamini laughed nervously. A little bravado came over him—the shining shilling at last!

'The biggest one I ever saw, worth at least a bob,' he bantered with the clerk.

'I've seen bigger,' the clerk said lazily, with a kind of finality. You couldn't argue with these fellows, he thought. They'd pay sixpence, only half of what the rat was really worth and pocket the rest. What could you do? Take the rat back? That was their threat if you pressed for more.

'Mumble, mumble-der-der—one hundred and ninety-five Quarry Street . . . Where did you get this rat, boy? There's no such address . . . Quarry Street ends at number . . .'

'It's mine. What the hell you care? Just pay me my money and let me go.'

'Just you run along now, and . . .'

'You're a thief, a nasty thief!' Jamini shouted.

'Oh, so I'm a thief, am I? We'll see about . . .' The clerk started coming to the counter where the rat lay. Jamini snatched up the rat and hurled it across the desk before he could get out. The pens lined up on the ink-stand went flying and the ink rolled over. It forked out two long black splashes on the ledger.

'You want the rat. Take it!' the boy screamed as he ran out of the Sanitation Department and headed down Knox Street.

'Come back here! Come back here at once, you little rogue,' the clerk called, chasing after him. Jamini turned, still running. 'Go to hell, you dirty thief!'

The afternoon moved slowly as he lingered about the Square. No shilling, no show, but he would wait for her. There were times when she would go with him to the sea, or to the hills of St Ann's at the end of the tramcar line. But now he knew that it would be useless to ask that of her. What bad seed of tropic sleep had sown itself into him he did not know, for even when she did run away to the hills with him, they fought each other before long, with her telling him that he would grow up to be a disgrace to everyone. 'Even you?' he had asked her, but she did not reply.

The sun was falling low behind the hills of Laventille as he wandered about the Square counting off each fifteen-minute chime of the Trinity Church. The shadows along the rails of the Square moved up with the chimes, and finally he saw her enter the Square. His heart leapt and all the anxiety of waiting fell flat as he saw her. She had entered the Square with someone who walked away when she saw him.

'You shouldn't wait for me like this. I don't belong to you,' she said before he could say anything.

'Why can't I wait if I want to? If you don't want me around, just say so, come right out and say so. Perhaps you don't want me to wait for you because you don't want me to see what a fool you making of yourself.' He knew that he should not have said that, he knew that it would precipitate everything. He wanted to tell her that whoever it was he saw her with could not love her the way he did, but he didn't say that, he couldn't say it that way.

'You shouldn't wait for me ever again, Jam, because . . .'

'Because what?' he asked. 'Because I saw Tommy running away when you came into the Square? You know how many times I've heard Tommy say what he would do to you if he had the . . .'

'Don't say any more,' she snapped.

'Is that why? Is it true then? You belong to him, then, is that it?'

A sudden change came into her voice, a sadness which he did not understand. She took his hand in hers, then said, 'It's all over, I don't belong to anyone. I'm not good enough for you—not any more.'

'Oh, no?' he said.

'Tommy . . . and what he told all the boys, it's true. He said he would tell everyone if I didn't do what he said. But it's too late now, he can do anything to me, I don't care.' She kissed him on his cheek and ran away crying.

'Wait, Lakshmi, wait for me!' he called out, but already she was running past the gate at Frederick Street. 'Wait for me!' he shouted again as he started after her. He couldn't understand what had happened to him in that moment. It seemed that he turned, and there she was running through the gate where he now stood. He was looking up and down Frederick Street, hoping that she did not go directly home, that she was somewhere in the street waiting for the tears to dry. He started running up Prince Street. His feet carried him along tirelessly. His heart sped, floated, climbed to frightening heights, stood balancing in mid-air, then fell crashing down and broke, for his mind thought it saw Lakshmi in a hundred faces crossing in the street. In the quick burst of laughter swelling out of a girl's throat, the fleeting back of someone's head in a tramcar, he thought it was she, and when the illusion broke, he was powerless to the dancing, running feet and the eyes of the street and the voice of someone calling, 'Jam . . . Jam . . . wait for me.' And he tossed his head about in search of the voice, but the voices and the eyes and the fleeting faces he thought were hers came closer and he saw that they were not. He wondered if she knew how what she had told him, had driven him in the streets, had picked him up like a dried-out blade of grass and tossed him about, letting her heart soar, letting his heart shoot up to the crests of mighty waves that broke and left him stranded in mid-air, then let him fall . . . feeling his stomach filled with the boiling of the sea below as he went falling through an eternal emptiness of waiting, falling, waiting. Forever in a second. Then crashing down into the sea that sucked him up again, toyed with him in its eternal rise and fall, in its eternal illusions of her face, the bright brown hazel of her eyes that he searched for in the faces sweeping past, but never, never finding hers.

The streets were empty of tears, empty of eyes like hers, and empty of love. The streets were cruel, the streets that did not stop their running, the streets that did not say, 'Jamini . . . she loves you . . . it's you she loves.' The mouths of the streets were dry and harsh and in their callous humming did not stop to speak, to say, 'We saw her come this way . . . quickly . . . we saw her that way . . . now hurry then . . . you'll find her!' The streets only wound him tightly as a top, dashed him down again with all their might, leaving him in an ugly, spinning, deadened dance. The streets that he had loved, the streets that had watched them as they loved, as they kissed each other in the doorways of closed shops. The streets went on, they did not know that love had died. The streets were light—light and filled with living feet. The streets were filled with laughing faces—faces that he did not see. The streets were empty of lovers who could not see his eyes and say, 'Yes, we know, we know that the streets are cold, we know that your heart is breaking, we know the gnawing of your soul.' The streets had forgotten, the streets that had hidden lovers in their shadows. Love was dead in the streets, dead in the eyes that did not know—the eyes that could not stop the clockwork for a moment and say, 'Yes, come . . . we will help you to find *your* pair of eyes.'

And as he ran like a wounded animal pursued by its hunter, he wondered where he could find a place away from the sweeping, fleeting, running eyes of the street, a place to cry. He wondered when he would fall into a throbbing, sobbing mass, when the running madness of his brain would trip his feet and swallow him up in the crescendo that was closing in on him, spinning the yellow ball of the evening sun into sharpened pinpoints that pierced at his eyes; making the streets and the houses dance; making the tramlines blur and double; cutting the streets into two separate floating images—and then the first teardrop splashed ahead of him. It lashed the sidewalk, it seized the hot pavement as it broke into a black wet many-pointed star, and he felt the rims of his eyes filled and weighted. Then the momentum of his running body broke against the white porcelain sink of the public lavatory and he cried, laving his face with cool water from the tap. He rubbed his fingers against the coarse grain cut out on the brass handle of the tap, his fingers twisting it until they hurt. He wanted to break it from the pipe. He looked at the pale, white sink, the thin long streak of orange rust traced out by the continual leaking of the water. He listened to the hissing sound it made as it escaped from the closed tap, making the silence of the washroom come to life, and then he heard a bird outside, calling from the Calabash tree, *Kes-kee-dee . . . Kes-kee-dee.* He looked up to the row of small broken glass windows through which the sound of the bird's call floated down. They were dirty, caked with the rust of dry earth, washed by the rains, old with dregs of the dry and the rainy seasons that had come and gone. The eyes that watched those windows, the ears that listened to the call of birds would come and go. A feeling of sadness ran through him as he looked at the windows, thinking of the Square, of how love had come and how it had died, and the world about him had an eternity that would never be his. He kept tasting the sweetness of the water as it mixed and thinned out the salt of his tears, still laving his face, so that no one coming in might know that he was crying, so that no one might know that the world had run away and left him all alone.

Rahim returned from his wanderings one day to find Kale Khan stooping over his charcoal brazier boiling some rice. With his eyes half closed, he blew through a hollow bamboo tube to keep the embers of the fire going.

'*Barp*, everything all right?' Rahim asked the old man.

'Yes, boy, everything all right.' And with that statement, that particular intonation, the old man dismissed him. His tone suggested that they had nothing else to say to each other.

'If is anything you need? if you ain't feelin' good or any . . .'

'Boy, come here, sit down, sit down,' the old man said as Rahim faltered. 'You make you own bed. You*self* have to sleep in that. I never work for nobody.'

The old man sat down on his haunches, his legs drawn up to his chin. He seemed thin, his body was like a bundle of sticks. He sat on his low stool, packing his old clay pipe. Rahim struck a match and offered to him. He nodded, sucking deep long draughts that hollowed out his cheeks. The flame darted in and out, in and out of the pipe like a humming bird flitting in and out of a flower.

'I ain't going to start now,' the old man continued, waving out the match with slow movements of his hand. It had already gone out, but he still waved it, with a fanning movement, as he drew the smoke deep into his lungs. In a tone of utter weariness he spoke his words slowly, softly, as if speaking out loud to himself, looking into the darkening corners of his room.

'You do you business, I still have two-two, three-three people this side, that side who know my work. That 'nuff for me.' He paused to put the match in a small shell he used as an ashtray.

'I is old man,' he groaned, 'but watch.' He stretched out one hand, palm downwards. 'Yes see, they ain't shakin'. Still have plenty strength to work. I workin' for *my* people when they come an' bring little little job, is all right. It don't have partnership in this kind of work—must work alone, otherwise bad business.'

'I hope that you ain't vex, *Barp*.'

'Vex? No, boy, what vex?' he laughed a little dry laugh. 'Whaaaat vex?' he repeated. 'Pathan can't vex with he own flesh-an-blood. Is just like if you put you hand in fire to vex with you own flesh-an-blood. G'wan, g'wan upstairs now,' he said softly. 'Don't bother you mind too much. Mustn't worry, mustn't worry 'bout anything.'

As Rahim left the room, Jamini was just coming into the gateway. In a fit of anger Rahim seized him by the shoulders. The boy could feel his father's bitterness in the twist of his clothes.

'Boy, where the *hell* you went to?' he shouted.

Jamini held his head down. 'Nowhere,' he said sullenly.

Rahim gripped his ear, tugged at it hard, so that the boy's eyes would meet his, and when they did, there was hate in his cutting stare. He stood motionless, looking Rahim straight in the eyes now.

'What the hell you mean, nowhere? Nowhere is a place? Every time I ask you where you went you could only say nowhere! nowhere! nowhere! You is a blasted vagabond or what? One 'er these days you go get yourself in some kind 'er mischief an' then go find out where the hell this nowhere is.'

Silence.

'You can't talk, you lose you tongue?' He shook the boy again by the ear. Jamini shrugged his shoulder. His ear hurt, but now a strange anger seemed to cripple him, deadening his senses. Rahim could pull his ear off, tear his hair out, he wouldn't feel it, he wouldn't budge.

'What you comin' to at all? You want to be a idler? Walk 'bout all over town? What the hell does go in your head at all?' He struck the boy on his head with his knuckles. 'Nothing—nothing, eh—nowhere—nothing.' His knuckles struck the boy's head. 'That is you name these days? Answer me when I talk to you, boy!' He grabbed his hair now, shaking him as he spoke, demanding an answer to his question.

Jamini looked at him hatefully from the corner of his eyes, his head hung backwards, to the side because of the way Rahim held him by the hair.

Nothing was going on in his head. Nothing, and everything. He hated Rahim. He hated himself for it. The two angers were fighting in his brain. They cancelled each other out leaving him deadened, painless, colourless. They left nothing in his brain.

'You think you is a man now?' and then disgustedly, disdainfully, 'Boy,' he said, 'you ain't *begin* to know what it is to be a man yet.'

The angers were clawing in his brain, they made a great noise in his ears, they blinded his ears now. And then, suddenly, Rahim did a strange thing. He let go of the boy and grasped a hammer from the floor and pushed it into the boy's hand shouting, 'You hate me, eh, you hate me, talk up, tell me? Here, take this hammer, you want to kill me, that is it?' He folded the boy's fingers about the hammer handle, saying, 'If you hate me so bad, come on an' give me a blow! Go on, hit me with it!' The hammer fell to the floor. Jamini would not clench his fingers around its handle. His throat ached, but he would not cry. The humming and the noise in his head spread through his entire body, and he felt limp and weak. Then Rahim hit him hard on the head, jolting him forward. 'Gwan, g'wan upstairs, you damn fool. You head only full with nonsense. After all the try we try to teach you a trade, you only know how to knock about all over town!'

'*Rah*EEM!' There was a loud angry shout from the old man's room. Rahim started at the suddenness, the anger in the old man's voice, the way he called, not Rahim, but Rah*eem*. In the silence, he could hear Kale Khan shuffling his feet into his wooden-soled slippers. He heard him reach for his iron rod walking-stick, he heard it drag across the floor, and then Kale Khan stood at the door. Rahim saw the anger, the disgust on Kale Khan's face.

'What wrong with you?' the old man asked. 'You turn animal, o' what?'

Rahim stood silent.

'You ain't have no feelin' o' what? You think that boy go respect you like father?'

'But *Barp*,' Rahim whined nasally, 'the boy only idlin' all over the place. He moomah tellin' he *day-in day-out* to stop quiet, to learn a trade. He can't stop in the house. Who know what trouble he go bring on we head?'

Kale Khan couldn't stand this snivelling.

'An' what the hell you put *hammer* in the boy hand for? What the hell *you* have in *your* head, eh? You want *me* to tell you?'

Rahim fell silent again. He felt ashamed that he couldn't answer the question. Why did he force the hammer into the boy's hand?

'You takin' out your temper 'pon that poor boy, that why you bring chile in the world? Tell me, to holler 'pon them, to cuss and damn them when you want to ease you own mind? I born long long time, don't think I is a jackass. I know just what goin' on. Whole day today you make jackass of yourself, now you want to take it out 'pon that po' boy.'

'*Barp*, I . . .' Rahim started feebly again.

'That all the sense you have in *you* head? I don't know what devil you have in you heart, what poison you have in you vein. A chile, you own own own chile.' Then, slowly, emphasising each word, each syllable, the old man said scornfully, 'Boy, I don't know what *kind* 'er man you is, ain't fit for *nothing*.'

And he walked back to his room, leaving Rahim standing alone and ashamed. He heard the old man say, 'Send the boy down after he eat he dinner,' as he turned and walked up the stairs.

Downstairs, later that evening, Kale Khan sat at his counter writing another letter to Hindustan. He expressed his joy over the freedom of India, pleading for help in the repatriation of his people. In his letters he continually told of the injustices to Indians in Trinidad.

'That you, boy?' he called, hearing Jamini's footsteps outside.

'Yes, Dada, it's me.'

'Come, come, sit down.' He sighed softly. And as he looked at the boy, he knew what he would have to do before the arrival of the envoy from India. Tomorrow, soon, as soon as he felt strong, he would begin. His blood, the whisperings of his soul had spelled out his course. His large eyes widened as he ran the envelope across his cracked tongue and sealed it.

'You want something to eat, boy?'

'No, Dada. Just finished dinner,' the boy said.

'Mustn't mind what Rahim tell you. You is good boy.'

Sitting in his room now, Jamini wondered how he had come to drift away from the old man. He felt a great sorrow fall upon him, a kind of guilt, as he watched the old man's movements, his pale face. He spoke so strangely. Jamini felt the old tenderness he used to know, he remembered those mornings of the rainy season when he nestled in his grandfather's arms, the days they went to the Square. What had happened to those days? Kale Khan opened his Capstan Navy Cut tin and rummaged inside. He took out four different coins and examined them in the light, then put them back. The fifth coin was a shilling. He handed it to Jamini.

'Here, take this, buy something for yourself with it.'

Jamini took the shilling. He could hardly speak. He couldn't understand why the old man had called him to his room. They merely sat in each other's presence, not saying much, but he knew that Kale Khan wanted him there, wanted just the sight of him so that he could summon up his thoughts, look directly at the closest symbol of the ruin that this land had brought upon them.

Another rainy season was upon them, and as Jamini watched the rain falling in the yard, he wondered if it was falling everywhere. Was it falling on the plains where Kale Khan rode in India? On the huts of his fathers? On the streets he'd walked?

A wet chicken came by to shelter itself from the rain. Kale Khan grabbed his iron rod walking-stick, which hung on the arm of the rocking-chair, struck it hard on the ground and growled, 'Git away, stupid bird, g'wan that side.' The chicken shot out from the cosy spot, half flying, half running, and went pelting out into the rain, then came to an abrupt stop, as it realised that it was once more in the rain. Then it clucked in an angry offended way, twisting its head round, looking at Kale Khan.

'*Barp*, you mustn't go outside in the rain, you know what the doctor tell you,' Rahim said to him softly, pleadingly, coming into the room.

'Doctor, Doctor, Doctor this, Doctor that,' he grumbled, giving way in the end. Something deep inside of him had broken. He was not quick to take offence now.

These days he went into his room to lie on his back on the bed-board, still listening to the rain falling outside, thinking, that it was *time*, only time was dying and nothing more. He started dying with it a million years ago. It warned him when it was getting evening, and his world settled about him with all the unaccomplished little tasks his failing energies kept him from.

And Jamini, thinking of his own wanderings in the streets and of how his heart had trembled in the dark, knew that he must stay close to his ailing grandfather. He knew that he must fill the old man's cup from the pipe outside, that he must go with him to talk to the crowds in Woodford Square and deep into the hidden towns and hamlets of the island, until the day when they would go to Hindustan—Jamini and Kale Khan.

12

THE JUMBIE BIRD called in the Calabash tree, it darkened the night with its *twee-twee-twee-twee*. The night was filled with curses and oaths hurled at the unseen bird, its *twee-twee-twee* calling out a message of death.

In the beds of the young, between the white sheets of lovers lying in slack nocturnal embrace, all around the Town Hall, through the Trinity Church, the Red House and Woodford Square went this fearful reminder, awakening the sleeping night with the *twee-twee-twee* of the Jumbie bird calling, measuring out Time for some unseen listener whose silent thought now played on violent acts, and arrant deeds, who feared that it came calling on this night for him.

Bird, go away, you are cast out of the stone bowels of your mother's insides. Bird, go away, you are the bastard child of devil and whore, drown your calls in the bottom of the Caribbean Sea; do not come perched in the Calabash tree with tidings of death crouched in anonymity.

Muffled voices in the pillows, sure that it was not for them, hurled curses at the unseen bird.

Come out here if you are devil or whore,
Come out here if you are spirit or stone.
I will plant a rock in your black throat.
Bird, show your face in this night you profane.

But the Jumbie bird sat in the Calabash tree on Frederick Street along Woodford Square. It came night after night with its message of death and its *twee-twee-twee*, its melancholy cry of *twee-twee twee-twee*.

Bird, why do you come in the middle of the night, to hide your black feathers in shadowy leaves? Show your face once, and death will be stuffed into your own throat. Bird, death does not hide in the Calabash tree, it walks on open ground, it fears not stone nor man nor light of day. What coward's eyes hide between the leaves, and will not take challenge on this night? Bird, come down from that Calabash tree.

The curses flew, the nights turned day, the threats went past the Jumbie bird's ear, but the Jumbie bird came each night to cry . . . to warn from the Calabash tree. Bird, here I am, come down with your wicked claws, scratch out your companion's name. Let us know for whom you issue foreboding calls of *twee-twee-twee* in these waiting nights. Bird, you're formed from the droppings of devils, the bitter gall of rubbed cucumber edges flows in your poisonous veins. Why come to these nights and blacken the moon, hiding in the Calabash tree?

But the Jumbie bird hid in the Calabash tree. For one pair of ears, for one sick soul lying alone somewhere in the night, one heart that knew the Jumbie bird calls would never cease *this* time for him.

The moon ducked under the clouds those nights, pulled the sheets of its haloed ankles tight. And in the darkness across Frederick Street, between the half-open jalousies, Jamini peeped, his eyes searching the Calabash tree in Woodford Square for the Jumbie bird's perch.

'An old man once threw a stone at the Jumbie bird and the next day he died on the Town Hall steps.'

A voice reminded him as he held his hands across his chest to press the loud flutter of his heart. He looked for the Jumbie bird in the Calabash tree, the Jumbie bird whose voice he heard, but never could see, the Jumbie bird that ran away by day and buried itself in the heart of the jungle, but returned with its reminder, its haunting *twee-twee-twee*.

The neighbours said, 'Is the ole man next do', is he the Jumbie bird calling fo'. He time up and he got to go.'

And Jamini said no, not Dada, as he heard its *twee-twee-twee*, as he searched the dark branches of the Calabash tree on those long nights that lasted forever, hoping each time it stopped it would end this mournful sound.

'I wish I were a spider hiding in that tree . . . I'd sting that bird . . . I'd . . .'

'I wish I were a scorpion . . . hiding in the grass . . . I'd cock my tail and . . .'

'I wish I were a centipede . . . with a hard black shell and a hundred feet . . . I'd . . .'

'I wish I were a soldier with a pointed sword . . . a powerful gun . . . I'd . . .'

'I wish I owned the Red House . . . with both those cannons, and those cannon balls . . .I'd . . .'

The neighbours said, 'The ole man old, an' he see he days, is time for he to pack up an' go,' and Jamini said no, the Jumbie bird's calling for someone else, not Dada. He said no, no, no, no, no, till the mornings came and the Jumbie bird left the Calabash tree.

The rainy season was almost over now. Everyone waited for the rains to end, but Kale Khan seemed to be waiting for something else. These days he sat dozing on his bent wood rocking-chair looking out into the rain, then, as if he saw some moving form out in the distance, he awoke suddenly, his eyebrows arched questioningly. As he sat in the chair dozing, it seemed as if a voice came calling him from somewhere out between the raindrops. He awoke again, answering, 'Yes . . . who that?' and turning his head from left to right, he saw no one there, and heard only the soft and silent pitter-patter of the rain drilling small holes in the dirt of the yard. He frowned at the grey light, cleared his throat, then let his head fall to the side and went to sleep again. Towards evening, he awoke, hooked the handle of his walking-stick to the crossbar at the foot of the chair, and dragged the chair into his room.

The following morning, Binti came into the gateway, her two-gallon cans in hand, her slippers shuffling, her funnel and measuring cup jingling from her waist. 'Rahim, Rahim,' she called up the stairway, but there was only silence, a strange silence, the old woman thought, the silence that falls across a home when the woman of the house has gone away. 'Jam, ay, Jamini.' But still there was no answer. 'No use in walkin' up all them steps,' she told herself, remembering the strangeness of the house when last she had found Rahim sitting alone in the darkness.

As she was leaving, she peeped into Kale Khan's room and saw him doubled up on the old sign-board. She could hear the low moans he made with each breath. They were short breaths and his chest rose and fell with each filling of his lungs. His nipples were knotted tightly as if he was freezing, and plastered to his chest were seven small spear-shaped leaves which had been soaked in some concoction, leaving them an oily green, the fine lattice-work of the veins on the leaves standing out in high contrast. Binti nodded her head pityingly and put down her cans. She took the coconut-husk broom which stood in the corner of his room and began, with her back bent, to sweep away all the bits of crumpled paper which had contained his snuff.

Kale Khan got up slowly, raising himself on his elbows and craning his neck around to see what was making the scratching noise.

'What you doin' there, old woman? Can't see I tryin' to sleep?' he said feebly, not once looking at her.

She stood up, adjusted her glasses, and wiped the perspiration from her forehead with the back of her wrist.

'G'wan back to sleep, li'l bit o' noise won't keep you awake.'

He stretched out on the wooden bed-board, turned his face away from the door and remained quiet for a while, looking at the walls and the peeling wallpaper.

'Old woman, you makin' dust fly outside there, you want to catch sick when that dust fly inside your nose or what?'

But Binti paid no attention to him; she went on sweeping, and when she was finished, came tip-toeing in to his room and started arranging things on the counter, pulling the rocking-chair to its accustomed corner, standing his boots upright under the bed, and picking up dirty pots and pans which he had left lying about.

'*Now* what you doin'? You think I could find anything after you hide them this place that place?' he asked, but she went on as if he was not there. She went outside to her cans, poured some coconut oil in the palm of her hand and came back into his room where he was sitting on the edge of the bed, his eyes closed, his hands grasping the bed-board supporting him on either side. She started slapping his head with the oil, rubbing it in well with the outstretched palm of her hand. As soon as he took in his breath and started to open his mouth to speak again, she passed her hand about his face and over his mouth, rubbing oil well over the skin of his face.

'Now don't give me no extra trouble,' she scolded him.

He sat resigned, disgusted, and finally began uttering sighs of relief, making soft ' ah . . . ah . . . ah . . . ah ' sounds with each rub, each squeeze of her tiny little hands on his forehead, his temples, into the corners of his eyes, the ridges of his brows, the back of his neck, along which she pressed her thumb firmly, sliding it slowly up and down, making it glide smoothly on the coconut oil. He looked up at her. Was it twenty, twenty-five years?

'You want specs to watch me with or what?' she asked coldly. His tired eyes looked into hers with the expression of a child who had done some mischief and was scolded. Then he hung down his head.

'No,' he said. 'No,' he repeated as she put her arm about his shoulders and let him down gently onto the bed-board and tiptoed out as quickly as she had come.

'Better he believe that he dream it,' she said to herself as she headed up Quarry Street.

And then the rain stopped suddenly that day. There was a light warm shower, and the sun came bursting through, and everyone knew that the rainy season had ended. Kale Khan seemed to shake himself free of the long sleep; he got up early in the morning, walked slowly out into the sun dragging his walking-stick behind him. He placed his hand over his brow and looked up at the clear blue sky, then went to the stairway and called to Jamini.

'Go market side and buy six white carrot, big like so.' He placed his thumb-nail about ten inches from the end of his walking-stick. 'When you get that, go to that butcher boy Taj. He is a rascal, that scamp, anyway, you tell him Kale Khan want three bone! Must have plenty marrow inside.'

He looked squarely at Jamini. There was only the faintest twinkle in his eye, but it was there, and it made the boy happy to see him this way again. Pointing to the handle of his walking-stick which had a small hole in the top, he said, 'You know what kind bone I mean, like so. Don't let that rascal take your money till you see how much marrow them bone have in them, and don't forget tell he who you is—understand?'

The boy nodded. Both he and the old man were smiling now, as though they shared some secret confidences.

'Get quarter pound mustard seed. Don't pick up old old seed that can't grow, must be fresh. Look, see them seed have colour like raw gold. Ever see raw gold, boy?'

Jamini shook his head questioningly.

'You mean to say you is jeweller son and Rahim never show you? Anyway, come.' Kale Khan took out a bright saffron yellow length of cloth. It was the most colourful turban cloth the old man had, it was also a colour he liked a great deal.

'Yellow like so, see? All right, now, g'wan, and come back quick quick quick, have plenty plenty work to do.'

After the boy left, he set about cutting up lengths of umbrella wire which he twisted into U-shaped handles. By the evening, he had the radishes hollowed out, and he pierced the handles into them. Jamini helped him by bringing water from the pipe in the yard and the old man first filled the radishes, then dropped a few mustard grains into each and hung them up in a row where the morning sunlight would warm them and make the seeds grow.

Late into the nights that followed, the boy heard the Jumbie bird in the Calabash tree. *Twee twee twee* the bird called, then he heard his grandfather's wooden-soled slippers, his iron rod walking-stick, *clop clop clank . . . clop clop clank*, as he went to the pipe, replenishing the water in the radishes which he drank regularly. That was medicine number one.

Medicine number two was now to begin. He shook out some coins from his Capstan Navy Cut tin and gave them to Jamini for car fare expenses. He lectured to the boy for the better part of the morning on the exact details of his requirements, pacing about his room anxiously in search of objects which would convey his description more vividly. Finally the boy left.

Late that evening Kale Khan was hunched over his charcoal brazier slowly turning some flat bread which he and Jamini would eat for dinner. With Meena gone, and Rahim seldom at home, the old man cooked for himself and the boy each day. He was used to it when Rahim was a boy. With his own two hands he had done all this before, besides which, he thought that no Pathan should have women hovering around him constantly. 'Otherwise grow up like woman,' the old man had said more than ten thousand times, and no one had questioned, or dared to debate this with him.

As he saw the boy enter the gateway, he rose up quickly, and a sudden dizziness shook him a little, his legs cramped from the stooping position in which he tended the fire.

'You get it, you get it, boy, eh? Which which place you went?' he asked anxiously. The boy's face was dark and burnt from the sun. His skin was oily and he seemed tired, and he felt that he had failed the old man.

But Kale Khan, sensing that he had failed, gave a loud laugh. 'Don't make face like if you moomah and poopah dead, come on.' The old man put his arm about the boy's shoulder and clapped him close.

'Come, sit down, eat. And tomorrow wake soon soon soon befo' sun get up, without *even* coming this side. That way you go have whole day to catch them.'

The following morning Kale Khan got up and went to the stairway. He banged on the landing with his iron rod. 'Boy, ay boy, Jam.'

There was no answer. 'Boy!' Still no answer. The old man smiled to himself. 'Good man, good man,' he said to himself. The boy was up and gone into the hills of Laventille. He had a good start this morning.

Kale Khan hung all the radishes carefully along his walking-stick, holding it in the middle. He opened the tap in the yard, and slowly, lovingly let a thin stream of water trickle into each one. The morning sun played on the shoots of the young mustard plants inside the radishes which were beginning to shrivel. He stroked the young pale green leaves which looked waxen in the clear light, then he went back to his room and hung them up one by one.

His heavy boots which had stood idle through the rainy season were covered with mildew and a strange bright orange-coloured mess. Kale Khan put on his spectacles, and took the boots into the yard. He hit the heels hard on the ground to shake loose any roaches or ants which might have crawled into them. It was a ritual which he never forgot since he was in the regiments in India. He hugged the boots one by one to his breast, and with a sharp knife, he began scraping out the small map-like growths of tropic fungus which were constantly on the move. The old man shaved along the boot leather, his eyes filled with a sense of victorious glee as the mould and the old wax and polish fell away. Then he began rubbing coconut oil into the dry leather.

A thin long shadow cast by the evening sun swept past, and the old man looked up. It was Jamini, carrying a large brown-paper bag in his hand, beaming when his eyes met his grandfather's.

'You get it? You mean to say that you really catch them at last?' Kale Khan asked, his face all lit up, his eyes as sharp as pin points.

'Come, put it this side.' He pushed away myriads of objects, files, tools, hammers, with his walking-stick.

'You know how to carry out orders good good good, make good soldier one day, boy.'

From the paper bag he took out, one by one, five pink snails, each the size of his fist. The slimy creatures pulled in their horns lazily as he set them side by side. They oozed a thick slimy fluid as they spread their groping wet flesh on the counter. He took up one of the hammers, broke them open, then he pulled them out with his gnarled trembling fingers and placed them directly into boiling water. He squatted in front of the fire, blowing into its embers, occasionally spooning off a grainy brown froth which he tasted, slapping his tongue on the roof of his mouth. Then he added salt in pinches which he ground slowly between his fingers, letting it fall gently through the vapours and into the broth. His hand circled about the pot quickly, sprinkling the salt evenly, then he flicked his fingers clean and covered the pot. He sat before the brazier, worn, waiting, his arms stretched forward resting on his knees, his head bowed between his legs, and when the broth was finally done, he drank it down.

Every other day the boy brought him a new supply and he repeated these actions in much the same way.

For medicine number three he said to Jamini, 'I want you to go Innis Drug-store and tell he send Kale Khan liver oil. Go on now, take money from there.' He pointed to the Capstan tin. The boy went to the drug-store at the corner. As he entered there was no one about, but he heard the rattling of bottles and phials from behind the counter.

'Y'ace, I'll be right there,' the chemist's voice called.

The shelf on which the statue had stood was empty, and as Mr Innis came out wiping his hands on his apron, he looked in the direction of the boy's stare.

'The old man's no longer with us. Got a bit tired of us, I dare-say.'

Jamini smiled a little bit uncomfortably. Mr Innis seemed the same. Time had not changed him, but the boy. Now they could laugh together about the statue of God.

'We'll just have to get along as best we can without him, won't we?' he said as he handed the boy a bottle wrapped up in brown paper.

Kale Khan set about opening it as soon as he got it. There was a blue label on the bottle with the picture of a fully-dressed man—necktie, jacket, hat and all—holding a fish as tall as himself by a cord strung through its laughing mouth. The cord passed over the man's shoulder, where he held it by both hands. The tail of the great fish touched the ground behind him. Kale Khan sat on his bed prying out the cork with a pointed file, blowing away the loose pieces as they broke off. On his counter lay a corkscrew which Rahim had bought for him, but the cod liver oil had stood on the shelves of Mr Innis' Drug-store so long that time, dust and the full pelt of many August suns had weakened the old corks. Unfortunately for Kale Khan, cod liver oil did not evaporate like many other medications which, as they partially dried out, were placed in the box of half-price specials.'

When the cork was all out, he placed the bottle to his lips and drank from it as though it were water, then he held the bottle up to the light to see how far the level had dropped. In earlier days, he used to measure it out with a tablespoon, but each time, he had to go out to rinse the spoon, then dry it. 'Mustn't make ants, boy . . . mustn't make ants come,' he would always warn Jamini when, as a small boy, he had dropped a crumb of food in his room. Now he could tell by the feel in his mouth the exact quantity he wanted.

Underneath his counter stood a row of five or six cod liver oil bottles which he saved, all bearing the same trade mark. He could get six cents for each empty bottle, but when he had a dozen saved, Mr Innis would give him a free bottle of cod liver oil for his collection which he considered more of a bargain, for, as he called it, 'a *round* dozen.'

As the mustard seed sprouted, as the snails bubbled and bounced, as he drank down the cod liver oil, measuring its dosage by the feel of his mouth. Kale Khan's face, his actions, his voice, all livened. His sandy-grey complexion disappeared, his wizened body, from which all the blood seemed to have drained, brought forth its oils and saps as he sat in the sun each day, for he treated his body these days with a love that he did not have for life itself. Like his boots, like his sword, so he treated his body, not with a selfish love, but more the love of an instrument that would be used to preform some task.

The steady return of the old man's health and vigour was not received with any grace or kindness from some of the superstitious neighbours who had sworn up and down that the Jumbie bird had come for him and no one else. In a way, it came as a disappointment to them. It seemed as it were, that the old man had promised them a slow and quiet exit. The Jumbie bird's cries had said as much, yet the old man hung on. Even the narrow escape of death will disappoint people sometimes.

Only Jamini was happy now. If he heard the Jumbie bird, he turned his back to the Calabash tree and went on sleeping. The neighbours complained that the old man was possessed by some devil coursing through his veins which had now brought him back from the grave to hurl more curses at them. Most firmly convinced of this was Bissoon, the fat Government chemist who sold recipes for home-made concoctions to anyone who had a fever, or who might want to start a small trade.

'They should put that fat old fool in jail-house and throw away key in the sea.' Kale Khan often shouted across the backyard fence loud enough for the chemist's ears. He was not surprised by the ridiculous rumours, he felt only disgust at what had happened to the minds of men like Bissoon who fell into a kind of mediocrity of mind in the hands of a government which used men like him, the clerks in the Red House, the Treasury boys who sold postage stamps, and all the rest who had some knowledge or learning. They were made to feel fortunate, they were looked up to as the great men in Trinidad upon whom some great honour was bestowed. Mr Salwan, Dr Gopal, yes, even men like them came under the whip and stroke of Kale Khan's tongue, and he laughed heartily at them as he went out to Woodford Square these evenings where a few people gathered, growing in numbers each day as word spread about the market place.

When Kale Khan put the question of returning home to them, they jumped at it.

'What we have to lose?' they queried each other. 'Man, let we go home. What we doin' here? We make other people rich all we life, now we days over. Khan Sahib talkin' sense.'

'Look up in them hills,' Kale Khan said, pointing to the hills of St Ann's and St Clair's where great mansions stood looking down at the city, and across it, straight out to the Gulf of Persia. 'Who livin' up there? Tell me, it have one single bungalow up there that own by any of we?'

'No, man . . . no. The only time we get to go up that side is when one of we boys is a gardener or a yard boy,' they grumbled, as the crowd grew larger with people who were headed home after their day's work.

'But you know what place it have reserve for we? Over there.' He pointed to the Town Hall steps with his walking-stick. 'That is we reward, we payment! I know it have a lot of worthless scamps who say that I want to make trouble. All I sayin' is this, what done, done and over for good. I only askin' for we to go back home. It have one week left before Hussay time, and that same day we Commissioner comin' from Hindustan. Let he see with he own own two eye what we doin' and how we livin', and befo' long we will be back in Hindustan.'

At the mention of the word Hindustan, the crowd roared, and Kale Khan stood smiling silently. The hair on his back and shoulders stood on end and tingled with this long-awaited feeling of glory.

In all the city squares, in the market place, into the little hamlets lost in the hills, buried away far from the ring of bicycle bells and the clanking of tramcars, the old man and Jamini went telling all that the time had come, that their spokesman, their restorer of justice was already on his way. He went to the Public Library and borrowed books, old newspapers. With his spectacles hanging down his nose he read one after the other reports of punishments, reprisals, fines, legislations which bound his people to the Island, laws which suppressed the learning of their own language, the passing on of their own culture and tradition, their festivals. He laughed at the small two-inch news item about the Princes Town Hussay in the old newspaper.

'Is only them who was there that night know what what went on,' he thought to himself, and again he addressed the crowd, this time in Arima, an island district, saying to them, 'We old people know what what thing happen. You remember what what Nancy story they tell you in Hindustan: so much so much work, how quick quick quick you could make money and go back home and be rich man. Remember how you run away from your family home? You never hold a cutlass in your hand befo', but you was young and you did want to show your poopah and moomah how you is a man and you run come this side, sun to wake you, work to kill you, rain to help you sleep, to help you remember days in Hindustan.

'We old people know what happen. Sometime we does forget, but is all you children who have to learn how to read and write. Read the history of your own people,' he clamoured out to the crowd that had gathered in the savannah at Arima.

Like fire-flies of the dark a few vendors had set up little stalls with sweetmeats and home-made delicacies. The gathering had turned into a small celebration, and the air was charged with a lively optimism which had died many years ago. In the twist of some of the faces in the flambeaux by which the old man spoke there was written a hopeless resignation. Faces that had not smiled for years were bursting forth as if new life had been rubbed into their old, old folds and creases.

'How much of you know they ain't allow we to vote for so long? And you know why? Because they allow them only who know how to read and write in English to vote. Now tell me, you think they ain't know that damn few of we did know how to read and write we name in English? Them laws was make to keep we tie down here . . . to use so long as sugar make money, and after that they say you could do what you please now. Who—tell me who—make enough money as long as they live here to pay a passage back to Hindustan?'

Kale Khan laughed with an angry irony as some of the younger folk questioned their parents and a strange anger rose in them now when the older folk said despondently, 'What you did want we to do? We come in bond for five years thinkin' we would make some money and go back. After time pass we still remain the same. Everybody say wait, wait, one day we will get a chance, so we wait.'

It was not long before the old man's name was on the tongues of another generation who had only vaguely heard of him and thought that he might have gone back to India, or perhaps died quietly somewhere. Out of the shadows and the night he seemed to appear with all the vigour and fire that had once dwindled to a slow smouldering ash. He blew life into that ash as he did into his charcoal brazier. Gently at first, so that it would not be snuffed out by a sudden rush of his lungs' breath. Then when he felt that he had touched the hearts of the people, he went finally to Princes Town. As he walked through the old sugar capital of the south, he knew that his words had found the almost forgotten yearnings in the hearts of the resigned, for the streets were thronged with people whose tempers had run so high, that the constabulary was on hand to keep order. After he left Princes Town, it was said that if Kale Khan had told the three or four thousand present to stand on their heads, they would have done it! At Police Headquarters, at Government House, his name was on the tongues of all. They wondered why they had not done away with this little sprig of a man long ago, for now it was too late, now they would have to answer to one hundred and eighty thousand Indians with the resentments of one hundred years of deprivation and abuse simmering on the surface, which required only the faintest spark to explode into a horrible nightmare. And now India's High Commissioner to the Caribbean was arriving, as if some mysterious force had planned it that way, on the first night of the Hussay!

The Commissioner's plane was due to arrive at Piarco Airport at two o'clock that afternoon. There was to be a sixteen-gun salute and an official welcome by the Governor and his dignitaries. The ambasador's title was one of greater rank than that of any colonial governor, and a sixteen-gun salute which was rarely sounded would blast the skies that day. Word rang out among the peasants. All along the twelve miles of country roads between Piarco and Port of Spain where carat huts stood like brown mushrooms off the main road, the Indian tricolor was hung on bamboo poles as tall as could be found. Children dressed in their best clothes, their hair combed and glistening with coconut oil, in the sun, lined the road with small flags to wave at the procession. Others were going directly to join Kale Khan at the airport.

Also at the airport was another welcoming party which consisted of a small knot of professional men, doctors, lawyers, and a few businessmen, with Mr Salwan, the city's most prominent Indian citizen, who, it was rumoured, was going to stand for one of the few seats in the Governor's appointed cabinet.

Everyone was surprised at the voluminous turnout at the airport. The Governor's party, Mr Salwan's party, airport officials, a few thousand Indians started arriving at Piarco. Mr Salwan was in such excitement over the response of the people, he could hardly contain himself. He went over to the Governor's party, took several bows, shook hands all round, then went about looking for one or two familiar faces among the crowd. There was some uneasiness in the peasants with whom he spoke. They knew him vaguely, for on rare occasions such as the birthday of Tagore or Gandhi he had gone into the countryside and passed out a few dollar bills to some of the peasants so that they would come to the 'India Club' and parade about. The club was located on Queens Park as an assertion of Indian dignity. It was hardly known outside of the small group of Mr Salwan's welcoming party. It was a place where a few nervous people met. People with brown skins, whose accent, dress and taste for whisky and soda seemed ridiculous. They would have looked equally ridiculous in Indian dress, or would have gone hungry at a wedding where the aroma from the great cauldrons coiled up to their nostrils and there was no silverware to pass the food from banana leaf to mouth. Their bones had tautened too long, they could no longer cross their legs and eat on level ground like their parents did.

Across from the runways there were at first two or three vendors with baskets slung over their arms doing a brisk business as they wove in and out of the gathering crowd. A few minutes later, there were handcarts with bottles of coloured cool drinks lying haphazardly on huge cakes of melting ice, and from among the carts there was a wild voice bawling out, 'Today-today we goin' back home! Come up an' cool down the body!'

Mr Salwan looked about at the milling crowds disdainfully, listening for the loud voice of the wretched little man who was beginning to embarrass him in the eyes of the Governor's party. He looked over to the Governor's stand, smiled sheepishly, bowed from the waist, then gave a cutting glance to the vendor. One of the uniformed officials of the airport was going past. 'I say, old chap, I mean, look here,' he said to the official.

'Yes, sir, what is it?'

'Couldn't we do something about these rogues and rapscallions? I mean, it looks badly, badly.' He shook his full round face, and the loose flesh of his mouth trembled as he spoke. 'You know what I mean, these chaps barking about, well, what will people think, I mean, well, you know what I mean?'

'I'll look into it right away, sir.'

'There's a good fellow.' He clapped the official on his back, a wide grin across his face.

Mr Salwan was chatting away with his colleagues in the little wooden platform when the official returned to tell him that there was nothing they could really do, that the man had his rights, he was not on airport property.

'You chaps are hopeless, hopeless,' Mr Salwan stormed as he stomped away in a huff and went to the vendor himself.

'Fellow! Fellow!' he shouted, but the little man went on calling at the top of his voice, 'Today today we go see who is slave an' who is master, get your soda, cold cold soda.'

'Now see here,' Mr Salwan shouted, finally catching the vendor's attention.

'Sahib want red red soda o' green green soda?' the little man queried.

With the frightening air of an authority that constables assumed, Mr Salwan asked gruffly:

'What's your name, sir?'

The little man looked about him. 'Me . . . who me, Sahib? . . . Sookiah! My name Sookiah! Look, look, Sahib, have 'um white white soda for big shot people like you. No like red, no like green, mus' like white.'

But presently, Mr Salwan's attention was turned to the entrance of the airport from where a great tumult of noise was coming. An old 1936 Ford convertible surrounded by a dozen drum-beaters was moving slowly into the airport. There was hardly a child left standing, they all ran toward the drummers and the car, and as they came closer, a figure could now be seen sitting on the folded canvas top at the back of the car dressed in a distinguished-looking turban of bright saffron-yellow, its tail of deep-red scalloped edge hung down in front of his chest.

It was Kale Khan, both arms outstretched to the cheering crowd. The first children to reach the car had hopped on to the running-board and were taking turns at pressing the horn which added to the din of the drums, and the foot-wide shining brass cymbals.

The car was heavily weighted down, its body pressed low over the wheels, and as it got nearer, Mr Salwan popped his fingers into his ears to block out the din and the drum-beating.

'Blast!' he said, as he stomped away to rejoin his welcoming party. Sookiah was still standing quizzically with a bottle of white drink in his hand.

The car and drum-beaters had reached the airport buildings now and Kale Khan stepped into the midst of the cheering crowd. He walked past the central gate through which all passengers must go, and as he went past the small stand where Mr Salwan's party sat, he cast a quick cutting glance along the faces.

'Well! What all you boys doin' here? You turn Indian overnight? Worthless scamps!'

No one replied. They looked to Mr Salwan who let his full weight drop to his chair with a low moan. Kale Khan walked along, swinging his walking-stick jauntily and now, in front of the Governor's stand, he said, 'Excellency!' and saluted briskly.

The Governor, a thin tall greying man dressed in decorous white uniform, his hat festooned with a bunch of red feathers, stood up and returned the salute. They smiled at each other and Kale Khan came walking back to a little party of men who had either been at the Prince Town Hussay, or who had led smaller uprisings in other parts of the island. All had stood their ground, but the Princes Town uprising was the only well manoeuvred little battle from which the peasants, despite losses, had gone home feeling victorious; among them Kale Khan was the greatest soldier, leader and stickman.

There was a loud '*Boom*' from behind the airport. The plane had been contacted and although it was not yet visible, the first gun sounded to announce its arrival. There was a concerted noise among the crowd. Kale Khan stood in the exact centre of the air terminal where a path led from the runway to the building. With both hands on his walking-stick, he leaned forward, his shoulders slightly stooped, the hanging end of his turban moving in the wind. His eyes drew together then relaxed as he searched the sky for the plane.

And then, there, beyond the hot air shimmering above the runway in the sun, beyond the bushes edging the airport strips, beyond the tall brown coconut trunks, above their deep green palm leaves, as if suspended in the cloudless blue sky was the tiny silver bird glinting in the sun. The crowd, fired by a wild excitement, started singing the Indian national athem in broken voices, husky voices, voices that had forgotten how to mould and carve a tune, yet singing on, mumbling on, with the words only. Kale Khan stood still, only his wild eyes pulsed and quivered with all the intense emotion welling up in him. His tongue darted out like a lizard's wetting his dry lips. He cleared his throat and moved his weight, still pressing upon the walking-stick in front of him, both hands clenched tightly to the handle.

As the plane neared, as it became larger and larger, there was a childish astonishment among the peasants. How many times had they seen a plane land? While ploughing in their fields they had heard a rumble in the sky, looked up from the soil for a moment and saw a minute object flash in the sun, then they went back to work again. It was with a sense of disbelief that they watched the great silver bird come rushing into the airport. Two small gusts of smoke scorched out as its wheels touched the ground, speeding up the airport as large as twenty of their carat huts.

The first person to get out was the Commissioner, a young man, perhaps Rahim's age. The large guns in the distance began firing, and he waved to the cheering, singing, and now sobbing crowd. The drum beaters, carried along by the frenzy of their own rhythms, began jumping in the air. Mr Salwan was leaning far over his platform, his stomach pressing hard against its rail, clapping his fat little hands, shouting above the tumult, 'Bravo! Bravo!' Then he turned around to his party and signalled them to do likewise. In the Governor's stand, there was only a stiff official air. They were all standing, waiting quietly. Kale Khan walked out slowly to meet the Commissioner.

A little girl darted out of the crowd with two garlands of bright yellow magnolias. She put one about Kale Khan's neck. The old man bent down so that she could reach, and kissed her on the forehead. She offered him the other garland for the Commissioner, but Kale Khan took her small hands in his, so that she could garland the Commissioner herself. As the little girl placed the flowers about the Commissioner's neck, Kale Khan saluted. The Commissioner then shook hands with him, placed his arm about Kale Khan's shoulders, and the two walked on into the crowds.

To Mr Salwan's disappointment, the Commissioner walked along in this friendly embrace while he paid his respects to the Governor's party, and then along the paths the crowds fanned out to allow him to greet all the people who had come to welcome him.

In the evening there was a small gathering at the Governor's mansion. Again Kale Khan was there, as if defying Mr Salwan or any of his party to get close to the Commissioner. But the old man tired easily these days, and later on, he only smiled as he watched Mr Salwan and his colleagues edging in on the Commissioner's attention. He knew that after the Governor's official welcome was over *he* would accompany the Commissioner to the new Indian Embassy. As Mr Salwan and his friends spoke to the Commissioner, Kale Khan could tell that they were not saying pleasant things about him, for he caught them casting furtive glances at him, as if making sure constantly that he was not within earshot of their conversation. The Commissioner listened, he smiled, he nodded, and when the function was over, Kale Khan left with him for his new residence.

They talked until Kale Khan had covered the complete history of the indentured Indians in Trinidad, asking the Commissioner to come to the Hussay festival the following day to see with his own eyes how faithfully they kept pace with their mother country, how they had never forgotten their homeland, and how true to the minutest detail they tried to preserve their heritage, their culture, their marriages, feasts, religion, and festivals.

It was late. It was dark. They were both tired, the old man and his grandson. It was the kind of darkness which light does not drive away. Kale Khan lit the cup flame. It was still dark. The boy thought he heard him say 'Let me rub you down for the last time.' He wasn't sure. He didn't dare to ask. He thought that he didn't hear what the old man said. He waited sitting on his bed, tired. The old man poured some coconut oil into a bowl. The boy had undressed. He waited. The old man's mind seemed fumbling, wrapped up in itself. It broke and he said, 'Yes, now what . . . oh yes, coconut oil . . . what else, let me see . . .' He stared at the boy. His state went straight through the boy, then their eyes met, and he smiled. 'Ah . . . oho . . . ready, boy?' The boy's body had taken on Pathan proportions. The old man looked at him, pleased. His arms and legs were filling up with the muscle of manhood. His limbs had lost the gangling growing slenderness. He had the deep-set eyes of Kale Khan, their rims dark, almost blue-black. His nose was straight. The old man liked the boy's smile most of all. It made him dilate his nostrils a little together with a light that burst forth from his eyes. It was vigour and character that the old man liked in the boy's face, for he saw in it the continuity of his strange race of men. The small mole on the boy's cheekbone was dusted with only the slightest down of hair, his skin bronze in the lamplight:

'All right, boy,' he said as he started smearing the boy's chest with the oil. And he thought:

'These are my bones. This is my flesh, my flesh that must never die. Boy, you have my hands, and my face, you walk with my feet. Yes, this is my blood.' The boy felt that some strange mystery was going on in the old man's mind. He did not know what.

Kale Khan stood up and finished off by rubbing the oil into his own hands as though he were repeating some prayer which the boy did not understand.

Still Jamini could not ask, still he was not sure, if the old man had said, 'Let me rub you for the last time.'

There were footsteps in the gateway. The boy looked up to Kale Khan.

'Who that?' the old man called coldly.

'Is me.'

'Me who, you ain't have a name or what!'

'Is me, *Barp*, Rahim.'

'Oho, an' why you walkin' on soft foot like thief in the night? Come, sit down. G'wan upstairs, boy,' he added to Jamini. 'It have *big* Hussay tomorrow, plenty thing go happen.' Jamini nodded to Rahim and went upstairs.

And after he had stretched out on his cot, he heard the Jumbie bird calling in the Calabash tree. His heart leapt, and he had strange feelings in his insides. Kale Khan had told him that a boy will sometimes feel strange emotions because he is growing up, but the boy could not help but feel that there was something mysterious about his grandfather's actions since the end of the day. He covered his head with his pillow and went to sleep thinking that his father was downstairs, and that there was no need to worry. Still, the Jumbie bird hid in the Calabash tree.

Rahim had not seen his father for several days. He wasn't as worried as he had been in the past, the old man seemed to reach out from the depths of darkness and death in a miraculous way. He was himself again. The dream that he had dreamt so long ago was taking shape. Each speech, each little gathering and finally yesterday at the airport . . .

'Boy, where you does keep yourself these days? Nobody ain't know where you does go, where you does eat, I don't even know if you does sleep here or what. I think I hear somebody say they see you at the airport yesterday . . . you was there or no?'

'No, I wasn't there, *Barp* . . . I don't know, I felt as if I didn't have no business to go there yesterday. I hear 'bout what happen and I was glad but I still can't help but feel that I can't understand. Well, we ain't nothing, the whole world full of small small people like we. If we wake up in the mornin' and see day break, sun shine, rain come an' go, that's 'nuff.'

As Rahim rambled on, Kale Khan got up to get his pipe. From time to time he would put in, 'So?' or 'So!'

'A man does come in the world, and first thing he do is to bawl out. He learn that he have this that work to do, he have to find out what work make for he. It ain't have no difference where he is, where he go, what thing he have to find out he could find out wheresoever he is, Hindustan, Trinidad . . .'

His back still turned to Rahim, the old man was now filling his red clay pipe by the light of the small cup-flame on the counter as he spoke.

'If you did grow up in a big big country instead of this pissin-tail piece of ground you might'er see what what place a man have in this world. You grow up here and all the stretch your mind could stretch is to see what what place you have to find for yourself. A man have the whole world with he, he can't spend his life runnin' up and down like blind mongoose lookin' for snake. He have to have some respect for everybody else. Where he brother is trouble, is he trouble. Is a kind of selfishness that a man have inside of him when he could see what what troubles he own people have and still so busy with his own life that he can't even think 'bout them.'

'*Barp* . . . the world is a big place . . . who is me? I is nobody, I . . .'

Kale Khan turned around angrily and dashed his pipe to the floor. The tobacco scattered with the broken pieces of red clay.

'You is *my* son, that is who the hell you is! You is my flesh an' bone. Is my blood you have inside of you. Because of that you is something, otherwise you would be nothing. Is I who make you, is I who give you my hand and my foot. I give you my own own finger an' fingernail, and I give all the fine fine design you make up in your filigree work. Where you think they come from—God? Is *me*! First time you twist a wire an' I see how your hand move I know that you was my son. When that car roll in Piarco Airport I did want you right there sittin' down beside me. Where the hell you went to? You think that is know I didn't know that when the day come after all these years that you wouldn't be there? I know it long long time, boy. I see that too in you eye. You bring up with woman when you was still small, you get soft heart. I try to break you away from that old woman but it look like if *one* minute too long to leave Pathan with woman. It have something that does melt their heart and now, and now . . .'

Kale Khan's hand was trembling as he snatched angrily at his cup of water on the counter. 'You heart turn like water!' He turned the cup upside-down and let the water fall to the ground.

But his deluge had not ended, there was still some storm in him.

'I bring you up to give a good kick in they backside to low-minded people. I did want you to have a heart like lion, hard like a stone. I did want you to pick up a stick in Hussay time and swing it till you feel a fire burnin' you up. You does worry too much.

'I try to tell you that you have to do what your blood tell you, but your ears hard! You never listen. You sittin' 'pon your back-side an' lettin' your head full up with confusion. Where the hell you goin'? I remember long long time when that boy was still small I tell he that God dead. You was vex with me. I tell he that befo' he have to find out that it ain't have nothing, nobody in this world to bring even a cup of water from the pipe for you.

'I look at you face and . . .' He held Rahim's face between his fingers, staring into his eyes, his thumb touching the mole on Rahim's cheekbone. He stood still for seconds that way, as if he wanted to erase the mole with his thumb. Rahim could feel the small pressure of the old man's thumb as he watched him, waiting. It seemed that Kale Khan's mind had strayed far in that dead silence, then like a flash of lightning it returned, and placing his hand on Rahim's shoulder now he said slowly, 'It take the whole world to make you. Must never say that you is nobody. I kill you dead dead dead with my own two hands befo' I think that you come in the world and go out from it without doing something befo' your life finish.'

The old man paused. 'You hear anything from Meena?' It was not really a question, and when Rahim did not answer, he went on, 'Well, a man got to have some shame. I glad to see that you still have that left. When that gone . . . well, anyway, is your lookout.'

13

IN NO place but the tropics are life and death so close. There is a violence that shifts from hour to hour. In the mornings, as the first rays of warm sunlight touch the grass of Woodford Square, the dense dew tumbles into the earth. Soon after there emerges a powerful pungence of the earth in its convolutions as the rich moist air escapes, carrying with it the heady odours of purple poui, the sickly sweet scent of a calabash that had exploded its thousands of sticky seeds, and the smell of damp dew-soaked bark. The earth is a milling of life, of lust. A million buds have burst open in the early morning and everything stands erect, seething with a kind of defiance, an avaricious hunger, a violent urge to possess the earth, to swarm into the streets and houses, the asphalt road, to come piercing through the crevices of loosened floor and floorboard.

But in an hour or two, the great amber ball of the sun flies down from the skies and lashes its whip at all this vigour. The morning grass that stood firm now withers and turns brown. The thin long red-tongued petals of the hibiscus shrivel and turn purple in the sun. The pungent aromas of earth and blue begonia blossoms are burnt out, the soft-shelled calabash pod is scorched crisp to rattling, and tropic sleep, a crushing sleep which nothing aspires to awaken, comes pelting down from a sky of crystal blue with its sheets of white heat until all the verdure, all the juices, the saps, are stunned and stilled.

Keeskeedee! Keeskeesdee! Keeskeedee!

Jamini was awakened by this call of a bird perched in a tree across the street in the square. He could see the bright yellow of its breast, the light brown of its back and tail, and when it opened its beak to call again, he could see the pink of its throat, and its little pointed tongue.

The huge bells of the Trinity Church south of the square began striking and Jamini jumped out of bed with a sudden fear, a strange anxiety of having slept through some important event. He wound a towel about his waist, snatched up a hibiscus stem, with which he brushed his teeth, and ran down the steps two at a time.

As he stepped into Kale Khan's room, it was empty. The room was swept, it was neat, and everything on the counter was arranged with a sense of orderliness. His eyes flashed under the bed. The old man's boots were gone, only his wooden-soled slippers stood on the floor. Jamini rushed out into the yard and banged on a rusty galvanised sheet which was the door to the shower.

'Dada?' he called questioningly.

'Your Dada get up soon soon and done gone,' Rahim answered from the shower.

The boy felt a pang of sadness clutch at him. Kale Khan had gone off to the Hussay and left him. Rahim turned off the water in the shower.

'I have the fire make already, boy. As soon as I come out we will fix something to eat and then go to see the Hussay in St James.'

'All right,' he said despondently. He could not help but feel that his grandfather had purposely left him behind and gone on alone. They would never be able to find him in all that milling and excitement. The boy could have gone with him into the homes of the people who built the floats, and in the yards where the drummers prepared for the road. He could have got up so close to the large drums, that they would boom against his chest until his heart felt as if it were tumbling through his body, and if anyone not knowing him were to say, 'Who is this boy . . . what he doin' here?' there would always be someone else who would say, 'He Kale Khan grandson, man . . . you ain't know he? . . . He poopah have a jewel shop in Frederick Street.' And then, 'Ohhh . . . I thought he was just some boy come in from off the street to get in the way.' And they would pat him fondly on the head, leaving him to roam about the yard through all the ceremony and chanting that went on before the dazzling floats were launched out on the road.

The boy felt uncomfortable as Rahim prepared their food. He felt that his father was trying to do everything Kale Khan would have done, or Meena, if she were there. He hardly knew what reply to make when Rahim said, 'Well, we goin' to see Hussay together.' He wished only to get away, to get started.

When they got to St James, he disappeared in the crowds while Rahim stood talking to some people. It was still early in the afternoon, yet he felt that time was running out as he looked everywhere for Kale Khan. Each time he saw a turban bobbing up and down, he ran ahead to see the face of the man wearing it. People looked at him as he stared them in the face then turned and went away. In the food stalls where people had begun milling he roamed back and forth. Perhaps he might see one of the old men who was at the airport with Kale Khan yesterday, but there was no one he knew, no one he could ask. His pace slowed and he began to feel that standing in one spot would be as good as running back and forth. But this lasted for a few moments only before he began moving about again.

The sun was going down, and he was tired. He turned into one of the small streets in St James in complete dejection, and there was Lakshmi. She had evidently seen him first and was coming toward him.

'Jam,' she called, and when she reached him, 'You hate me, don't you?'

'No,' he said, 'not hate.'

He wanted to tell her that something was going on that he could not understand. He wanted to tell her that he had never stopped loving her. He did not know quite what had happened to her and he knew that if he should ask her, she would tell him. He knew that Tommy had made love to her. He felt that he would want to know all, everything, all the visions he had created in his own mind of their love, ghosts that had haunted him and filled his soul with an anguish that he thought he would never be able to drive away. The loneliness and the longing he had felt on those days, those weeks when he wept silently on his cot in the gallery, burying his face in the pillows so that no one should hear his sobs. He knew now that when he had been with his grand father planning and travelling about from one end of the island to the other, it had penetrated the deepest corners of his memory, and had helped to blot out the anguish of his soul.

The boy looked at her now, wanting her with a strange hunger, the hunger that a man has for a woman immediately after she has betrayed him with another. But she had not betrayed him.

They held hands, they walked. They could see the Laperyouse cemetery. There was always silence there, and dead bones. They kissed. Not spontaneously, she offering her lips when he wished, he offering his. Their lips missed, stumbled for a second, then met. They walked on, his arm about her waist. She knew that he wanted her, she knew that she would give herself to him. She felt the strangeness of his desire, desire without love, desire like a debt that they owed each other. They passed an old woman cleaning an overgrown grave. They could smell the damp green roots she pulled from the wet soil. They walked past groomed graves, monstrous mausoleums. They could hear the Hussay drums beating through the air. Their hearts were cold. He stopped walking. She turned and asked, 'Here?'

'Yes,' he said. 'The grass is tall here.'

She sat down in the grass. It grew as high as her shoulders. With her head down she began unbuttoning her clothes. He turned away from her as he undressed. He felt her arms close about him. He felt her breasts touch his naked chest. They were soft, limp. The passion that could tauten them was absent. They closed their eyes . . .

The boy felt his cheek against hers, wet with her tears. They went back to the Hussay crowds.

'I have to find my grandfather,' he said.

'Yes,' she said, 'I know. You're going to go away with him and I won't ever see you again.' She was standing with her hands behind her back under the awning of one of those small shops in St James. He looked back at her, then turned and looked ahead as he walked on. He did not look back again.

The half-moon that marks the date of the Hussay was already in the sky and darkness was falling across the hills.

The boy shuttled about the crowd in which excitement grew by the minute now, for it would not be long before the Hussays would be launched out on to the streets. The night was clear and from the brilliance of the stars in the heavens it was certain that there would be no rain. The night air was filled with the smell of small fires kindled by the drummers to heat and tauten their drums. All attention was drawn to a small knot of people who had just arrived, the Commissioner, his party, Mr Salwan, and his colleagues.

Jamini pushed his way through to see if Kale Khan was among them, and not seeing his grandfather among the faces, he almost plucked up courage to ask if they had seen him, but Mr Salwan was driving off the people, shouting at them, 'Get away now. What will His Excellency think of us? Go on, go on!'

There was a tumultuous clattering of drums not far off, and the crowd slackened. Some ran to the corner of a small street where three of the half-moons had come dancing out on the street, glittering with the foil of various colours, frills, streamers, their outermost edges mounted with knives, daggers and the shapes of outstretched palms. The sturdy men circled the moons about, swishing the air as they passed close to the on-lookers. Then, one by one the eight floats came rolling on to the road; magnificent miniatures of a fairyland architecture with domes and minarets, oriental archways, studded with gems. Each Hussay had its moons, its drummers, and its stick players who cavorted, danced and parried, each to the rhythm of its own drummers, each a vast thunder of sound that covered the others. Large bronze cymbals crashed and shot out points of light as they vibrated, and the boy went from one Hussay to the other searching out the faces of the band of stick players.

When he reached the last one and did not find the old man there, he started back again to the foremost Hussay, a white one, its interior corridors and passageways lit by small earthenware lamps. The thousands of onlookers had gone into a bacchanalian frenzy. Men who were not stick players drew their handkerchiefs tightly between their hands, skipped over them, then held them over their heads, dancing, strutting to the maddening rhythms, jokingly imitating the stick players, challenging them to battle, then dancing away. Women and children threw handfuls of rice on to the creeping, crawling procession.

The boy was almost at the first Hussay when he heard a loud *crack*! *crack*! *crack*! The drums stopped short. There holding the stick that struck the ground, was Kale Khan, stern, his face drawn with anger.

The boy tried to force his way closer in, but the crowd restrained him, for the other stick players had moved to the sides to make room for the two stick fighters.

The drums started again with that ominous rhythm that would carry the fighters along. Kale Khan moved his body in unison with the drum beats. His saffron-yellow turban, its tail hanging down his back, shivered as he picked up the rhythm, at first with his feet, then the rhythm mounted in his body, his waist and hips were now part of the movement. He threw his wire-bound *lathi* high into the air, straight as a spear, caught it as it came plummeting down, and as it touched his hand, as he slapped his fingers about it, he smiled, not to the crowds, but to himself.

His opponent, a younger man, was striking the ground with his stick, keeping the rhythm of the drums this way. Then the man, their sticks extended, circled about each other. The ends of the sticks touched and they drew away. Kale Khan came walking in with a fast *crick-crack crick-crack*, and the younger man, who was not quick enough, could only parry each blow of Kale Kahn's lightning *lathi* as it drove him back until he was up against the crowd. But instead of following up his advantage, Kale Khan circled away. As if some great heat within his body was consuming him, his face and forehead broke out in a profuse sweat that put an edge of deeper yellow about the rim of his turban. He took the bright-red tail of his turban and wiped away the sweat which had trickled into the corner of his eyes.

His opponent was back in the middle of the circle again, jutting his *lathi* in the air. Kale Khan was slow to move in this time, for the dim-lit images of faces and Hussay seemed to melt and dissolve before his eyes. He dried them again, almost forcing them to focus. The tall white Hussay, the anxious faces of the crowd settled before his eyes, and he went walking in again, his *lathi* swung now above his head, now it hit the ground, and his opponent was down on his knees. Kale Khan struck out, and the man broke the blow with the pad of his left hand. As he did so, he fell onto the side and Kale Khan, instead of crashing down on him, was seized by a watery image of the people and the moons that danced about him. He could not tell where to strike, and as he circled back, stomping his feet harder and harder on the ground to retain the rhythm of the drums, he began to see a double image of the ground and the faces that surrounded him.

He saw the Commissioner's face among the crowds, then it was gone, and he could hear the Commissioner's voice of the evening before, saying that he was not sent to Trinidad to revive old quarrels, that the past was dead and over, that India was no longer at odds with the British, and that India wished that they would settle here and try to make this place their home. And when the meaning of his words struck Kale Khan, he felt a great physical jolt that sent him spinning, plunging into nowhere. He felt a horrifying loneliness seize him . . . there was no home, no land peopled by men among whom he could walk and feel that it was his world, his home, a world that did not leave him alien and a stranger in the streets.

As if some great fire flared up in the bowels of his being, he began sweating. He was tearing off his shirt and now, feeling the muscles of his arms, a wild fever swept through him. His mind was telling his body that it was filled with all the saps of his youth, and the drums he heard were the drums of his old home town. 'Who this pissin' tail boy think he is?' the old man murmured to himself and then, as he started walking into his opponent with his lightning *lathi*, the whole image he saw before his eyes dissolved again—the voices of his *chelars*, the voices of Princes Town that clamoured for Khan Sahib, all rolled away to be replaced by faces that seemed angry with him, faces that laughed and cheered his opponent, and his *lathi* falling still for a moment gave his opponent the lead.

The man came in with a *crick-crack-crick*. Kale Khan jumped in the air, and as he came down to earth, he felt the bones of his knees and ankles hurt as though there were no cushioning tissue between them. He had fallen back into the crowd parrying all the way without a single second which afforded an opening, and in a moment of swift decision, as his opponent's *lathi* was coming at him, he ducked and let the man go plunging into the crowd. Now he was back in the centre of the ring again, and his mind slipped once more; he could hear the Commissioner's voice telling him that he had done wrong by inciting his people to rebellion, by sowing discontent among them, by promising them that they would go back home. He could hear him saying that this was their home and that he should have tried to help them to make this place their home rather than set them against it. He heard the Commissioner's voice ask him '. . . and how many people in India do you suppose know of your existence?' And the old man's heart broke like the calabash that had shrivelled in the sun, its hundreds of seeds of anger of death spilling forth.

But his opponent, who had been pushed back into the circle, was vexed and humiliated by his last fall into the crowd. He held his *lathi* and stood shaking it as if to ensure its strength.

'*Barp . . . Barp*!' Kale Khan heard Rahim's voice call out and looking about, his eyes again went dull.

His opponent was walking in on him. Kale Khan struck ground first, his stick came up first, and at that moment when he was going to come crashing down on the man's head, he saw his face. It was Rahim's face! He held his stick in mid-air.

'*Barp*! . . . Somebody stop him!' Rahim called from the side of the circle of people who would not let him through. Before Kale Khan's eyes could focus again, as he stood transfixed, his *lathi* poised in mid-air waiting to see if he was not indeed going to strike down his own son, a blow came crashing down on the side of his neck. His eyes instantly turned up in their sockets, and he staggered backwards twice, his *lathi* still in his hand. His eyes seemed to be trying to force themselves back to centre, then he fell backwards, his right leg jerking with the spasmodic reflexes of a slain animal.

When he fell to the ground, he felt as though he were standing close to one of the great yard-wide bells of the Trinity Church, there was a fantastic explosion of sound in his head, a ringing rumbling sound. He could see only a dull red flame-like blast before his eyes. The deafening intensity was dying slowly as he writhed on the asphalt road, but too slowly, his ear-drums would break with the continued *gongggggg* . . . swimming and crowding the canals of his ears.

And then as the sound softened, his boots, which pointed upwards as he lay dying, fell to the sides and his feet lay flat on the black pitch road. The old man's turban had sprung loose as his head struck the ground, his hair the selfsame silver of the moon. A thin stream of blood escaped from the corner of his mouth onto the saffron-yellow cloth of his turban, his blood the same deep red of its scalloped edge.

And now only the distant drums could be heard, the slow beat of dead rhythms muffled in the dawn as the Hussay wended its way to the salt-water of the sea where the ceremony would end.

They laid Kale Khan down on the old signboard in his room. From the counter Binti took a small green phial, its red label stamped 'Innis' Drug Store,' the swirling letters of the chemist's hand spelling out 'Water of Rose.' She removed the cork, passed the bottle left and right below her nose, then poured some of its contents into her hand and started anointing Kale Khan's feet, his hands, and then his face. The rose water brought into the room a strange smell of freshness, the freshness of the dead.

Binti sat at the head of the old man's bed, bent over him, looking at the half-closed eyes, the stilled dilation of his nostrils that strained to work, a wicked temper on his face. She shook her bracelets up her arm, put her hand gently on the old man's forehead and moved it around slowly until it cupped his chin. She ran her thumbs lightly across his eyebrows, placed them into the corners of his eyes close to his nose, then arched them outwards. She lifted up his head in both her hands. Rahim came and moved the wooden block, then she placed Kale Khan's head in her lap.

Her *orhani* had fallen to her shoulders, and the tiny bun of her grey hair hung loosened, ready to tumble down into a thin small string behind her head. The profile of her face pointed to the old man's feet, her eyes looking along his body. She took the corners of her *orhani*, and, working it under her spectacles touched it to both corners of her eyes. As she finished, she drew her breath quickly through her nostrils, saying softly, 'Rahim . . . *Barp* gone?' asking as though she weren't sure that the old man was really dead.

'*Barp* gone an' leave we, Rahim.' She looked at her son through the thin lenses of her spectacles, the old man's head still in her lap. Her eyes seemed large, ready to push themselves through their sockets.

'He gone an' leave all we by we-self.' And now, turning to Jamini, 'Jam, . . . your Dada gone, boy.'

The boy held his head down as she spoke to him. She turned

her face to look at the old man again. There was something like a conversation going on between her and the dead man. She passed her fingers across his lips, then stopped and listened as if she were saying, '*Barp* . . . so you gone . . . so you gone and leave we alone.' And then, stopping the movement of her fingers which were passing through the old man's bright silver hair, she listened, as if to hear Kale Khan say, 'Bin,' for that is what he called her then, then when love and life were not so old and tired. 'Bin . . . one day I shall make you a necklace of filigree that even the spider in his web will envy.'

And then with an upward sweep of the back of her hand, she stroked his face fondly over and over again, saying with her hands alone, with the small show of affection in the darkened room, 'Go to sleep . . . sh . . . sh . . . sh, go to sleep. Don't talk now, *Barp* . . . I will rub your forehead for you till you sleep away.' For it was so that she remembered him, the way she had loved him then, with caresses until he fell asleep. Time and all the Hussays and the stick fights slipped away. Anguish, all the pain and the quiet loneliness of years of Quarry Street . . . all these slipped away on quiet feet. All the world had run away to hide its face in corners of the night as Binti touched her lover's face, for he was young and close to her again as she had known him once, a long long time ago, and had never let the picture of their tender moments run away from her.

No one talked in this room filled with images, memories running past, carrying with them an incessant noise that blotted out the quiet of the dawn, its silence whispering that morning was coming. They heard the calling of the old man's voice; they heard the laughter of his throat. Although he was stretched out still and lifeless, they could not believe that he was really dead. Rahim looked outside where a chicken scratched the earth. There was something moving about the way the bird clucked and waited for its daily handful of corn, perhaps a few curses, and a threatened blow from the old man's walking-stick. How long, Rahim wondered, how long would the chicken come clucking and scratching before it understood that Kale Khan was dead?

Seeing that the dawn was coming up, Rahim reached into his pocket and took out two silver shillings, one old and worn, with Queen Victoria wearing a veil and crown, the other new and bright, King George's silver shilling. He looked about the room, and softly, as if telling a secret that death should not hear, he whispered to Jamini, 'Boy, is you the old man did like so good good good, better take this money and mark he name on it.'

Jamini got up from the block of wood on which he sat.

'An' when you come back, see if you can find a piece of string,' Rahim added, his voice again just above a whisper, his jaws working up and down, his temples swelling in and out, as he pressed his teeth together again and again.

As the boy left the room Meena began sniffing, and Binti, looking at the old man's half-closed eyes began drying her tears with the corner of her orhani. From the back of the shop they heard the slow blows Jamini struck on the coins, spelling out the letters of Kale Khan's name and the date of his death. Between the blows of the hammer came the solemn beating of the Hussay drums still headed for the sea at sunrise. Meena listened to the hammer blows, the drum beat, and she could already see the handing over of the lettered coins to the poor, forty days later. She would make a little offering, feed six or eight of the old men who slept along the Town Hall steps. Some people would say that the old man did not believe in all that nonsense, but she didn't mind. She said to herself, 'Everybody have to make they peace with God some time . . . don't mind what the old man say in he living days, in the heart of hearts he did have he own God. He have to bury like he own people.'

Jamini came in with the coins. No one could read the small letters, nor the numbers of the date, but they saw small blue-white glints from the deep little wedges of the chisel cuts as the boy reached over the old man's body, touched his eyelids closed, and placed the lettered silver shillings to weight his eyelids down. It was then that Meena cried out:

'*Barp . . . Barp* . . . you gone and leave we all alone. Now who go tell we what to do?'

The silence returned to the room slowly when Meena's cry died down to a soft sobbing. The return of the silence made Rahim uncomfortable. He felt that someone should say something, anything, to quiet the sounds of the drums coming from farther and farther away, but still coming, reminding them of Kale Khan, his violence, his death. He wanted to say, 'Sun coming up, it look as if morning done break already,' but he couldn't. Afraid that his voice would break in the sentence, that the sentence would in some way insult the presence of death's companion who had seen the last of mornings, who would see no more suns nor dawns. He turned again to Jamini.

'What about the string, boy, you bring it come with you?'

Jamini took out a wad of white flour bag string from his pocket. It still had kinks of the stitches it had been in a flour bag, and sprang back like elastic as he ran it between his finger and thumb-nail to straighten it out to its full length.

No one smoked. No one wore perfume. The wind outside was dry that morning. Yet in Kale Khan's room there was the sweet smell of black tobacco which the old man had smoked. It would never leave his walls. It mingled with the scent of Rose Water, the scent of the old man's life and death were walking in the room.

Now the string was straightened out, and Jamini started winding it first below the joint of Kale Khan's largest toe. It sunk deep into the flesh making a thin white ring below the toe-nail. The boy then held both feet together and the thin long soles of the old man's feet pointed upwards. Then he wound several more turns around the other toe so that the old man's feet would not jog about when they hoisted his bier on to their shoulders to take him to his burying place.

Back in his corner, the boy stared at the profile of his grandfather, the mole on the old man's cheek gone dry, lit by the feeble tongue of flame which had in time past spun a halo around the old man's cheekbone. He could hear Kale Khan saying in his slow and tired voice:

'Boy, night-time too long, day-time too short. Did old people never get time to sleep.' He wished the old man did not have to wait through the long night before they would take him to his grave where he would sleep a long and never-ending sleep forever. He was glad that God was dead, glad that Kale Khan had told him so. No angels pelting down from God's right hand would wake up Kale Khan. No messenger with roughcut voice and curling fingernails would stomp upon the old man's chest and ask him to recite from the Koran. No one would wake him up and ask him now to measure out his deeds. No one should ever ask him this, not Kale Khan, they should let him sleep, sleep, sleep for ever.

The boy kept staring at the dry and sandy colour of the old man's face, the dust of death's erosion. Death, quickly wasting away the skin of the face. He remembered someone saying that the hair would grow for several years, the beard, the bright grey-silver of the old man's head. He thought of the old man's long cold sleep against the earth, stretched out on the bare ground with his feet set close together. Yes, all this was so, but Kale Khan's voice would still be heard, the throbbing of his throat; these things Jamini could never feel had stopped. Kale Khan would move again to fill the night air with his muffled coughing, the *clip-clop-clopping* of his wooden slippers, the ringing thump and clank of his iron rod as he went to the pipe outside to fill his empty hollowed-out radishes. The boy felt his nostrils go empty. His liver and his heart, his bowels and his being felt as though they were seeping out of his body through some deep and draining wound that weakened him, seizing him with a vast and overwhelming loneliness. He listened to the slow thuds his heart was letting fall, beating out the slow *clot*, *clot*, *clot* of his grandfather's wooden-soled slippers slapping up against the living flesh of his heel . . . and he kept murmuring to himself, sobbing deeply within his breast.

'Dada . . . Dada . . . why didn't you teach me about death? Why you didn't teach me everything so that I wouldn't feel this way. You gone to sleep, and who will take us back to Hindustan? Who?'

He caught himself shaking his head as he repeated over and over:

'*Who*? . . . *Who*? . . . *Who*? . . .'

Time would change, water flow, night turn to day. All this, the world—the purple flowers of the poui along the hills of Laventille all go to sleep, but the old man would never die. Jamini would always remember him at night. He would remember as he lay on his cot in the rainy season, or when the Hussay drummers came running from St James and halted in his room, their feet still soaking wet with dewdrops from damp grass across the length of the Grand Savannah. The drums would come and pound upon his ear, he would hear them beating, pounding, calling, saying:

'Boy . . . boy . . . ayyyyy boy . . . boy . . . you ain't did hear that Jumbie bird? Coming and bawling, waiting night after night in that Calabash tree? Must try and understand, boy, is me who it was calling for. Time does come when all o' we have to go.'

Yes, he would remember when the raindrops came down, dancing in their frenzied steps at night, *tip-tap-tapping*, hopping along the rusty arched grooves of the galvanised roofing. He wanted to remember beyond this time, when time would scrub him clean of all the things he'd seen. He told himself that he would remember this odour of rose water, this sooty burnt-out smell of coconut oil the lamp gave off, the smell of exhaled black tobacco that dulled the picture posters on the walls, building up continuously, layer upon layer until the garish colours smoothed and blended with the hushed and brooding quiet of this room. As he had chiselled the letters of Kale Khan's name upon the silver coins, so Jamini hammered upon his mind the taste of death, the smooth grey iron handle of the walking-stick that the living hands of the old man had polished, the silken silver footprints rubbed out on the soles of the wooden slippers. Yes, these he would want to remember. These things he would want to hold before his eyes when darkness fell across the length of Woodford Square and the fine trickles of water from the fountain, ragged threads of dancing spray breaking past the surface, made lonely sounds, the fountain held in an inverted cone of yellow lamplight in the empty square and now and again the old man's coughing from across the square as they choked and spat, then turned their face to the wall, along the darkened archways of the Town Hall steps.

Outside the old man's room several of his friends were gathering. At St James the Commissioner had told them the same things that had driven Kale Khan to his violent death. A torrent of dejection had fallen upon the waiting faces, they were seized with a kind of stupor. They carried on the Hussay ceremonies in the true spirit of his historical beginnings, one of mourning and sadness.

The old men stole glimpses at the dead body of Kale Khan, and when Jamini had placed the silver coins on his eyes, the sight of his face with the two discs of white broke something in them; they huddled together in a little knot below the awning, for now they knew that their lives, too, had come to an end, that all they had done and hoped for had become meaningless.

There was a steady flow of footsteps through the long gateway as the hours of the morning moved on to daylight. More and more people came to take a last look at Kale Khan's face, to offer their sympathy to Meena and Rahim, and Binti. Kale Khan's friends had settled down into a small crowd outside the room. They sent for coffee from the all-night stands along the market place and ran small errands to the drug store, or to the ice factory, or they helped with the grotesque coffin chest which was stuffed with ice and replenished as the hours wore on.

Footsteps, and still more footsteps through the gateway; the slow, sometimes hoarse murmuring of the old men outside the room. Jamini was looking at the large ice box in which they had placed his grandfather, a large case made of metal that rang with a dull timbre as they manoeuvred it into the small room. It was painted by the undertakers with ripples and knots so that the ugly chest would seem to be made of wood. After all the rentals, all the moving from one place to another, the ugly brown paint had fallen away from the cold of the ice it had housed so many times, leaving a dull metal-grey in spots. On the top of the great brown box was a glass lid which opened over the face. The lid had served little purpose, for each time someone came, it was covered over with the condensation on the inside so that it had to be opened, letting the ice-cold air of the box escape. A small gust of the cold air, touched with rose water, had swept past the boy's face when he first looked at his grandfather in the box. Now he sat watching a bucket which had been placed below the box to catch the melted ice. He found himself waiting for the drops of water to fall into the bucket, counting them. A fresh supply of ice was brought in and the massive lid of the refrigerator box was lifted off by two of Kale Khan's friends. They emptied out a large bag of broken ice and spread it around the box. One of the men took an ice pick and began breaking up the pieces which were too large. The boy placed his hands over his ears. He could not stand the sound of the ice falling against the tin box. Each stab of the ice pick seemed to pierce him.

There was the sound of several people approaching the gateway. The hoarse whispering outside stopped suddenly, and the little group broke up in a strange way.

The Commissioner, with Mr Salwan and a few others, had

arrived. The old man looked at them sullenly without saying anything. Some of them moved away. Binti was seated on the old man's bed. Her eyes caught the Commissioner's. She pointed to the box.

'You come to see he face, he inside there!' she said acidly, then looked down at her hands which came to rest in her lap.

Mr Salwan was reaching over the Commissioner's shoulder whispering something to him. The Commissioner gave him a cutting glance. Mr Salwan smiled foolishly and tried to put on an air of reverence.

'*Mai* . . .' the Commissioner said softly, 'I came here this morning to see *you*: to tell you that I am truly sorry for what has . . .'

'You ain't see me from the time you come in this room? You must be have plenty plenty more work to do, like that!' She pointed to the ice box again.

'*Mai*,' the Commissioner started again, 'a great many things have happened here as well as in Hindustan. Who are we to judge each other? In Hindustan we have been so wrapped up in our own troubles, we knew nothing of our people abroad. I am here as a stranger in your midst . . . I . . .'

Binti hated the Commissioner's slow droning explanation.

'You don't know nothing . . . you was right when you say that. You wasn't born when they start bringing we here as slave: What you talkin' 'bout? The dead done dead and gone, leave that alone. The old man do what thing he have to do. It ain't your business what he do. He own man. He had like a spirit inside he that come talk in he ears, and that make what happen to he. Write your letter to Hindustan and tell them anything you want. It ain't have nobody to blame.

'That man mind,' she said, shaking her finger in the direction of the ice box, 'was like the world. Somebody start spinning it like a top and it go and go till the winding run down. Which which place it go, which which thing it do nobody could explain, and that is all.'

The Commissioner, feeling that he was caught in a situation far beyond his knowledge, beyond the rash statements he had made immediately upon his arrival, left Binti now. He moved silently to Rahim and Meena to tell them he was indeed sorry for what had happened.

'You went too far, man. You never should'er tell the old man that Hindustan ain't we country any more,' Rahim told him.

'Yes,' he said, lost in thought, 'yes . . . that was wrong.'

Like Binti, the boy too felt that there was nothing more to be said about Kale Khan. It was no use trying to apologise for him nor try to explain what drove him. The only thing that mattered now was that he was dead. The drops of water falling into the bucket below the ice box brought a finality to the boy's mind that nothing could erase as he waited for the morning to come.

Towards the first light of day a slight drizzle came down and the old men who still hung about outside came into the room and huddled close together. They sent for coffee as they used to in time past, but they drank from their tin cups as if lost in deep thought and the boy wondered what they could be thinking, but looking at them yielded nothing of their thoughts. There was only the faint rasping of their ragged beards as they rubbed their faces meditatively. Between the fine drizzle large drops were ringing on the galvanised roofs now, a rhythm still irregular, but growing towards one vast sound that the rain made when all the drops became full blown and drove across the roof-tops. The old man's lamp, a small tongue of flame from a cup, was placed at the head of the box. It sputtered as the wind came up with the rain, and looking upon all these images, the boy felt strangely as if he had been through all this before. Slowly, it came to his mind that he had dreamed of his grandfather's death a long time ago. The most fearful detail of all was the rain, and the water which had collected in the old man's grave.

As they carried Kale Khan's body to its resting-place, his bier borne by six of the old men, the boy walked solemnly through the narrow pathways of the vast cemetery knowing that when they got to the grave it would be filled with water. It seemed odd to him that no one else had anticipated this for there was sudden surprise on all the faces when the bier arrived at the grave. No one knew what to do. Rahim looked about confused, as if to say, 'Well, how often in a man's life does he have to empty out a grave?' There was nothing like an old can lying about the cemetery that could be used; and the watchman's house at the cemetery gate was quite far away.

'I think I know what to do,' someone finally broke in. It was the taxi-driver who rode Kale Khan into the airport not too long ago. He had brought Rahim, Meena, Binti and Jamini to the cemetery in the same car. 'I used to have a can in the trunk of the taxi to keep gas in . . . let me see if it is still there,' he said, going to his taxi.

There were some whispering in the crowd. 'It ain't good for a man to go down inside a grave before he time come . . . is not a good sign, man.'

Binti grasped the edges of her skirt, pulled them in front of her, and standing at the edge of the grave shouted to the crowd. 'All right, all you blasted fools . . . all you blasted coward give me a hand if you 'fraid . . .' There was only stillness and dead silence.

'Come on . . . come on . . . is dead you 'fraid to dead?' she shouted in her shrill little voice.

'*Mai*, don't make no row . . . *I* going down and empty out the water,' Rahim offered.

'Damn fool and them . . .' she muttered as he took her by the arm and led her down from the moulds of earth heaped up around the hole.

The taxi-cab driver returned with a gallon can and gave it to Rahim who had gone down into the grave, trying to empty out the water with his cupped hands. It was slow and most of the water fell back as he tried to throw handfuls above his head. Now that he had the can, it went faster. He filled it with the red muddy water and handed it up to others above until the floor of the grave was empty. Even as Rahim was helped out of the grave, there was still some reluctance from the men who stretched out their hands to reach for him. The bright red dirt of the cemetery when wet was slippery as moss. One false step and the two men who helped him up would topple into the hole as well.

Binti stood by, clicking her tongue on the roof of her mouth.

'You mean to say that soon soon soon after a man dead . . . he body ain't have time to get cold yet and everybody 'fraid he . . . not only 'fraid he, but 'fraid he go carry them with he?'

Although her voice was not with great power or strength, the old woman's posture as she stood on the large mounds of red earth beside the gaping hole, the cold grey rain sky cast behind her, made her seem suddenly to possess the fire that Kale Khan had had in him.

'Who 'fraid . . . who 'fraid . . . and 'fraid for what?'

One of the bearers came forward. 'Come on, all you boys, what we waiting for? Is we who have to bury Kale Khan.' And so saying, the six men moved through the crowd carrying a dozen planks of wood. Two of them went in first, the others lifted the old man's body out of the coffin and lowered him to the others who placed him gently on the red earth. Now they began wedging the boards about two feet above the body and when all but his face was covered they waited for everyone to take their last look. Rahim, Meena, Binti, Jamini looked down at the face of Kale Khan for the last time, and Binti looked around at all the faces about the grave then nodded.

'All right . . . put the last two pieces of wood in they place and all you boys come on up,' she told them.

Meena began crying, her bosom jerking with deep sobs. Rahim put his arms about her and kept whispering to her, 'Meena, Meena, don't cry. The old man live he life in the only way he know how. He gone to rest now . . . sh . . . shhh.'

There were sobs and crying from many others, the sound of people blowing their noses. Binti surveyed the faces around with a sternness that would not break into tears. She looked at Jamini, and the boy, as if feeling the strength she had within her, felt like clasping his arms about her and crying, allowing himself to tumble into a torrent and weeping that would clear the tightness of his chest. Meena's crying had quietened down now, she held a handkerchief across her nose and mouth as Rahim left her side and went to Jamini.

'Is you the old man did like so good, boy, better you throw the first handful of dirt on he,' Rahim whispered in the same tone of secrecy he had used since the old man's death.

The boy stooped down to pick up a handful of earth, and he could smell the raw odour of the white planks mixed with the smell of wet earth.

'It's me, Dada . . . Jamini, the one you always liked so well.' And so saying, he threw the handful of earth, carefully aiming it to the far corner of the pine boards so that it would not land above the old man's body. He threw the earth trying to scatter it so that it would not land with one heavy thud upon the planks, then turned and wove past the people who crowded close to the edges of the grave, wincing with each thud of the earth that Meena, Rahim, Binti and the old man's close friends threw in. And now he could hear the sound of shovels striking hard into the thick wet dirt, he could hear the thick wet clods of earth falling heavily on to the white planks as he walked away, counting his footsteps. And when he was forty paces away, he looked at the spot wondering if the terrible angel from God's right hand would come flying down when the last person got this far from the grave and rap on the white pine boards to wake up Kale Khan. He wondered if God was really dead.

As they drove home from the cemetery, Binti was the only one not overcome with grief. If she grieved, no one knew it. She seemed to possess a new strength, a new violence to take hold of Rahim, Meena, and Jamini's lives.

'I went to see that big big headmaster at Queen's Royal College. I ask he to let you come and make lesson there,' she said to Jamini. The boy looked out of the window of the car as it moved through the rainy streets.

'*Mai*, you know that is a place for rich people children only. Why you gone and do a thing like that?' Rahim asked.

Meena too seemed surprised at the old woman's words. Apart from the cost of the school, Meena wondered how she had managed to get an interview with the principal. Looking at the old woman's clothes, her worn slippers, the utter poverty of her dress, Meena wondered if her mind was not slipping. But when Binti explained, it did not seem so impossible.

'The headmaster have a cook that I does sell my vinegar to . . . he have a yard-boy, a Indian yard-boy, who grow up in Princes Town. Well, I tell them my troubles and they say they go talk to the headmaster, so when the man say he go talk with me, I tell he my troubles and he listen. It have some good white people in this island, you know. Anyway, I want you to forget about your Dada now, boy, forget all the things you and he plan together. All of that is old dream for old people like he and myself, you must promise me to try and make good lesson and stay in that school,' she said to Jamini.

It did not surprise Rahim now that Binti could have done what she said, but he still wondered where they would ever get the money to send their son to a school like that. The old woman rummaged about the draw-string of her skirt, taking out a small cloth purse of gold sovereigns which she had saved throughout her lifetime. She handed it to Rahim, saying, 'Take this. It have 'nuff to send the boy to school with for the first year and for you to start your trade again. Buy what what thing you need, and it have a room behind the coal shop in Quarry Street. I want you and Meena and this boy to move out from Frederick Street and come to live with me. Is true that my eyes ain't close yet, but I know that I ain't have too much time left.'

In the following days before the boy started going to school he helped Binti around the coal shop. He thought of how the other boys would jeer at him when they found out where he lived. He thought of his father and his father's trade, and the little room they now lived in behind the coal shop on Quarry Street. Binti was raking up the coal into her bin, and as the boy watched the scoop she used, the one with the 'Blue Nose Butter' trademark, he remembered how it was long long ago, and how worn it had now become, worn down like all else around him. He wondered how far down its wearing would reach before the old woman too would die. As he watched the shining surface of the white worn metal, it evoked in him that lustre of Kale Khan's walking-stick, the smooth lustre upon iron that the touch and use of living hands keep in a constant polish. And a feeling of sadness, of vast loneliness fell upon him as Binti raked away the fine metallic dust of coal that had come and gone. He thought of the coal men and of the silence of the jungles; he thought of the thick long vines that hung from the tall trees to the ground; he thought of the shafts of sunlight cutting through the trees; he thought of how they fell in a forest silence that no one heard; he thought of the long journey of the trees that went to coal, that came to touch the 'Blue Nose' scoop; he thought of the pale soft white ash still holding its shape, resembling the solid black coal which had had all its substances drawn and dried, waiting for the gentlest gust of air of spoken words alone that would suffice to make it crumble into a small mound of soft white dust. He thought of all these and he was afraid of something in the world that dwelt quietly beneath the surface of all things, that moved slowly at morning, evening and night throughout the still dead silence of the hot and lonely abandoned streets of two o'clock afternoons. He was afraid of that all-levelling force that dwelt somewhere, slowly devouring the world and all that moved and loved.

When the sun came up in the morning, the old woman was the first to rise. From his room behind the coal shop, the boy could hear the sounds to which he was becoming accustomed. They were no longer bird calls nor wind in the trees. He heard the old woman place her feet in her slippers, then, as if she were stretching her body, he heard her sigh, and then she was moving about. Later on, he could hear her at the pipe in the yard gargling water in her throat, then spitting it out. Then it was time for him to get out of bed and help her in the coal shop. There were always a few early customers who needed some coals to get the breakfast fires going, perhaps an onion to fry their eggs with, or a few tomatoes to throw into the hearth. After this first round of sales, Rahim helped her to arrange her ground provisions in small mounds. Binti went over the lot of small heaps, adding one here, removing two from another heap. Then Rahim began hanging up some of his jewellery above the produce where people could see them. In time he thought he would get a small signboard that simply said 'Jeweller' with a large hand, its index-finger pointing to the gateway so that people would not have to disturb the old woman if they needed him.

On one occasion, Meena had offered to sell the set of jewellery he had presented her at their wedding, so that he could buy a signboard and get a small glass case with a mirror below, but Rahim had refused with the feeling of guilt a man has when he knows that he has done wrong and has not the heart to accept kindness from the person he has wronged. When Meena tried to reassure him that soon things would be better, he could not find the conviction he once did in her words. It seemed as though he wanted to refuse her even that, until one morning when he was awakened by heavy rapping on their door.

Still half-asleep, he opened the door, to see who it was.

'Morning,' a man greeted him. Rahim did not know whether to be annoyed or not. He was simply flushed with the kind of embarrassment one has when half-asleep, trying to talk to someone who is wide awake.

'I went to your old place to look for you.' The man smiled as Rahim pushed his tousled hair from his face, slowly coming awake.

'Yes, . . . business was slack . . .' Rahim started out feebly, '. . . so I decide to come out here and see if I couldn't . . .'

But the man, sensing that Rahim was groping for words did not press him to go on.

'About two years ago I brought some stuff from you, remember?'

Rahim looked him over carefully. From his speech he could tell that he was an American, but that was all. 'No, man, I can't remember. People does come and go here. So much people pass through my shop, is hard to remember one face from another. I know it go sound funny to you, but all of the American people who used to come in my place look like the same person.'

They both laughed at this.

'Well, here's the story. I want to make for me one of the finest sets of jewellery you ever made.'

Rahim was completely awake now, and Meena could hear the conversation between them. He was so delighted with what the man had just said, his first thought was what he could offer him by way of refreshment.

'We ain't have coffee make yet, but if you want I could send the boy down to George Street and get something for you.'

'Thanks,' said the man. 'I'd like to, but I can't. My ship's pulling out soon and I have to get back. We're on our way to South America, and we'll be back in two weeks. You think you can manage to get the work out by then?'

'Oh yes . . . yes . . . yes,' Rahim said. 'Sooner than that, if you want.'

'No, sooner than that would be too soon. Rahim, I want you to put everything you've got into it. My daughter is getting married when I get back and I promised her that I would get her the finest work from this area. Now how much of an advance would you say you need, fifty, a hundred?' The man took out a thick leather wallet and pressed some bills in Rahim's hand.

'Look, I could give you a receipt if you want. Write anything on a piece of paper and I will sign it to say I take such-and-such money from you.'

The man winked at Rahim. 'I'll take your word for it,' he said. 'I've got to run if I want to catch that ship. But the seventeeth, don't let me down now.' And with that he was off in a taxi which was waiting for him.

'Meena . . . Meena, wake up!' Rahim called, filled with excitement as he entered the room, only to find that Meena was already up. 'You hear, you hear what that man say 'bout my work?'

Meena, just as excited as Rahim, tried to tell him again what she had always known.

'You is the best jeweller in the island, Rahim, only you, you is the only one who can't believe it. It take somebody else to make you believe.'

But Rahim felt an old, old pride welling up in him again. The kind of feeling that emanates from the marrow, the kind of feeling a man is convinced has gone dead and dry in him. It was this feeling that almost drew tears to his eyes, for it was like coming to life again, and he plunged into his trade with the little tools he had, feeling that reward at the end of the day that only loving accomplishment could bring. As he lay in bed those nights rehearsing all the small details of design, the subtleties of wiring and soldering, the new shapes and forms that came cascading through his mind, he felt that he could go on and on, carried along on the wonderful tide of this new hope. No more did he wonder whether there were people in the vast world who paid a casual glance to some fragment of his work. Now he knew that his dreams, all the way down to the little jewel boxes housing some brooch, some pin, were something real and that in these thoughts lay his reward—that fleeting glimpse of our eternity that he had felt whispering at his fingertips. This was so, and the world had not forgotten him. Somewhere someone would say, rotating a piece of his work, 'I wonder who made it . . . I wonder if the jeweller in Trinidad ever thought that his handiwork would come this far.' These things he knew were so, and there was nothing in the world that could change this, nothing that could take this away from him.

In the afternoon when he blew out his blow-lamp and threw water on the River bridge, for Prince Street, offered a view of sunset upon the city that was everlastingly beautiful. The sun seemed caught behind the Red House, and long horizontal shafts of light came piercing through the trees of the Square striking the low-lying areas of Rose Hill and Quarry Street, which wound serpentine to the top where there was, as if seated at the mount, a small church looking out at the last rays of each evening's sunset.

As he stood at the rail of the bridge one afternoon, watching the splendour of day's end, he could see Jamini coming home. The boy was dressed in the uniform of the school, white shirt, blue serge trousers, monogrammed cap, and a tie of the school colours. There was something about his son dressed that way that gave Rahim a sense of pride. The boys who wore that uniform seemed to suddenly acquire a strange dignity. Whether the boys knew that they should conduct themselves in a particular fashion, whether the atmosphere of the school gave them this bearing it was hard to say, but Rahim was well pleased as Jamini approached. There was a tired look on the boy's face, but it was some distance on foot to the Grand Savannah where the school was. When Jamini was close enough for Rahim to see his face, he knew that it was not just fatigue, but something else that gave the boy's face its downcast expression. When he came and stood beside him on the bridge, Rahim placed his hand on the boy's shoulder asking him, 'What it is that have you looking so worried?'

The boy looked down to the sea at the mouth of the Dry River. He shrugged his shoulders dejectedly. 'Nothing, just tired, that's all.' But he knew that Rahim had seen through him.

'Tall me,' Rahim pleaded again. 'I is your father. If you can't tell me what wrong, who you go tell? You know it ain't good to have things bottle up inside you.'

Jamini held his head down examining his fingernails as he leaned against the Dry River Bridge.

'Is the school? Is the school that you don't like?' Rahim asked finally, and from the boy's reaction, something like a wince as Rahim struck upon the truth, he knew, he knew that he would have to tell.

'It's not the school so much, it's the boys. I just feel as if I don't belong there. All the boys are English boys. They have different clothes to play football in. They can come back on their bicycles to play cricket or . . . I don't think they want to have much to do with me.'

'But it have a couple of other Indian boys besides yourself?'

Rahim asked, not as a question, but with the implication that the boy should have no reason to feel this way. Jamini shrugged his shoulders as before. 'Yes,' he said finally. 'There are three or four others, but I don't know, they talk and act just like the others. I don't think I belong there. I feel as if I'm in gaol every day. I don't like the way the yard smells, I don't like the way the classrooms smell . . .'

He looked up at Rahim who was smiling. 'And you like the way it smell down by the sea?'

Jamini was flushed and now he looked at Rahim, surprised, for he had indeed run away from the smells of chalk and ink and gone down to the sea several times when he could not stand the coldness of the boys or when he felt that his clothes were not neat enough to go to class.

Rahim's smile broke into a wide smile now as he clapped the boy on his shoulder, shaking him fondly.

'So you think I was born big. You don't think that I was a boy one time, too? That I did get tired of school too, and run away to the sea? But that ain't all. Something else troubling you, tell me what it is?'

And so the boy told him, rambling, disconnected, confused. He told him how he was watching the 'Blue Nose' scoop, how he thought of Binti and then the silence of the forests and the black coals and the return of everything to the earth. But he felt that he could not make himself understood. He looked at Rahim questioningly, silently pleading, his eyes asking, 'Do you understand . . . did you ever feel this way . . . do you know what I mean . . . how I feel? Do other people feel this way?'

Rahim understood. He understood perfectly. He could not remember a time when he was more happy. He felt that this was indeed his son, a boy, growing into a man each day, that his lust had called from the unknown. There was a sudden feeling of joy that flooded Rahim's heart as he looked at the boy's face, thinking that this was his own flesh, his own blood, beginning to feel the wild storms and movements of the soul that Rahim too had felt, until slowly, secretly, in his work he had found something which snuffed out all the thoughts that had once told him that his life was meaningless. As his skill and his craftmanship had grown under Kale Khan's firm hand, he felt that satisfaction which he knew would endure beyond all else, that of creation, of work with his hands that spelt out the petals and leaves of beauty in his work.

'I know that you don't like this trade, and that is why you *must* go to that school. I know that it will be hard for you, but you have a chance that plenty people don't have. A man have to find a work in this world, he have to do something that great—I don't mean big—I mean something that only he could give to the world. You wonder why they teaching you all kind of things in the school, you wonder what use they have? That is because you have to look and look till you find that *one* work that make for you, a work that it ain't have nobody else in the whole wide world could do like you. That way you could put something in the world that it didn't have before. That is the thing I find in my work, and although you don't like my trade, must always remember that it have that something in it for me and that is what I want you to find out, because if a man can't find that something then he life finish!'

Rahim stopped to light a cigarette. The sun was down with its vast array of oranges. The treetops in Woodford Square were a great flame of fire that seemed to burst out of the sky, and deep down below the Dry River bridge, they could hear the faint coursing of a small thread of water flowing down to the sea. The boy remained silent, listening as if his mind was shaking and sifting Rahim's words back and forth, putting them into the kind of context that he could apply to himself.

'If a man could find that, then he could look at a hundred of them 'Blue Nose' scoop, he could watch at how everything does come and go in the world and still know that he life have something special that go last forever and ever.'

Up Quarry Street where the road began to climb, they could see Binti. The old woman was looking down the street, her hand placed over her forehead shading her eyes from the blatant burst of light through the trees. The boy remembered seeing her that way before when he was still quite small and he wondered how everything had become so bewildering in so little time.

'Now come,' Rahim said. 'What I telling you won't make sense right away. Put it in your mind somewhere and let it rest there for now. Day by day, if you look hard enough you will find that work that made for you. It ain't have nothing else in this world to make a man feel happy like that. That is why I want you to go and learn. Ask plenty question, and listen good to what everybody have to say, examine it careful careful and try not to give up before you find that something that the world have for you to do. What you say?'

Jamini was still for a long while, as if waiting for Rahim's words to run through his mind and then he looked up.

'Yes,' he said, 'I will do it . . . I won't give up.'

'Good man,' Rahim said, beaming. He clapped his arm around the boy's shoulder holding him close to his side. 'Good man, good man,' he said, as they both walked up Quarry Street.